Dearest Paula—
Hope you enjoy

STRANGER'S DANCE

this Montana
story!
Love—
Stephil

Troy B Kechely

Though historical events and businesses are detailed in this book, the main characters and the story itself are the creation of the author and completely fictitious. Any resemblance to any real persons, living or dead, is purely coincidental.

ACKNOWLEDGMENTS

I thank God for the gift of an imagination that allows me to create my stories. Also my deepest appreciation goes to Anika Hanisch for her patient coaching and editing of this novel over the two years it took me to complete it. I must also thank the dozens of family and friends who read early drafts and tolerated my bouncing ideas off of them. Without all your help, this would have never been completed.

A special thank you also goes to the wonderful and helpful people of Deer Lodge and Avon, Montana; the staff at the Montana Territorial Prison Museum, and those who make a living off the land on Three Mile Road.

To all the strangers who wander into our lives,
who touch our hearts, and change our souls.

CHAPTER 1

MAY 1935

The sharp ring of hammer striking steel filled the shed, echoing off the walls and roof. With each impact a tiny fragment of granite flew away from the large grey slab resting on the wooden frame. Even on the solemn day of its installation, Frank knew the gravestone would draw compliments. It was almost done.

The block had spent millions of years beneath the earth; it took only a day to free it. Frank and his father, Clay, quarried the slab themselves from a cliff seven miles north of Avon, Montana. Months of work, sweat, and steel had transformed the rock into a thing of beauty. Rough edges transitioned into a flat face, smoothed with the steady cuts of a brushing chisel. The surface now displayed words and ornate flora, befitting the woman whose grave it would mark.

Frank knew he did good work, but that was all that it was—work. The stone's real meaning was lost on its maker. His occasional stone carving commissions meant one thing: food and shoes for his wife and his father, and that at a time when the ranch was barely able to pay its yearly taxes to the state, as well as the loans at the bank.

Pausing, straightening his six-foot frame, Frank stretched his sore muscles, both knuckles and spine popping and crackling as he worked out the kinks. Hours of leaning over the granite head-stone had taken a toll. At that moment, Frank's three decades felt more like five. With a large horsehair brush, he made two sweeps across his work to clear away the larger bits of stone. He blew gently across it, ushering away the finer dust. A glimmering cloud formed in the sunlit doorway.

The chiseled letters on the six-hundred pound block were deep and would be visible for decades, if not centuries. But the subject of the stone's dedication, the departed wife and mother, was the last thing on Frank's mind. It was the rose that held his attention. If he felt a flash of pride, it was over this: the stone petals did appear as smooth and fine as the real thing. Frank's face hardened, and he pursed his lips as he looked for any remaining imperfection. He glanced at the detailed sketch he had made before starting and pondered whether to make a few more delicate taps on the leaves that flowed off the rose's stem but decided against it. In his mind, he heard his late mother's words: *If something is already beautiful, no point in trying to make it more so.*

Vivian was never one to compliment Frank's work, saying she was sure flattery would go to her son's head. She'd been a tough woman, as women needed to be if they coped well with life in a remote mountain valley. Still, Frank missed her. A year before, when Vivian was very ill, and they all knew she was not going to recover, she'd given firm directions to Frank. Her own stone was to have nothing but words and dates. He'd done that for her. The stone he was finishing today, for a Deer Lodge matriarch, was a far more elaborate affair.

The sound of heavy hooves and jingling harness penetrated the walls of the shed. Through the open door, Frank saw the two Belgian draft horses lumber by with his father Clay at the reins. The team pulled the flat bed wagon loaded with fresh cut lodge pole pines. A rare break in the spring rains allowed them to repair fences. That required new rails to replace the ones damaged by weather and livestock. The lodgepole pines were sturdy and straight; they'd fit the bill.

Frank didn't like letting his father fell trees alone, but the stone-carving had to get done. It was a busy time of year made more so by the stonework. They still had to feed the cattle, since frost and an occasional snowstorm visited their small ranch easily into June. Branding was done, but it would be a few more weeks before they turned the cattle out into the foothills to get fat on their own. Meanwhile, they completed the never-ending fence repairs whenever they could.

The stonework always came like spring rain—a little too much all at once, followed by none at all. For years, Ross Funeral Service in Deer Lodge had contacted Frank whenever they had extra orders that they could not fill, or when demand for his talents came their way from Butte or Helena. But with all the ranch management falling to Frank now, he could only hope to complete three or four stones a year. He might be able to do more if he had pneumatic tools like the high-end carvers did. Chisel and hammer were all he had, so that was what he used.

Regardless, this particular stone was complete. Content with his handiwork, Frank dusted and packed his tools and sketchpad into the covered box that kept them clean and dry. The tool set was a mix of well-used chisels, some of which Clay had pilfered back when he worked up at the mines. Most of the tools were a generous gift from an old Italian stonemason who had stopped in Avon after working on a building in Missoula.

Frank, only thirteen at the time, was waiting for his mother who was in the mercantile. Free to explore the town, he had dallied at the rail station and met the stonemason. The boy was fascinated by the thought of carving rock. The old man must have found his enthusiasm and questions heartening and gave the tool set to

Frank. He claimed the set was too worn for his purposes, and he didn't want to pack it all the way back to Chicago. When Frank showed the chisels to his mother, she assumed he had stolen them. Vivian dragged him back to the depot by his ear to return them, only to hear the stonemason repeat her son's own summary. She apologized to the man and, for the first time ever, to Frank as well.

Taking off his leather apron, Frank walked outside into the bright afternoon sunlight. He shielded his eyes with a callused hand, then focused on the hillside to the northwest of the homestead. A black shape a few hundred yards away caught his eye. A black bear, perhaps? There were one or two around, scavenging after the long winter hibernation, but the movement wasn't right. Almost a coyote's gait, but much larger than any he'd ever seen, and coyotes weren't black as coal. A wolf? There hadn't been a wolf in the region in more than twenty years. A dog, then. If so, it was a big one, and strays didn't usually wander into this valley. Ranchers would shoot them on sight if they were near their herds. Dogs were chicken killers and pests. There was little use for them unless you had sheep and one very well-trained canine.

Frank watched the animal, wondering where it came from. The dog stopped suddenly, as if it knew it was being watched. It turned and looked directly at Frank. Even with the distance between them, Frank felt the stare, the sensation that can only be experienced when looking directly into another creature's eyes.

"Frank, ya mind givin' me a hand?" Clay shouted. His father was struggling to get the team settled down so he could unhook them from the wagon. Frank walked across the farmyard to help, looking briefly back toward the dog. Nothing but empty field. The dog must have disappeared into the timber. Frank rubbed the ever-present stubble on his chin. He thought nothing more of it and began helping his father.

"How'd they do?" he asked as he grabbed the halters of both horses to calm them. They'd owned the team only a few weeks, and they still occasionally acted like they weren't accustomed to regular work.

"Well enough, I suppose," Clay said, adjusting his hat and wiping his brow with a plaid handkerchief. "David was actin' like the laziest damned horse I ever seen."

Clay unhooked the long wooden tongue that connected the horses to the wagon. He lowered it to the ground, maneuvering around the animals and equipment by instinct and sheer muscle memory. With the horses free from the wagon, the two men led them into the barn to remove their tack. Clay was taller than his son but had a gentler look about him. Though Frank could recall a time when his father had been a steely fellow, short tempered at home and with other workers at the mines. That had been Clay's solution to dealing with their too-small ranch—he worked for years at the numerous silver and gold mines at the head of Ophir Creek, just up the road from their place.

"It's no wonder Goliath is as strong as he is," Clay said petting the horse. "David slacked in the tugs a bit more than usual even for him. My arm's sore from havin' to smack him on the ass with the reins." Clay rubbed his left shoulder and laughed. But Frank grimaced at his father's assessment, concerned about having an uneven team. The two Belgian draft horses had cost nearly every spare penny they had after their last draft team got too old to pull. These new ones were Frank and Clay's main work force. Back east, some farms had tractors now—if they still had land that yielded during such dry years—but everyone in this region still relied on horse and mule.

The great neck yoke and huge leather collars still needed to be removed. Clay slipped the large metal hames off the collar, leaving them resting on David's shoulders and still attached to the harness. Stretching over his head, Clay unlatched the buckle at the top of the collar to remove it from David. He handed the collar to Frank to hang it in the tack room. Coming back, Frank watched his father pet the horse. The animal looked back with large deer fawn eyes.

"They worked fine before, might be a little peaked is all," Clay said, back paddling a little. He'd likely picked up on Frank's silence, the undertow of concern. "Sure is a prince; I swear this horse knows he's good looking."

"Pretty won't cut it here," Frank grumbled as he removed Goliath's collar. His father's newfound compassion for the animals was more frustrating than the horse's poor work ethic. Clay hadn't always been this way. He used to whip horses mercilessly when they didn't do what he wanted. Frank inhabited a sensible middle ground: he was not unkind to livestock, but did regard them as tools. His father had taught him that long ago. It was still a true assessment. Wealthy folks in New York might have pets, but animals here needed to earn their keep. That wasn't a merciless sentiment; it was the nature of things. If they didn't work hard—if everyone didn't work hard—there would be no food. "We can't feed anything that doesn't earn its keep," Frank said as he pulled the last of the harness off Goliath, its tangled mass resting on Frank's shoulder. Clay did not reply, but Frank heard him whisper something to the horse. In a tenuous silence, his father removed and hung up David's harness and began grooming the animal.

Frank followed suit, putting away Goliath's harness and brushing down the larger of the two horses. He stewed as he worked. He considered himself a decent man. If he ever raised his voice, which was rare, he had damn good reason. He wanted to shout at his father at that moment, but he didn't. It was still impossible to argue with him anyway; that much had never changed. The men led the animals to the side corral just off the barn.

Clay spoke once more, obviously trying to soften his son's concerns. "I might a been exaggerating a bit," he said. "David ain't crow bait. Give 'em some time; I know they'll be a cracker-jack team. Besides, we can't afford another." He paused only long enough to let Frank assess this as his final word on the matter. Then he asked if the headstone was complete.

"Yeah, the rose was tough," Frank said. "But it looks nice. I'm sure that they'll be happy with it."

"After a fashion I suppose, given the circumstances. Did you know Marge?"

"Why?" Frank gave him a confused look. He poured out a scoop of grain for the horses. Even a benign topic could turn tricky with his father at the helm. "I think I met her once at one of Mother's Ladies' Aid Society socials; can't say I knew her."

"Nice gal, used to play cards with your mother," Clay said. Frank ignored this. The stone was a stone; it wasn't the person. Clay asked if they needed to deliver the slab to the cemetery.

"No," Frank said, grateful to discuss something entirely practical. He explained that John, one of their neighbors, had to drive to Deer Lodge the next day. John had a truck and was happy to haul the stone in for them. Though Clay had a '29 Ford sedan, the car certainly wasn't suited for hauling the large headstone. They hoped to afford a truck someday. For now, the car, the horses, and the generosity of their neighbors would have to do.

"Just gotta brace it so it don't crack," Clay said and chuckled. Frank had to agree with that observation; John had a habit of taking turns and bumps too fast. Earlier disagreement set aside, the men took care of a few final chores in amicable silence. Horses groomed, fed and watered, both men looked up when they heard Abby's voice calling from the house.

"Frank, Clay—you get washed up for supper now." She brushed her long brown hair aside from her face. Frank gave his wife a curt nod. He watched her pull a few shirts off the clothesline, then walk back into the house. The clothes basket was almost as big as she was. They had married the day after her eighteenth birthday, almost five years ago. Abby was still lovely, still a fine individual. Really, everything would be easier if she'd been unfaithful or contentious. She was neither of those things. So, it was strange how he found himself unable to conjure up an ounce of what he'd felt when they married.

Frank regarded women as intelligent; he thought well of allowing them to vote. There was no thinking otherwise with Vivian as his mother, and this was agreeable so long as women understood the order of things, that men were by virtue of their minds and physical form, better suited for certain work and certain decisions. Abby respected that notion as far as Frank could tell. She was a good wife, a fine cook, and she worked as hard as any man during branding and haying in the summer and cattle driving in the autumn.

There was just one flaw, one burdensome fact they never spoke of, but its weight now clouded every look, every conversation. In Frank's landscape, marriage presupposed family. As was the case for many modern couples, they'd married out of affection. But Frank married equally for the continuation of the ranch. Everyone in the valley questioned why he had no children, just as they had questioned why Clay and Vivian had had only two—Frank and a sister who died in infancy. The hope of any ranch was in generations. As it was, there would be no one to care for the Redmonds' land within another thirty years. Hell, there would be no one to care for him and Abby, in the way that Frank had cared for his own mother as she passed, in the way that he completed the work of two men on days when his father grew tired. It was not, in Frank's mind, unkind to regard Abby as inadequate. It was pragmatism.

The duel in his mind was murky, for as much as the land demanded stewardship, the land also demanded that a man regard the spoken word as solid as any written contract. An oath was the one thing that a fellow could give and keep at the same time. Frank had vowed to care for Abby. This too was paramount. So, he cared for her, but without heart. They were hardly lovers; they were workmates, as dull in conversation as a pair of hired hands. He took from her, at times, only what he needed. She did not begrudge him that. She was a good wife. That was what made his present thoughts so grinding.

The horses cared for, Clay headed in first to wash up. Frank stopped at the screened porch that jutted out from the two-story double-plank house. He felt uneasy, like he'd forgotten something, or like someone was watching him. There was nothing on the hillside where he had seen the dog earlier. It must have headed south towards more populated areas. He shook off the feeling, then went inside.

The smell of stew and fresh baked bread greeted him. Abby was pulling a loaf from the big black Monarch wood stove—the hulking heart of the plaster-walled kitchen. Her stained apron wrapped around the pan to protect her hands, she flipped the loaf onto the cutting board. With a quick shake, the loaf popped out of the pan. She wiped her hands on the apron, then smoothed it out over her faded blue-checked dress. Silent, she carried on with her tasks while Frank washed up. He dipped his hands into one of the two water buckets on the counter top and rubbed them together. Store bought soap was a luxury; he used very little to get the day's grime removed. After drying his hands on a threadbare towel, he took a metal dipper from the second water bucket and took a drink.

Frank sat down with his father and wife and waited. For years, he'd known he was outnumbered on the matter of whether a hypothetical deity might require their acknowledgment at every evening meal. He respected that Abby would defy any creature over three topics dear to her heart: the existence of one overly-involved God, the welfare of her saddle horse Jane, and any happening within the boundaries of her kitchen. Supper prayers overlapped both topics one and three; Frank was careful to avoid conflict on the matter.

Abby leaned over the Dutch oven sitting in the middle of the table. She dished out a steaming bowl of stew for each of them, then bowed her head and whispered a short prayer of thanks. Frank politely abstained when Clay and Abby said their amens. If praying brought Abby some small pleasure, he would not take that away. The food was good; Frank recognized that much, in gratitude to Abby.

"Did you finish the new stone?" Abby inquired as they began to eat. Frank knew she had been alone most of the day caring for tasks in the house and barn: collecting eggs, feeding chickens, and the constant cooking and washing. Talking was the last thing Frank wanted to do during dinner, his mind mainly on all the work yet undone. He answered her, though, knowing that Abby's days were very solitary, and that she craved the conversation.

He told her it was complete, that it looked fine, then nodded at Clay and added, "That was my last slab; we'll need to head up to the quarry in the next few days and get another down here while we have time." The three discussed this plan and commented on all the equipment that needed maintenance and when they might run the fence line together to make repairs. It was businesslike conversation, but peaceful enough.

That night, as the sun dropped behind the Garnet Range, the trio retreated into sleep. Frank drifted off thinking he smelled rain in the air. The fragrance was only a taunt. The clouds forming over the mountains passed by without leaving a drop. Hot, dry days were coming.

He felt Abby get up first. The windup alarm clock on their small dresser was rarely necessary. Abby woke on her own at five most mornings. As usual, Frank stayed in bed a while longer, knowing that this was the time Abby took to read. There was one great advantage of raising beef cattle: they didn't require four o'clock milking. Frank tried to go back to sleep but couldn't, his senses now awake. The sound of the porch door opening and closing told him that Abby had gone to the outhouse, and the same sounds announced her return a couple minutes later. He heard the creak of Vivian's old rocking chair as Abby sat down. She was reading. Perhaps Thoreau or the Bible or Emily Dickinson.

Frank had always marveled at the little shelf filled with her books. There were at least a dozen from her girlhood and a few precious ones that were more recent gifts. Frank could read, but he saw little use for the skill. Did reading help him brand this year's calves? Would it help him mend a fence line? One day, in their first year together, Abby herself had admitted that the book called *Walden* had not prepared her at all for a life as remote as theirs.

"Why read it then?" Frank asked. "And why read a book by some dead woman poet?"

He'd never forget Abby's reply. "So I don't forget how to speak English."

"None of those books have regular English in them."

"Precisely," she said.

She was the educated one, the girl who had moved West with her parents when she was fourteen. If she hadn't married Frank, she would have become a schoolteacher. She never lorded this over him, though he teased her once for having some preconceptions about rural folk. "I may not be book smart," he drawled. "But I ain't no hayseed either; I can read. I just know a better use for a newspaper when I'm done with it." She laughed. She called him witty and sweet back then.

The rocking chair creaked, and the old clock downstairs ticked away, both counting off time till Frank knew he had to leave the warm bed and start another day. Soon the rhythmic creak of the chair ceased. There was a clatter from the cast iron pan on the stove, the smell of coffee. He rose then, switched the alarm clock off before it could ring, wound it and set it back on the dresser, donned his trousers and suspenders. Downstairs, Frank and Abby regarded each other with polite nonchalance as they completed their respective morning chores. It was too early in the day to talk. But Clay had a way of disrupting the perfectly functional wordless truce.

"Good morning, everyone!" he declared as he came downstairs. Frank looked up from his coffee, raised his eyebrows.

"Good morning, Clay," Abby said. She smiled at him, always more likely to cater to the old man's moods. "You're sure chipper this morning."

"Well, I'm not buzzard food yet," Clay said. "So that makes for a great start." Clay adjusted his suspenders and headed out to care for his morning ablutions.

Abby filled the tin plates with eggs, bacon, and diced fried potatoes. With a subdued thank you, Frank accepted his plate and ate. For whatever reason, prayers were not required at the morning meal. Thank God, indeed. He could feel Abby's eyes on him, but Frank maintained a solid stare at his breakfast.

Right then, mid-bite, he realized he wanted to leave. He'd never considered it quite so clearly. There it was. Clay sat down with them, and the old man and Abby chattered away. Frank heard their voices but none of their words. They talked. They chewed. Silverware clattered. Frank could hear only what had become a chant in his mind: *Got to leave, got to leave.* How could he? Impossible. For now he had to settle for the coming day of working outside, free from the confines of the tiny house. But the leaving he needed was much more than departure for a day of work about the ranch. *Got to leave.* The sheer distance he needed was as broad and permanent as his certainty. It was time.

After breakfast, Frank worked hard and fast, grinding away at every task as if his effort could drown out the restlessness. He and his father unloaded the lodgepole rails from the wagon, fed the cattle, tended the pigs, turned out David and Goliath and the ten saddle horses into the corral next to the barn. *Got to leave.* Frank had sensible, justifiable reason to divorce Abby. But how could he abandon his father? Yet the thought was incessant. He had to run, and far.

The sun was climbing high over the continental divide, and it quickly burned off the morning's frost. The day grew hot, more than normal for late May. Frank and Clay were thankful that they had unloaded the fence rails earlier. The heat this early in the year concerned them both. In their little corner of the world it was common to have snow storms all the way into June. They'd had rain this year, but the snow was fast melting from the high peaks. Stories of drought across the nation and massive dust storms weighed on the minds of everyone who lived off the land.

The fence rails unloaded and the animals fed, the two men retreated to the equipment shed to dismantle and clean the sickle mower. They needed to find out if any parts needed replacing prior to haying season. The equipment shed's plank siding had plenty of gaps, so the light breeze blew freely through the walls, providing some relief from the heat. In the shadows of the steep-pitched roof, the men maneuvered carefully around the dormant machinery. Frank could say one thing for the task: it demanded his entire attention. That was a welcome respite.

After a few minutes of puttering, he determined that they needed to replace several of the cutting blades. One of the connecting rods that drove the sickle bar was also cracked. That was an unexpected find. They'd have to take the rod into Avon to see if the local blacksmith could repair it. If not, they'd need a replacement from the regional equipment dealer. It was yet another cost that they could not afford. Frank looked at the cracked connecting rod, then at his father. The old man whistled then muttered, "Shee-it." Frank grunted his agreement. The two rallied and decided that, for the moment, they needed to sharpen the blades that were still decent and install replacements from their own inventory. They could do that much themselves.

It was about noon when John Fredrick stopped by with his flat bed truck. The man was a flamboyant presence wherever he went. He announced his arrival from the top of the drive, blaring his horn and swinging his hat out the window. John and his family lived up the road about a mile. Like Clay, John had got his start working at the mines up Ophir Creek back before they closed in the twenties. Nowadays, John was a jack-of-all-trades, nabbing every day laborer job he could find, from working on the logging crew for the railroad, to acting as foreman for all the new construction work on the highway. He and his wife Patty had ranchland as well, but, like the Redmonds, struggled to pull all the sustenance they required out of the land alone. After all, they had four children to feed.

John's odd jobs had provided for them well enough; he had paid cash for that '29 Ford. Being one of the few people along the road to have a truck, he was popular, even though his personality was irritating to most. Frank liked the man, though. He counted John a good friend even if he was loud, maybe even because he was so boisterous. Frank didn't like to speak, but John did. That made for easy conversation. Put a nickel in John and let the show begin—the man didn't care if all you did was nod and laugh from time to time. Even if John got rowdy down at the Avon bar now and again, he was a decent man, a hard worker who was gone on jobs for weeks at a time. And here he was, ready to help with the stone whether he got paid for it or not.

Using a skid frame, the three men muscled the finished headstone onto the flatbed and strapped it down tight. Frank gave John the connecting rod from the sickle mower as well. Sure, John was happy to drop it off with the Avon smithy. "Thanks. Take it slow," Frank said. "If you can." His words were drowned out by the engine. John honked the horn a couple times and waved his hat as he pulled out of the gate at the end of the drive. Dirt kicked up as the heavy truck struggled in a patch of loose gravel. John's laughter carried over the ruckus.

Abby had been standing on the porch watching. Frank noticed her shake her head and sigh as she headed back into the house. He knew she was thankful for John's help, but didn't care much for his reckless character. Usually, her disdain for John didn't bother Frank, but it did right then. *Got to leave.*

Frank and Clay returned to their work on the sickle blades. They had already removed the bar and popped the rivets that held the blades, then begun sharpening or replacing each blade as needed. For over an hour, they carried on with that task. Clay seemed to be getting tired, though the old man would never admit it. Taking a break, he stepped out of the shed. He stood in the bright sunlight of the barnyard, hands on his hips, stretching. Frank watched his father for a moment, then returned to his work. He stopped when he heard Clay speak to someone outside.

"Well, hello there, stranger. Where'd you come from?"

Frank immediately feared that railroad tramps had wandered up to their place looking for an easy road stake. He wouldn't put it past his father to treat such folk with more hospitality than was wise. Not taking chances, Frank clasped a hammer and stepped outside. No hobos. Instead it was a large black dog with a few patchwork tan markings, a splash of white on its chest. The beast sat between the house and the shed, panting steadily in the bright sunshine. Frank's first instinct was to grab the shotgun. He started toward the house, but Clay reached out and touched his arm.

"Hold on, son," his father's words were calm. "Don't think this boy's gonna cause trouble." Indeed, the dog was ignoring the chickens not twenty feet away. He also displayed no intention of attacking one of the barn cats who glared at him from under a stack of scrap lumber. The dog glanced at the cat and then returned his attention to Clay and Frank. For several tense seconds, the three held their ground, sizing each other up. It was the biggest dog Frank had ever seen, as big as a two-week old calf. The mongrel's long shaggy hair made him look larger still. The winter coat was shedding out, giving the beast a ragged appearance.

Frank had no doubt that it was the same dog he had seen the day before. Standing this close, the gaze from the dog's brown eyes was even more powerful. Despite his scruffy coat, the dog had a calm confidence, almost a regal posture, neither fearful nor threatening. Regardless, Frank had never trusted dogs—both for their reputation as chicken thieves and also for the fact that he had been bitten by one when he was a boy. He still carried the scar on his left hand. To Frank, dogs were unpredictable creatures with large fangs—a combination best avoided whenever possible.

"Must be the dog I saw yesterday when you got back from cuttin' poles," Frank said.

"You saw him. Where at?"

Frank pointed to the hillside, not taking his eye off the dog, "Didn't think much of it."

Frank groaned when Clay made the first move of friendship. "Ya thirsty boy?" his father asked and walked towards the hand pump by the barn. The dog cocked his head to one side and wagged his bushy tail, raising the dust around him. "Come on, you look hot."

The hand pump by the barn was fed from a deep cistern next to it. The top of the cistern was covered by thick wooden planks, with a section of fence around it to ensure no animals could fall in. It took about twenty cycles of the pump handle before water started to flow into the stone and cement trough. The dog observed from a few paces away as Clay took one of the buckets hanging on the fence, filled it, and set it down on the ground. Clay's guest walked up to the bucket without a fear in the world and began to drink. The animal seemed to be little threat, but all of Frank's instincts said to get rid of it, either by intimidation or shotgun. The old man wouldn't stand for that though. Frank could only hope the mongrel was passing through, long gone in a day or two.

After drinking his fill, the dog trotted towards the road, stopping to sniff one of the gate posts and lift his leg on it. He finished the job with two quick scratches with his hind legs, flinging grass and dirt into the air. Without a backward glance, he trotted on down the road.

"Didn't even bother to leave us a tip," Clay said, shrugging his shoulders. Too hot, too tired to debate the matter, Frank followed his father back to the shed. As they crossed the yard, he looked towards the house. It seemed that Abby hadn't seen the visitor, and he was content with not telling her.

CHAPTER 2

MAY 1935

Stepping into the morning air, Clay surveyed the mist hanging over the lower portions of the valley. A thick layer of frost blanketed the ground, and Clay's breath lingered briefly in a silver cloud. He buttoned up the heavy black canvas coat to fend off the cold. The frost and mist didn't concern him though. The sun's rays would melt both within minutes of touching the land. The road to the quarry would be dry by the time he and Frank got the team hooked up and the cattle fed. Spending a day up the mountain breaking out granite slabs was a nice change from the routine of ranch work. Even with the demanding labor involved, Clay enjoyed trips to the quarry.

Frank came out of the house, and the two headed to the barn to get David and Goliath ready for the day. As they walked, Clay looked northward to the twenty-foot tall fir up the hill, at the grave that lay beneath the tree's branches. It had been just over a year since Vivian had passed away, and the pain was still keen. Instead of burying her up at the Blackfoot City cemetery up the mountain or down in Avon, Clay insisted that Vivian remain close by. Though graves were only to be inside state recognized cemeteries, a few dollars in the right pocket turned the necessary heads. Now

Vivian's spot on the hill was deemed part of the Blackfoot City cemetery even if it was technically half-a-mile away. It was hard to say which was worse, her passing, or how she'd struggled in the years before. For almost three years she was ill—pneumonia most of the time, always with the first rains or first snow. Every trip to Deer Lodge or Helena, each stay in a hospital and every doctor appointment drained their limited funds—and what little hope they still held for her complete recovery. The financial hardship seemed to mock the family's grief, a little salt in their wounds. Within a month of each other, Clay lost his wife and then lost the last of their savings when the bank in Deer Lodge went under. Then cattle prices collapsed. All this sadness in the past year, and yet Clay found himself nursing the smallest, most delicate hope this spring.

He felt more like laughing than crying over it all. Vivian's death told him of his own brevity. And rather than find that brevity unkind, he had begun to wear it lightly, found it reason to disregard the hell-holes that all the banks were falling into. None of it mattered. So... why worry about the land, the ranch's loans, the nasty creditors? The whole mess of them, they were all gonna die someday too. The ranch would probably die. Though the land would live on. Death was a fine and soothing consolation that all the frightening hardship would cease. It had to.

But Frank saw his mother pass and took it as reason to worry more, which gave Clay his one and only worry now: *his son*. Clay knew that Frank could not understand why his father did not live in fear. Clay knew what Frank thought of his old man. He thought his dad was slipping off the rails. Funny. Clay felt more sane and content than ever.

He hadn't yet told the boy in plain speech what he found so obvious. To grow the ranch's income, to thrive, they needed to lease or buy more land. But all of the good parcels in the valley were taken. It was mathematics then. There would be a time when they couldn't afford to stay. That was the answer. The answer was not to work harder. They'd done that. Were still doing that. The answer was that they could not stay. The question was how to get Frank to see that fact.

Clay looked at his son, at Vivian's grave, at his son again. Frank seemed heavy with even more than that lately. More than the creditors. More than the fact that neither man would not humble himself to accept government assistance, or the fact that refusing such assistance likely destined them to selling. No, his son was stewing about something more. Clay's boy was angry.

Looking once more at the grave, Clay didn't think anymore of money. Or of Frank. He thought of Vivian, and doing everything he could to stay close to her for as long as he could. Then he set his mind solely on the task at hand: getting the draft horse team ready for a long day up the mountain.

It took half an hour to get the team hooked up and ready to go. Clay stood on the wagon and watched as Abby came out of the house. She handed Frank a tin bucket with a cloth towel tucked into it, covering their lunch, along with a tea kettle and two metal mugs. Having had Vivian to mentor her for a few years, Abby always packed the lunch with bare necessities plus a little something extra. The natural spring up at the quarry provided fine drinking water. It was a small and much appreciated luxury to have the fixings for tea as well. Coffee was reserved for mornings and when company came over. Tea was cheap, and Abby made sure to keep a good stock on hand.

Goliath stomped impatiently. Clay gave him a soft whoa, tightened his grip on the reins, and looked at Frank. The exchange between his son and daughter-in-law consisted of a brief and perfunctory transfer of the lunch bucket. Not a word, not a single touch. So that was it. The kid wanted out. Frank seemed to think he could hide it, but he never had a poker face. Bet Abby could tell. Yeah, she could tell. The girl looked so sad.

Clay shook his head in frustration. In his thirty-three years with Vivian, they'd had their share of grievances, but these were quickly resolved. It hurt Clay to see Frank and Abby continue to grow more and more silent. They didn't hurl cruelty at each other, at least not to Clay's knowledge, but they'd sure developed a knack for a steady and controlled indifference. Seemed that could be more dangerous. Frank accepted the lunch tin and turned away. He hopped onto the wagon and stashed the lunch tin under the seat. With a crack of the reins, the flatbed lurched forward, thick leather tugs tightening. They were off.

It had been such a relief when Frank married. For a while, Clay and Vivian had wondered if their boy would ever find a sweetheart. He was a good kid, never took to drinking or fighting. But in some ways, the boy was troubling for how little trouble he caused. Frank was a loner. Of course it was easy to be that way in this country, but the boy focused so hard on work, whatever task you set him to, he rarely spoke with anyone other than his parents. In what little spare time he had, Frank spent it drawing in a sketch pad Vivian had given him for Christmas or carving figures and reliefs, scenes and scrollwork, out of any stone he could find. Clay about near gave up on Frank being sociable at all. Abby changed that, at least for a while.

Clay drove the team toward the lower pasture. After feeding a load of hay to the cattle there, they headed out on the two-track leading to the quarry. It was a familiar road. The quarry was one of the few perks of their particular acreage. Back in the 1800s, a dozen or so mines sprang up in the area. Granite blocks from this quarry were used as foundation stones for bridges and other railroad structures to service the mines. The quarry had been short-lived, as more convenient sources were found and railroad construction diminished. It had been abandoned with little warning, exposed granite left with drill holes in the ledges and freshly broken slabs still on the ground. What a find for a budding stone carver. The quarry gave Frank his start at gravestone carving. He was only 17 when he carved his first stone for a family friend. Word about Frank's ability spread fast, and the carving became a critical source of income even before Ross Funeral Services began hiring him. Frank carved those stones, kept his family alive, and honored the dead. It was beyond Clay's fathoming how that honorable young man became the sulking brooder now seated next to him.

The quarry road branched north off the main track up to Blackfoot City, a remnant town near the last mine to close in their valley. That mine had kept Clay and Vivian alive when they first arrived in Montana. They'd traveled there from Minnesota shortly after their marriage, sparkly-eyed and naïve with their plan to run a ranch of their own. It was tight scrounging for years, with Clay working at the Ophir Creek mines, until they were able to purchase the parcel of railroad land at the mouth of Illinois Gulch. They were late-comers to the valley compared to some of the other families, but they hunkered down and made it their home. When the gold ran out, the valley reverted to quiet ranch land. The miners moved on in pursuit of gold and other elusive minerals, leaving the marks of their pillage. Even along the remote quarry road, there were waste rock piles at smaller mines along the creek. The dredge tailings were evident along every waterway, all the way down to Avon.

Clay was happy to leave the mining life and root himself in one place. Miners moved on, but ranchers viewed themselves as the land's stewards. Aside from the mine waste, the only other trace left of the miners was Blackfoot City. The almost ghost town was once the location of the first post office in the county. Now only a few people lived there in the rundown buildings still standing, subsisting off of small gardens and piss-poor gold panning. The burg had burned down three times over its short life as a mining town. The last time was just after Clay moved there in 1912. Coming from an Irish family, Clay had blended into the mixed pot of humanity that toiled there while the mine was still running. Aside from a few clap-trap buildings, the Blackfoot City cemetery on the hill was the only permanent reminder of the once booming town.

Though not steep, the path up to the quarry took a good thirty minutes by wagon, the road winding its way up the side of the mountain. Their journey ended at a flat area where an exposed granite outcrop jutted out of a bunchgrass meadow. Unhooking the team from the wagon, Clay walked them over to the makeshift corral that he and Frank had built years ago so they wouldn't have to leave the horses hooked to the wagon all day. They would use the horses later to hoist the slabs up onto the skid sleds that would drag behind the wagon. The stones' weight and the downhill road were too much for the horses to control, given that the brakes on the wagon were marginal. Better to let the friction of the ground and wooden skids limit the speed of their descent.

As Clay walked back from the corral, he saw Frank pull the tools they needed from the back of the wagon. As they walked to-gether, Frank talked about what he wanted to accomplish during the day. The trip up to the quarry had been silent. It was good to chat with the kid, even if it was only to discuss how to wedge the next stone slab. The two climbed a footpath up along the granite ledge, returning to the spot where they had worked last autumn. There were already half a dozen holes cut into the rock in a line running almost a foot back from the front face of the ledge. Frank wanted at least another dozen holes before they started driving the wedges into the rock to force off the slab.

Soon the quarry rang with the sound of hammer on steel as they took turns, one holding the plug drill, and the other striking it with the hammer. It was an action of pure trust, as one missed swing would result in a crushed hand or worse. After three hours they had the holes Frank wanted. Placing feather wedges in the holes, they made a single strike on each one, going down the line and then back up again, over and over. Slowly the pressure on the rock grew till a slab about eight feet by three feet by eight inches thick split off and fell to the ground with a resonant thud.

Well over three thousand pounds as it was, the slab needed to be broken into manageable-sized pieces. Then the horses could drag what was immediately needed onto the skid. The remainder could be hauled on another trip. They decided to wait until after lunch to split the slab and drill more holes in preparation for the next visit. They were hungry.

Clay built a small fire near the wagon to boil water for tea, then sat down in the shade of the flatbed to rest. He took off his drab tan hat, revealing a mop of white hair matted with sweat. While tending the fire, he spoke with Frank about ranch business. Should've been easy topics for the kid, but he seemed distracted, staring out over the valley and losing track of the conversation. Clay was about to confront him head on, ask him plain about Abby, when Goliath whinnied in alarm. Both men looked at the horses, then followed the direction of the animals' anxious gaze. On the road, trotting at a relaxed pace with his tongue lolling out, came the black and tan dog from the day before.

Ignoring the two men and their small fire, the pup headed straight towards the spring and started drinking. Both men and horses watched as the dog took three licks of water, paused for a second, and then took another three laps, repeating the movement till his thirst was quenched. Licking his chops, the dog looked at Clay and then walked towards him, stopping in a patch of shade at the end of the wagon.

"Ya lost, stranger, or ya just passing through again?" Clay asked. Where had this dog come from? How had he survived the winter?

"Think it's one of the Price dogs?" Frank asked. He took a sip of his tea and continued to ponder out loud. "Don't think it's Quigley's, they only got one, and I know he ain't the Grangers'. Maybe the Hart boy picked him up at the hobo jungle by the rail stop."

Yeah, Frank had no poker face at all. The only time the kid spoke at length was when he was nervous or scared as hell. Might be both this time. Frank really didn't care for dogs. Clay acknowledged Frank's suppositions. He shook his head in uncertainty. "Might belonged to one of the squatters at Blackfoot," Clay said and rubbed his chin. "Looks a bit thin though, I suspect he's been ranging as a loner for a while."

Clay tore off a chunk of his sandwich. "Ya hungry, boy?" The dog tilted his head and sniffed at the prospect: a bite of homemade bread holding several slices of roast beef along with a good helping of hand-churned butter. Careful, hesitating, the dog approached Clay's outstretched hand.

"Watch yourself, might be rabid," Frank warned Clay as the dog closed the distance. The mutt paused just long enough to sniff the offering before making a quick but gentle grab at the food, swallowing it whole.

"Didn't even bother to taste it, did ya?" Clay smiled at the dog, then turned to Frank. "Ain't worried, don't look like a bone cleaner to me, just a stranger scrounging. Anyhow, the Good Book says we're to feed the hungry." He tore off another chunk and handed it to the dog. This time he didn't pause but took the food willingly, shaking, grateful in a starved canine way. Clay offered the last of his sandwich after taking another bite himself.

"Don't think God was talkin' about some mongrel," Frank said. "If ya complain about being hungry later, won't get no sympathy from me."

Frank's face grew red as he spoke. He was clearly not done grousing about the dog.

"We don't need another mouth to feed, especially a useless mongrel," Frank said and threw a small stick into the fire to emphasize his point.

"Didn't say I was planning on taking him in," Clay said. Though now that he thought of it, the idea grew on him. A dog could help with cattle-moving, might be nice company too. He reached out his hand and scratched the dog behind his right ear. The pup moved closer to his food source. He seemed more than willing to spend some time with them now. "We ain't flush, but we're getting three squares a day. A few scraps won't break us," Clay said, getting a little pleasure at goading Frank on.

"You fed the thing! Now, it'll follow us back!"

The kid was out of line. Clay went for the jugular. "Last time I checked, my name's on the deed," he said, smooth and sweet, but he looked Frank in the eye. "If this pup wants to stick around, then we're gonna have ourselves a dog."

Father and son glared at one another across the campfire. Smoke from the crackling embers climbed slowly skyward. Frank took the last gulp of his tea and tossed the tin mug back into the lunch bucket. He stood up, but never changed his gaze.

"If he stays, he's your problem," he said. "And if that mongrel raises a lip towards anyone or anything, he's dead!"

Clay and the dog watched Frank walk away toward the granite slab. Clay let the threat slide. His son only threw fits when it was pretty clear he'd lost an argument. Petting the dog, Clay recalled an incident back when he was living amongst miners. He had once embraced a very callous, almost malicious attitude toward animals. The adage was: Never show kindness to a horse or dog, as they will just as soon turn around and kill you if given the chance. Being young and wanting to impress the other miners, Clay took on that attitude and held it till one unfortunate day.

There was a man whom Clay worked with often and considered a friend. The fellow lost his temper during an argument with a mine foreman. Instead of walking it off, he hurled his anger at the first creature he saw: an old bitch dog that had been living off boomtown scraps for a while. Clay knew folks had been feeding her. He hadn't paid her much mind till his friend unleashed his rage on her. A kick to the ribs sent the dog sprawling

to the ground. Clay could not forget her yelp at the first impact, the whines and cries as the man repeatedly kicked her. The
urge to save the poor mutt was certainly just as strong as if the
victim had been human. Without any thought or deliberation,
Clay rushed over to the man, spun him around, and landed a fist
square on his nose. The fellow never spoke to him again, and
Clay felt little loss over that. Looking down at the injured mutt,
Clay had felt empathy for an animal for the first time. Taking his
coat off, he wrapped it around the dog and picked her up and
carried her to the small cabin he rented with Vivian. They tried
their best to tend the dog, but she passed away during the night.
Clay sat on the floor next to her, petting her softly as she took her
last breath.

It felt much better to pet a dog that seemed happy and well,
even if a bit scrawny. "Don't worry about him," Clay said to the
dog, jutting his chin in Frank's direction. "He gets grumpy sometimes." The dog leaned into his hands, clearly enjoying the affection. So then, the pup wasn't motivated solely by food. Clay gave
the dog a final ear scratch, then got up to help Frank partition
the giant slab. The dog crawled under the wagon to sleep in the
shade.

The argument didn't come up again as Clay and Frank labored.
That was how they were, father and son. They might have their
heated moments, but the ranch demanded that they drop whatever bone they were chewing, drop it and get back to work. It was
a truce strapped together by single-word task-related commands.
Wait. Now. Lift. Here. Once more. The tension was still thick.

It was near evening when the slab was finally broken up into
manageable chunks, three of which were cinched onto the skid
sled. With sunset approaching, they only had time to drill a few
more holes in the granite ledge before quitting. Once done with
that final task, they loaded up the tools, and hooked up the horses. The dog was sniffing one of the slabs when the team's first

trudging steps jerked it forward. The sudden movement startled him. With a jump back and a deep bark, the dog watched as the wooden skids slid across the dirt, leaving two parallel trails of furrowed earth. After his initial fright, he regained his composure and trotted alongside the wagon on the long road home. Clay laughed at the dog's antics; Frank stared straight ahead. The horses continued their long, slow stone-dragging trip down.

Clay allowed the silence his son seemed to require, but he spoke once as they made the final turn onto their drive. "Son, Abby's a fine woman," he said. Frank stared at him with a look of confused derision. *That's right, kid, your old man's off his rocker. Go ahead and entertain that notion.* "Just thinking of what a nice sandwich she made," he added for good measure. Frank made no reply, and Clay was fine with that.

Back at the ranch, the men stopped at the stone shed, untied the skid, then moved the wagon to the barn to unhitch the horses. As they tended the team, Clay kept an eye on the dog. The mutt trotted to the horse trough to get a drink, then wandered over to the corral to sniff noses with the saddle horses.

The draft team cared for, Clay and Frank headed to the house just as Abby stepped out onto the porch to greet them. Likely about to inform them of a supper kept warm in the wood stove, she opened her mouth then stopped. She'd seen the dog trotting off behind the equipment shed.

"Whose dog is that?" she asked. She held the door open for the men, while looking past them in the direction of the shed.

"According to Clay, it's ours," Frank said.

So, to Frank he was "Clay" now, not Dad or Pop or Old Man. Clay smiled to himself. Them were fighting words.

"Ours? How'd that happen?"

Clay described their encounters with the dog, while Frank stomped inside and washed up. "Figure if he's here come morning, he's ours."

"Let's hope he's long gone tomorrow then," Frank called from the kitchen sink.

Abby dished out food as the men sat down. "A dog might be nice to have around," she said, obviously warming up to the idea. "At least we would know if someone was—"

The dog's barking interrupted Abby in a first-rate case in point. All three of them went to the window and saw John's flatbed truck still far off in the distance. They returned to the table and gulped a few bites of their meals, knowing dinner would be neatly suspended once John arrived. At least he spared the horn-honking showmanship when it was this late at night. The truck rolled to a stop in front of the house.

Clay stepped out to the screen porch with Abby and Frank following. They watched the dog circle the truck, intimidating barks making it very clear to John that getting out would be done at his own risk.

"See what I mean," Abby said to Frank with a smile.

Frank charged at the animal. "Go on, dog!" he shouted. "Get!" The beast stopped barking and backed off, but remained watchful. John stepped out of the truck and kept the dog in the corner of his eye as he shook hands with the men and tipped his floppy-brimmed black hat to Abby. The fellow did his best to stay on Abby's good side. Everyone knew that Abby was dear friends with John's wife Patricia. Everyone also knew that Patty once hit John on the head with a frying pan when he came home from the Stockman Bar painfully drunk and with a trace of lipstick on his face. Who knew what other stories the women shared with each other?

"When did ya get a dog?" John asked. He tucked his thumbs under his brown suspenders that held up his baggy pants. That and a shirt that was one size too large, gave him the appearance of a scarecrow in desperate need of more straw.

"It seems today," Frank said. "He's a stray. I was hoping he was one of yours."

"No, not mine, never seen him before," John said. "Damn big dog, though." John gave a sheepish grin to Abby, tilting his head in apology. "Pardon my French."

Wanting to get back to the meal, Clay changed the subject and asked how the delivery went in Deer Lodge. John let them know that the sickle part would require a replacement; the smithy didn't think a weld would hold. They'd order the part from Helena, but it would be three days before it came in. "And it'll cost seven dollars," John said with a grimace. The price was steep, easily a week's wages for a day laborer. This was the curse of keeping old equipment. Parts were growing rare and expensive. John hurried on to let them know that the gravestone was well appreciated. He fished in his pants pocket and pulled out an envelope. "Here's the money, and they even included another fifty cents for getting it done early."

Frank took the money, counted it out, and handed the fifty-cent coin back. "Keep that, for your troubles."

Clay's stomach growled, but John kept talking. He accepted the coin, then told Frank about a construction project he had found in Deer Lodge. "The prison is building a new hospital. Want me to see if there's any stone work?"

"Yes, do," Frank said. "Any money would help, especially with needing that sickle part."

Clay saw his son smile, such a rarity of late. What was that about? It was more than the money. They were not in such dire straits that they needed to leave the ranch for work. Not yet. That lifestyle suited John, but he had a larger family to care for. Besides, Frank had always stuck close to home—that was why he only took the stone carving commissions that could be completed in his own workshop. Frank loved the land as much as Clay did, having grown up in the valley. Glancing at Abby, Clay saw her put on a half-hearted smile. Yeah, the girl knew what was happening.

Abby sped the conversation along. "John, we were just sitting down to supper; care to join us?"

"No, thank you, ma'am. I should get going. If I don't get back soon, Patty will think I stopped at the bar." Their neighbor left then, the dog escorting his car part of the way, loud barks telegraphing his departure. Back in the kitchen, Frank gave Abby the money. She pulled out a small clay jar from one of her cupboards and tucked the bills inside. Since the bank crash, she'd concocted about a dozen hidey-holes in the house where she kept their funds from the livestock and Frank's stone carving. She kept the books too, having proven herself far more accurate than both Frank and Clay combined. This was unheard of amongst the ranches of the valley. Women raised kids and kept house. They didn't handle money—unless the woman was Abigail Redmond.

After supper, Frank tended the horses, leaving Clay to care for the chickens and pigs. After locking the chickens inside their coop, Clay hauled the scrap bucket over to the pigs. That night, the scrap bucket contained a real find by a scavenger's standards. Without refrigeration, the Redmonds and most other ranch families kept a quarter of beef hanging in a small screened-in box frame off their porch. A small amount of meat and a gallon of milk could fit in a sealed box sunk in the cold creek too. Neighbors took turns slaughtering a pig or steer and then shared the quarters. That practice minimized waste. But some spoilage was inevitable. Abby regularly shaved off the outer inch or so of the beef quarter and tossed it in the scrap bucket. Today was such a day.

Feeding the nasty scrap to the pig was the most sensible option. The pig would turn the mess into good meat and fertilizer for the garden. The dog, on the other hand, would give Clay nothing in return. Nothing but a doggy grin. Suddenly that seemed more valuable. The pooch had followed him to the pigsty and sat now, not begging per se, but staring. It was a very effective stare. Clay looked around to make sure Frank was not nearby and then summoned the dog, who came close and sniffed the pail. Clay reached in, pulled out the meat, and tossed it to the mutt. Then he poured the rest of the contents into the trough for the sow and her eight piglets. The dog gobbled the meat and looked at Clay, expecting more.

"Sorry, stranger, I'll see what I can scrounge up for ya tomorrow." The dog sniffed at Clay's hands and the now-empty bucket. Finding nothing else, he trotted over to the equipment shed, stopped at a bit of old straw, turned around a few times, and then lay down. Clay chuckled at how well the animal had settled into the routine of the ranch. He headed toward the house, where he met up with Frank, who had also finished up his chores.

"Where's the dog?" Frank asked, looking around.

"He found a mule's breakfast in the shed." Clay pointed to the black shape just inside the open shed door.

"If he's here come morning, I won't have much say on him staying, will I?"

"No, don't reckon ya will," Clay replied.

Frank shook his head and headed inside. Clay hesitated at the top of the porch steps and looked back. The dog was curled up in a ball on the straw, but even from across the yard he could see the canine eyes watching him and Frank. "See you in the morning, pup," Clay whispered so Frank wouldn't hear, but Clay swore the dog's ears perked up.

CHAPTER 3

MAY 1935

The dog enjoyed the comfort and warmth of the straw. It had been weeks since he felt content, felt safe. With no fear or concerns for his survival, the dog relaxed and drifted into a deep, dream-filled sleep. Not all the dreams were good, though. One was terrifying. It had haunted him for many nights.

The smell of blood filled the dog's nose as he sniffed and licked at his human, hoping to wake him, but nothing worked. He didn't know how the man had fallen, only that he was down and not moving. Finally his man stirred, groaning in pain. The dog licked at him, but still he didn't get up, only shifted his head some, trying to raise it.

They'd been walking along the railroad tracks, and now the sound of an approaching train filled the dog with dread. He nuzzled the man more forcefully, trying to rouse him. Stepping back, the dog gave a high-pitched bark. That seemed to bring the man nearer to consciousness. The train drew closer, its light visible as it rounded the bend. Both fearful and protective, the dog ran down the track, barking at the train, trying to get it to stop. It kept coming, faster than the other trains that carried heavy loads over the mountain pass. This one must have been pulling empty cars; it was closing the distance fast.

The dog rushed back to his human, barking at him to get up. The man lifted his head. His confused look turned to terror at seeing the oncoming train. He made a feeble attempt to push the dog away from the tracks, but the dog leapt forward, latched onto his sleeve, then lunged backward, trying to pull the man out of harm's way. The sound of the train grew louder. The dog felt his beloved human's fingers on his fur. He doubled his efforts; his desperation filled him with strength.

It wasn't enough. The man looked at the train and then back at his dog. Their eyes locked. They had depended on each other for more than five years, the hobo and his dog. With his last ounce of strength, the man pushed his canine companion away, sending the dog stumbling down the bank of the rail bed just as the train arrived.

In an instant, his human was gone.

The nightmare startled the dog awake, the vivid memory haunting him. The black interior of the shed hid him from the faint light of early morning. Curling up tighter into a ball, the dog wrapped his tail around to cover his muzzle as he tried to return to sleep. A door creaked open somewhere. The dog raised his head. He spied a small, dull grey figure leave the house and walk around the corner, only to return a few minutes later. He could tell from how the person walked that it was the woman. For two days the dog had watched them, testing whether they would welcome him or not. There was more movement, doors opening and closing. A faint light glowed in the house. The dog laid his head back down with a whine. The dream made him think of his old master.

He had traveled for miles up the mountain pass, following the scent of his human after the train had taken him, but the scent faded as the day went on. His human was all the dog had, all he needed, as they traveled across the country from hobo camp to hobo camp. Together they cared for one another, the man sharing with him any food they could find, the dog protecting him from those that preyed on tramps.

The dog hadn't seen his human fall. He had been exploring in the meadow just off of the tracks, hoping to catch a field mouse near the retreating patches of snow. After the accident, the dog ran after the train as fast as he could, barking the entire time. But the train continued to wind its way up the mountain. Unable to keep up, he slowed to a trot and finally a trudging walk, watching mournfully as the train sped away.

Two more trains lumbered by during his slow ascent of the pass, one going back down the mountain and the other heading in the direction in which his human had been taken. As the dog followed the tracks, he came to a long curved bridge, a spider web of steel elevating it from the deep ravine below. Smelling water, the dog made his way down the hillside to quench his thirst. While drinking, he caught a familiar scent. Following his nose, he found one of his human's shoes near a concrete footing for the bridge. Sniffing the shoe, the dog whined and renewed his determined pursuit.

Crossing the drainage, the dog climbed the hill and started sniffing around the tracks until he picked up the trail again. He had not gone far before the rails were swallowed by a massive hole in the side of the mountain. The darkness made him hesitate. The scent demanded that he go into the tunnel, but he couldn't. Fear of the deep dark and layers of other strange unknown smells prevented him. Confused, the dog paced back and forth at the opening until he saw a narrow road leading up the side of the hill. Running up it, he tried to follow the tracks that now lay deep below in the mountain. He could hear their path, the rumbling when another train entered the tunnel and when it exited on the other side of the ridge. Climbing onward, the dog fought giant snow drifts that lay scattered between the protective boughs of sprawling fir trees.

Finally cresting the top of the mountain ridge, he saw two strings of rail cars on side tracks far below. The sounds of men talking rose to his ears, filling him with excitement. They would help him find his human; they had to. The dog ran down the hill to the rail yard at the opening of the tunnel. Hope of finding his human gave him new energy. Focused on the scent, the dog ignored the men who were setting the brakes of a boxcar and working on the large water tank at the mouth of the tunnel. With his nose taking deep breaths, the dog darted back and forth, picking up scant hints that his human had been there. The dog smelled blood, too, but it was faint. Tracking the odors as best he could, he traveled across the rail yard until the scent trail stopped. Backtracking until he picked it up again, the dog followed it to the same spot where it had ended before. Sniffing around a set of tire tracks, he struggled unsuccessfully to determine where his human had gone.

A rock flew by his head. The men began yelling, and the dog jumped back, confused by their hostility. Other rocks followed, one striking him on his side. He yelped and ran for his life. The rest of the rocks fell short, as the dog dashed to the northwest. Soon the noises of the men and rail yard were all but gone.

It was after dark before the dog doubled back to the rail yard to try once more. Slinking from shadow to shadow, the dog moved closer. His senses were on high alert, but the area was quiet. The workers had retired to a small shack at the edge of the yard. A whiff of smoke rose from a pipe jutting out of the shack's back wall. Relying more on his nose than his eyes, the dog searched back and forth until he picked up the faint traces where his human's trail ended. The dog stood in the quiet dark for several minutes, his floppy ears lying flat against his head. He didn't know what to do. For the first time in his life, he was alone.

His grumbling stomach forced him to start walking again. He did need to find food, and his nose would have to guide him. The dog thought better of trying to befriend one of the men in shack, but the smell of food encouraged him to sneak closer. Sounds of laughter gave him pause as he made his way around a stack of barrels. A whistle blew, and another steam engine made its way through the tunnel. The dog crouched low to the ground, disappearing into the shadows. He watched as the men left the shack, taking their lantern with them. The shack was dark.

Waiting until the men were a safe distance away, the dog crept to the door of the building. They had left it unlatched; it opened with a nudge of his nose. Darting inside, he immediately found the stew on the table, even in the darkness. Ignoring all else, the dog put his front paws up on the table and ate greedily, oblivious that the door had swung closed behind him. After devouring everything, he made one last sniff of the room, then realized his exit was blocked.

The men were returning, and the dog began to panic, looking everywhere for a way out. The door was closed. The small window next to it was too high to jump through. Tensing, the dog heard the click of the door latch. The light of the lantern flooded in as the door swung wide. Seeing his opening, the dog rushed out in a blur of black. In his haste, his shoulder rammed into a man's leg. The impact made the man stumble backward. Curses echoed across the yard as the dog sprinted away—his stomach full, but his heart heavy with not finding his human. At least the angry men showed no sign of pursuing him very far. Exhausted, the dog found a hiding place under a dense spruce tree a few hundred yards north of the train yard and lay down. The sounds of the forest kept him on edge, but eventually he couldn't keep his eyes open any longer.

There was no hope of finding his man. He knew that much. The next day, and for the next four days, the dog followed the railroad down out of the mountains. He was wary of approaching the small towns, and stayed clear of the highway, which the railroad began to parallel through a narrow river valley. Leaving the rails behind, he wandered further to the northwest, following the smells of small ranches that dotted the valley. He observed each one from a distance before venturing closer or moving on. He avoided any properties where other dogs were already present, not having the energy to challenge them for a place in their pack. Other dogless ranches gave him a reception similar to that of the men at the rail yard. One rancher even shot at him as he ran away.

Growing more and more hungry, it was the smell of a carcass that drew him away from the main road and back up into the mountains. A fatality of the winter, the frozen deer was only recently exposed; the spring sun melting the snowdrift that had encased it. Many scavenging animals had visited the find already. The dog could smell them as well as the decaying flesh. Not having eaten in a week, the dog didn't care about who else might have laid claim to the feast. Devil may care; he ran over and ate as much as he could.

As he gorged himself, a new scent caught him. He raised his head and saw the dark shape of a bear approaching. Behind it trailed two cubs. Taking another quick bite, the dog considered holding his ground, but the bear's roar and half-hearted charge was enough to send him scrambling for his life once again. Licking his chops, he watched from a distance as the bear and her cubs moved in and began their own feast.

Realizing he had little chance of claiming the deer for future meals, the dog trotted off to the west and soon broke out of the trees into an open field on a hillside. He heard a noise in the distance and looked toward a small homestead. A man was staring at him. Feeling vulnerable in the field, the dog sprinted to the tree line and watched the ranch. He snuck in later that evening, caught the scent of that night's meal and examined several tracks around the house. He determined that there were three humans living there, and most importantly, no dogs.

The generosity of the older man over the next two days convinced him to stay. He had not experienced any human kindness since losing his master. The comfort of a loving hand and the warmth of food in his belly gave the dog peace as he curled up on the straw. The nightmare and the memories were troubling things, but he could rest here in this shed. That was good enough for now. His present curiosity about these new humans gently eclipsed his sadness. He could see in their faces that they were burdened by something. Perhaps they needed him as much as he needed them.

Forgoing his chance at a little more sleep, he sat up and observed as each human visited the little shack that smelled like piss. As activity increased inside the main house, the dog stood, stretched, and then patrolled the area, marking as he went. Soon, the two men came out of the front door. The dog scurried into the barn and watched. Both men appeared interested in his whereabouts, but the younger one seemed angry about the matter. The older man reminded the dog of his past human. He even whistled to him in the same way. By force of habit the dog came out of the shadows and trotted over. As he approached, the younger man glared. That made him uneasy, but the prospect of food and affection kept him on his course toward the older man.

The dog wasn't disappointed. The friendly one handed him a thick slice of bread wrapped around a piece of burnt bacon. As the dog ate, the men exchanged forceful words. The dog didn't care. He had food, and the old man's hands rubbed his ears. How good that felt! As the men left to start their day's work, the dog tagged along. He stayed close enough to rush in for ear scratches if the old man offered, while maintaining a respectful distance from the younger one. He was not a bad man, the younger one, but he would require more training.

CHAPTER 4
MAY 1935

Abby normally loved this time of day, the early cool. But nothing felt familiar or comforting that morning. Frank was leaving and she really couldn't tell whether he planned to come back. The flapjacks were almost done, the coffee simmering. Pancakes were a splurge, such a lot of flour and milk to make them. It was Frank's favorite breakfast. In truth, there was no warmth in the gesture, but it should be done. She was a good wife; she would not give him reason to say otherwise.

More than anything, she wanted to know his plans, but that would require asking him. The thought of initiating such a conversation was still more frightening than living with the uncertainty. His mood had migrated from his typical reticence to subterranean rage in the past week. The only time his countenance had lightened was when he learned of the possibility of a job in Deer Lodge.

John had returned a second time to let them know there was indeed a stone carving commission. In fact, the new prison warden had asked about Frank by name. Apparently, her husband's craftsmanship had become fairly well known in the city. John provided few details. A job. For the new warden. Maybe it was for the hospital, but he didn't think so. The new building was wood frame and stucco; it didn't require any stone masonry. The pay would be five dollars a day for two weeks or, as John quoted the warden, "as long as the job takes."

It was an outlandish wage; Abby wondered if the dealings were questionable. The last warden had been incredibly corrupt; who knew what the new one might actually rope her husband into. But, Abby could tell Frank found the mystery job captivating rather than a cause for concern. Good old John would give him a lift since Frank wouldn't need a car once he was in town. The warden had already arranged for lodging near the work site. Everything was settled. Except nothing was clear in Abby's mind.

Three days ago, the men had made all the arrangements as she watched. While they deliberated, Abby realized she didn't exist—even to Clay. As kind as her father-in-law was to her, even he seemed taken in by the dollar signs and the excitement of the whole affair. Frank had left for days at a time when selling cattle, but this was different. Didn't Clay understand that his son might not come back?

As Frank and John and Clay plotted and gaffawed and back-slapped, Abby grew tired of trying to get a word in edgewise. She turned back to the bread she had been making. She beat the dough with all her unspoken frustration. She wondered for a moment if her hurts might be communicated somehow through the bread. She wondered if Frank might take a bite of the bread and realize, "Oh! The past years have been hard on Abby, too." *Let him take this bread and know,* she thought as she set one lump into a pan to rise. *Was that sacrilegious?* Maybe. She beat the other lump of dough even harder still.

That was all three days ago. The warden wanted Frank to start as soon as possible, so John was coming to pick up Frank after breakfast that very morning. Abby poured Frank's coffee. How she wanted to ask—or rather scream at him to fess up. Maybe even if he yelled at her, it might be better than this devastating silence.

41

She also thought of pouring the entire cup of coffee on his head instead of setting it down by his plate. But she didn't.

She mustn't scream, mustn't lose composure. What if she gave way to her own upset, and that itself drove him off for good? She would not be the one responsible for forcing Clay and her to subsist on the ranch alone. She persisted, holding to the hope that Frank's ill temper would pass. Perhaps a week or two away from the ranch would do him some good. Deep down, she knew it would not. Perhaps the greater question was whether she should be there when he came back.

After Frank and Clay had finished breakfast, the two sat at the table discussing which repairs would wait till Frank's return. Abby left to gather eggs from the chicken coop. As she walked to the coop, she glanced back at the house, her mind still on the chasm between Frank and her. Lost in thought, she almost stepped on the dog. Her scream was not one of terror, but of genuine surprise. Abby dropped her wicker egg basket—thankfully nothing in it yet—as she stumbled over the hound. The dog, startled by her reaction, spun around looking for whatever had frightened Abby. He gave three deep barks, obviously ready to confront the unknown threat.

Abby composed herself and smiled, even laughed as she realized the dog was searching frantically for whatever had scared her. Poor unwitting dog. Abby heard Frank and Clay come running out of the house. Both looked concerned, though Frank's attitude quickly turned to rage. As usual.

"Why you son of a—." Frank started towards the dog ready to wring its neck. The dog cowered and looked for the quickest way out of the situation.

"Wait!" Abby shouted, first through laughter, than through her own sense of outrage. "Stop!" Of course, now Frank was acting the part of the caring husband—only as an excuse to hurt another creature. Abby stepped between Frank and the dog, her husband towering over her. "The dog didn't do anything, other than surprise me," she said, placing a hand on Frank's chest. It was the first time she had touched him in months. "Let the dog be."

Abby looked back at the animal, who still crouched low, looking even more confused and concerned. Despite Frank's intimidating presence, she found herself smiling once more at the dog. Frank was not amused. Abby stepped back, but kept herself between the dog and Frank. Clay asked what had happened, and Abby explained the situation as best as she could, laughing once more. Frank stood there with his dour face.

Clay walked over to the dog, who wagged his tail at Clay's approach. "Don't know where ya came from, boy, but you're sure settling in," he said.

Abby walked over to the dog and joined in petting him. "He really ought to have a name, don't you think?" she asked. The dog finally relaxed, leaned against Clay's leg, clearly enjoying the affection from the two of them.

"He's got a name," Clay said with conviction. "Stranger. That's what I called him that first time I saw him, and that's what he is."

Frank shook his head in disapproval of the entire situation. "I suppose the mongrel's here for good," he said. "Not that I've a lot of choice in the matter."

"No, I don't believe you do," Abby said. Her smile was tight, her eyes serious. There were a lot of topics she might avoid discussing with Frank, there were many times she felt afraid of him lately. But the dog had given her a reason to stand her ground. She picked up her basket and addressed the animal, "Well, Stranger, how about you and I go tend the chickens and let Frank pack his tools?"

Without a second glance at Frank, Abby headed towards the coop, and found herself humming a happy tune along the way. She hadn't touched Frank in a long time, and she also had not laughed in many months. That, too, felt very good. Stranger followed right behind her, his tail swishing back and forth as they went.

John arrived just after eight. Abby was back inside by then, mending two tears in the wicker basket, small damages suffered during that morning's scuffle. She paused in her work, listening to Stranger barking and, in the distance, the rumble of the truck. Frank came in, grabbed his bedroll with his clothes wrapped up inside. Without a word to Abby, he donned his coat and hat, then went out to the porch where his tool box sat on the stoop. She followed him and watched him load up as soon as the truck came to a halt. That razor edge tenacity Abby had felt earlier, that tough resolve, it dissipated then. She'd felt, for a moment, quite strong without Frank, had even entertained the thought of his departure as a relief. Not so as he left like this.

Frank would not suddenly warm in compassion toward her. She knew that. Still, she touched his arm as he finished settling his things in the back of the truck. "Leave a note at the mercantile?" she said, offering the statement more as a question. She stood at his side. Frank looked straight ahead, steely. Still, there he was, with his day old beard and that thin scar on his chin—the one he had earned finally standing up to a bully when he was a boy. There he was, just Frank. He must still be in there. "Just a quick message at the McAllister's or the post office. Let us know how the job is going."

This was the easiest way to convey messages to ranches in their valley. McAllister's being one of the few ranches north of Avon that had a phone. From there, ranch children attending school in Avon often acted as messengers, bringing phone messages and letters up into the valley each day. Abby waited for a moment, expecting a response, but didn't get one. "I'm not the only one who might wonder if you are well," she added. Frank nodded then, glancing at her and Clay from the corner of his eye.

"I'll leave a message once I know when the job will be done," he said, then climbed into the cab.

The truck muttered and spit down the dirt road till all Abby could see was the plume of dust rising against the foothills. Clay headed to the barn to get the team hooked up for the day. Abby closed her eyes. Breathed. She heard Stranger approach, felt the dog leaning against her legs. Looking down, she smiled once more. "Looks like it's just you and me," she said. The dog's tail swayed back and forth. She scratched the old mutt's forehead. He had no idea what burden she carried, had no idea how the morning's events might affect him if she and Clay had to leave the ranch. If they left—when they left—Stranger would be a stray once more. Poor animal. For now he looked up at her with a ridiculous grin and bright, happy eyes.

Perhaps he wasn't so unwitting. The dog shadowed her the rest of the day, as if understanding she needed a little company as she worked. Whenever she went indoors, he curled up by the porch. Abby would find him still there, minutes or hours later, waiting to accompany her wherever she might go.

They made the best of that day—Abby, Clay, and Stranger. Abby helped her father-in-law with the horses, helped unload another stack of lodgepole fence rails, held the horses and removed their tack and brushed them down, just as her husband would have. She simply did all those things in addition to her usual work. Like Clay, she was exhausted. They ate their evening meal in tired, but friendly, quiet. Clay announced it was time to hit the hay. That was that. No discussion about Frank, no care for each other's bruises. Perhaps it was best that way. Abby had no energy for difficult conversation.

Her physical exhaustion was apparently irrelevant to her mind; sleep was one elusive comfort that night. No easy escape into her dreams, happy or otherwise. She could hear Clay's occasional snoring in the bedroom on the opposite side of the stairwell. Odd to think how she usually couldn't hear that; Frank's snoring easily drowned out his father's. She used to find that funny, found it comforting. Used to sleep through it easily enough. In the past couple years, she'd grown to find the snoring obnoxious.

That night, it was the relative silence that got her nerves on edge. She tried to pray, but her mind only raced from one fearful possibility to the next. Conceding that she'd find no slumber that night, Abby left her bed and snuck downstairs, avoiding the creak on the third step. She lit a candle, added some kindling and a log to the embers in the kitchen stove. With a couple strong breaths into the firebox, the kindling lit and warmth radiated from the old Monarch. Bringing Vivian's old rocker a little closer to the stove, Abby wrapped a blanket around herself, sat down, and opened her Bible. The light of the candle barely illuminated the pages. Abby closed her eyes, didn't even try to read. She sat there, wondering at it all.

Her mother had given her the Bible shortly before they moved to Helena from Ohio. It was one of the few possessions her parents had managed to bring across the Atlantic when they left Scotland. That, and the old wall clock that ticked away above the mantel. For as long as Abby could remember, her parents had moved often. Her father had been a railroad track inspector and repair foreman. They moved every few years to follow his work for the Northern Pacific Railroad. It was her mother who advanced Abby's education when the many public schools she attended fell short. Both her parents encouraged Abby to read and learn as much as she could, her mother emphasizing literature and poetry, while her dad insisted on her being skilled in mathematics. These were rare opinions in that day, but Abby was grateful for her parents' stringent training, though even she wondered at its usefulness in her present life. Her family's last move was within Montana, from Helena to Garrison. Her mother had died of a fever a year after that. Abby, only fourteen at the time, began caring for her father, maintaining the home as her mother had. It seemed her destiny to continue that role, given how she now did her best to fill the shoes of the Redmond matriarch.

While living in Garrison, she met Frank, the tall but reserved man, who seemed so awkward when asking her for a dance at the Old Faithful Inn. She was seventeen, and Frank was older than most of the young men who had tried to earn Abby's favor. He admitted he wasn't much for courting, but he made time for Abby. Several months into that shy but well-meant courtship, Abby was at the Redmond ranch sharing Sunday dinner with Frank and his parents, when a neighbor boy raced up to the house. The child was flushed and frightened and asked for Abby. It was from his nervous stuttering mouth that she learned that her father had been killed when his car tumbled off the road on Priest Pass.

So, that was how Frank and Abby came to expedite their marriage. They did have fond feelings for each other. But the wedding day, itself, was doused with sadness. Abby married so she could have a place to live, honorably and not alone. Vivian and Clay, and certainly Frank, could not endure the thought of Abby living alone in her father's little house in town. How could she have ever told them plainly, that she wanted to be alone right then—perhaps for weeks, maybe years? She thought herself really ungrateful for harboring such a sentiment. So she said yes. And she walked herself alone down the aisle. She said her vows, and she heard Frank say his, and she saw townsfolk and ranch folk alike growing misty and soft over the bittersweet quality of that day. Women hugged her, and old ranchers nodded at her with sincere and kind looks. But Abby? A polite smile. She felt nothing at all.

Clay and Vivian walked her through the grief as they might have taught a child how to walk. Vivian taught her recipes, gently tricking her into remembering to eat. Clay taught her a few folk songs, then sang them off key, tricking her into laughing once in a while. Abby trudged through that first year, crept through that first winter, and arrived to wake one summer morning discovering she still had a family, still had a home. Discovered also that she had grown to love Frank.

After their second year together, Abby grew very concerned that she hadn't gotten pregnant yet. She confided in Vivian. "I'm not surprised," Vivian had said. "It was nine years before Frank came along. Clay's parents called it the Redmond curse." Vivian described the long history of the sparse family tree. They tended to have one or two children, if any at all. And all the men blamed their wives. Of course.

Vivian dropped her voice low and deep mocking them, "We pick barren women; it's our curse." She resumed her usual tone and added, "There are midwives who believe there can be problems with the men. I always thought that's what was happening in Clay's family. Makes sense, since he has a Redmond aunt with fourteen children." She paused, looked out the window at the men who were just leaving the barn, crossing the yard to the house. "Never told him that to his face, though," she said. Vivian encouraged Abby to be patient, told her she would have a little one soon enough. They never spoke of the matter again, delicate issue that it was. Still, how fine it had been to have Vivian around, to know another woman was nearby to soothe Abby's worries, to assure her that some things weren't her fault.

The clock on the mantle chimed four. Abby missed both of her mothers. She missed something more, too; she missed clarity. Right then, looking back, she saw her whole life as a steady unraveling of clarity. Life had been clearest when she was younger. Back East, life and God, often one and the same, were orderly, civilized, governmental. Church-going was as ubiquitous as obeying a state's laws. Still, her parents did not consider themselves particularly religious. They were both glad for the move to Montana, for the promise of solitude and space, a little more liberty. These were the qualities of the Western states—at least that was what you knew of the region if you lived in Ohio. Abby knew life would be very different in this new place, yet she was very surprised that God himself changed when they moved to mountain country.

The great Governor in the sky was still lofty, but now he was entrenched in the mountains themselves. And the weather. Rather than embodying structure and order, this god was feral, mercurial. God was a flower. God was the steely cold wind and also merciless heat. God was hunger and a much needed rain. Good luck at satisfying this god. Live right and well; things may still go poorly. Frank surely didn't bother with religion. Abby had been fond of him, not because he was religious, but because he was respectful and kind to her. Like Clay, he regarded God as a nonchalant energy, like electricity. Like thunder or sprouting wheat. There was no stopping or starting it, so why try?

Yet Abby, and Vivian, too, persisted in a belief that God was a being with some conversational interest in people. So they did pray. And when a traveling pastor came through the valley—this happened three or four times a year—and the church in Avon had a reason to hold a service, the women attended. Sometimes they successfully prodded the men to come, by holding out the promise of a pie or beloved roast chicken at the potluck afterward. Frank and Abby maintained a gentle, and unspoken, truce over the whole matter. He did not criticize her religious actions. She recognized that his empirical sensibilities, somewhat rare for where they lived, were also the reason he treated her with a very liberal tolerance. As far as he possibly could, he regarded her as an equal. All the recent tension and unkindness, this was something very new and very unlike the man Abby had loved early on.

Hard telling what it all meant. What stood before her now was the very real possibility that she and Clay would soon be running the ranch alone. They couldn't do it for long; she knew that from caring for the accounting for three years. Indeed, where would they go once they were forced to move? Considering that question, regarding it from a not-too-far-off distance, Abby realized a stunning fact: In all her life's trials, she had not personally chosen anything—the trials as well as the paths out of them. Someone else or some impossible situation had always dictated her next steps. In short, she found herself very ill-equipped to make a decision. As frightening as it was, it gave a strange thrill to her heart as well.

When her parent's clock chimed five, she still had no answers. The candle had burned clear down to a nub. What a waste; she had read nothing. No matter. The day needed to begin. She touched the hand-embroidered bookmark, a gift from Vivian on Frank and Abby's wedding day. She closed the leather cover and set the Bible back on her bookshelf. When Clay came downstairs, she was frying bacon and taters for their breakfast. The coffee was ready. "Sleep well?" he asked.

"Like a baby," she answered with automatic cordiality. She didn't even realize it was a lie till the words tumbled off her lips. Oh well, no sense clarifying the matter. Clay surely had enough of his own worries.

CHAPTER 5

MAY 1935

That first morning in Deer Lodge, Frank woke early to the sound of a truck passing by outside the boarding house. Eyes still closed, it took him a moment to remember where he was. The drive there had taken only sixty minutes, but it was plenty of time for Frank to chew on his thoughts and, one by one, set them aside. As mountains gave way to a wide valley, Frank had pondered whether he might look for more permanent work in Deer Lodge and mulled over the logistics of divorce. Meanwhile, John chattered away in the driver's seat, telling him stories about the past warden's business dealings. Warden Conley had held the position till 1921. He was ousted by the governor when there were fraudulent activities discovered in his handling of prison resources. Now the wardens were appointed by the governor of the state, so every few years a new one would come along. John shouted over the rattle of the truck on the slow washboard road and over the growl of the engine once they pulled onto the highway. Frank nodded, smiled, chuckled, and pondered other things.

What was the job, why the secrecy, was it something illegal? It was hard to imagine anything related to stone-carving being illegal. More likely the project was a town memorial of some sort, something meant to be unveiled on a certain date as a surprise. Maybe something ego-gratifying. The last warden was adept at spending public money on his own luxuries. Perhaps this one wanted to gift the town with a grand statue of himself. Frank, didn't care, even if it was such a frivolous project. He'd do it. He needed starting-over money, and five dollars a day for a couple weeks would surely do the trick. Plenty for himself, and a lump sum to give to Abby. He wouldn't send her on her way penniless. He would make sure she had enough to make it to Portland where she had a cousin. A clean start with family; that was what she needed.

When John turned onto the main highway to Deer Lodge, a dilapidated car passed them heading in the other direction. "Look," John called out. "Another tin-can tourist." The car was loaded with the family's belongings, furniture strapped to the roof and hood, children packed in tight between boxes in the back. The sight was becoming a common one as droves left the desolated Midwest in hopes of finding work. Someone should be standing on the highways out east, cutting them off, letting them know that there were few opportunities out this way. The federal and state construction projects were just enough to keep the locals busy. The car sputtered on, fading into the distance behind John's truck. Frank whistled and looked forward. He would not be humiliated like that. A few miles later, a brand new patrol car passed them. It reminded Frank that he needed to get a driver's license and register Clay's car—new requirements resulting from the state legislature creating a state highway patrol the year before. Ah, yet another cost that would nibble away at the proceeds of the warden's mystery commission.

Deer Lodge had the distinction of being the second oldest town in Montana, starting as nothing more than a remote outpost.

Now, it was a quiet cow town that happened to be the home of the state's only prison as well as a large locomotive repair shop for the railroad. On the way into town they passed by the Grant-Kohrs Ranch. Its massive operation vexed Frank, reminding him of his failing as a rancher. As John and Frank drove down Main Street from the north, they could see the prison's two red brick block houses rising up like castle towers behind the prison's grey stone outer wall. Armed guards walked along the top of the outer wall. John came to a stop in front of the tall stone and cement fortification. The imposing design was a throwback to when it was first constructed in the 1800s. In the far distance, some twenty miles off to the south, Frank could see the dispersing smoke plume from the copper smelter in Anaconda. As black as it was today, he figured they were running hotter than normal. He was thankful the haze never reached his ranch. John pointed to a single-story off-white colored block building across the street from the prison.

"There's the warden's office; go on in and tell him who you are," he said. Cautious, he added, "I'll let Clay and Abby know you got here. Leave a message for me at McAllisters, so I'll know if I need to come back down and pick you up."

Frank nodded. *If*, he'd said. So, John had caught on well enough. The man talked so much it was hard to tell if he saw what was happening to other people. Of course he did. It struck Frank that this might be why the man had so much to say. Bedroll over his shoulder and tools in hand, Frank gave a wave to his friend as he drove off. Then it was off to the warden's office. The north side of the building was new and housed the state registrar's office. The original building's exterior and column-framed entrance was as cold and bland as the prison wall that stood like a big brother across the street. Stopping at the door, Frank took off his weathered hat and tried to straighten his denim jacket and collar before checking his pocket watch and seeing it was a hair past nine. With a deep breath, he went inside, entering a short hallway with closed doors on either end. To his left he heard typing and a woman's voice behind the door. A sign on the door labeled it as the office of Administration and the Sergeant at Arms office. The sign on the door to the right declared it as the warden's office. That was where he needed to go.

Whatever confidence he had, dissipated immediately as he entered the office. Even Frank's good Sunday clothes would have looked ragged in this room. The dark-stained wood doors and wainscoting, metallic filigree in the wallpaper, rows of oak file cabinets, the well-perfumed secretary. It all smelled like a quantity of money Frank could not fathom. He could pass for a vagrant the way he looked. He needed to explain his presence and do so quickly.

The secretary looked up from her typewriter and asked, "Can I help you?" Her smile was sweet, but her tone made it clear she could have him escorted to the monolith across the street at a moment's notice. Frank stammered an explanation, said his name and the only details the warden had provided: "I'm here about the warden's stone carving commission."

That was enough to warm the woman's disposition. "So you're the famous Frank Redmond?" she crooned. Famous? That was odd. She didn't sound sarcastic either. "I'll let Mr. Jameson know you're here," the secretary said. But the warden had already overheard Frank's arrival. A booming voice came from a side room, "Let him in!"

With that, Frank was ushered through a rich mahogany door. The warden stood from his desk and crossed the room to shake hands.

"I'm William Jameson, I'm so glad you came, Mr. Redmond." The man had close-cropped grey hair, wise eyes, and wire-rimmed glasses. A well-read man judging by the bookcases—Abby would be jealous. But sturdy, too. He didn't look like a crook. He could be full of himself, though. The man's handshake was strong, surprising Frank, given that he assumed the fellow spent most of his time behind a desk. "Set your things down," the warden said, motioning to a wooden chair next to the office door. Frank complied, obeying automatically. Warden Jameson asked his secretary to fetch some coffee, then invited Frank to sit near his desk. Staring at the desk was a matter of comfort; as a craftsman, he could at least look at that object and understand it—the beveled oak, the flawless finish—it was extravagant, but it made sense. He let his fingers touch it in admiration. Frank didn't realize he was doing that till the warden's voice interrupted him.

"A fine piece isn't it?" he said. "A perk of taking over the job from a bad apple. Left all his belongings when he was ousted." Mr. Jameson sat down behind the desk and took a moment to admire it himself. "Those of us who hold this office, for the few years of our term, get to enjoy the luxury he obtained through deceit. A dubious pleasure, don't you think?"

Frank wasn't sure he was supposed to answer that. He began to open his mouth, looking for a word, but the warden spared him the trouble. "I'm pleased that a craftsman can admire another work of art," Mr. Jameson said. "Even if it is not in his own preferred medium."

The secretary came in carrying a tray with the coffee. She served the warden, then Frank. The woman departed and shut the door behind her. Frank was alone with the strange man. He had no friendly words because he was not practiced at such things. In Frank's world, a man spoke when he had information he needed to share, or he needed information that he did not have.

So he inquired, "Sir, why'd you ask me here?"

Mr. Jameson laughed—a quick staccato bark. "Straight to business, I like that," he said. "It wasn't easy finding you. Took me a week to convince the undertaker to give me your name and where you lived. I think they wanted the business themselves. I was planning to write you personally when, of all the luck, your pal came along snooping for work."

The warden paused for a second, and then he reached into his coat pocket and pulled out three one-dollar Peace coins, setting them on the desk in front of Frank. Suspicion bubbled up. What? Was this charity? Bribery—right at the outset? Astounding.

"That's for coming here on short notice, not even knowing what you are getting into," Mr. Jameson said. "It's yours to keep, whether you take the job or not. Fair?" Mr. Jameson stared at Frank with intense blue-grey eyes. There was a sincerity there that reminded Frank of his dad. Still, there couldn't be anything good in getting paid before completing a task.

"Sir, I believe we need to discuss just what it is you're hiring me to do," Frank replied, not touching the coins.

Mr. Jameson grew very somber at that moment, the fingers on his right hand tapping softly on the top of the desk. He knew Frank's mind, that much was certain. "It's nothing questionable, Mr. Redmond. I found you through the undertaker's parlor; I obviously need you to carve a gravestone." The man took off his glasses and rubbed his forehead as he continued. "I must have your utmost confidence. It's a very sensitive matter. I must know that you will tell no one about the specifics of your commission until I release you to do so. Am I clear?"

Frank sipped his coffee. He thought of leaving the office, but curiosity won out. The fellow was an odd stick for sure, but he was not lying. "I understand, sir," he said.

"Good," the warden said and then outlined the parameters of the job. That is to say, he described everything but the commission itself. Frank was to speak about the commission only with the warden. He'd be paid five dollars a day till the stone was complete. Frank would have complete privacy, completing his carving in a small utility shed within the prison grounds. A guard, the only other soul who knew of the project, would escort him to and from the workspace each day. Frank mustn't disrupt the routine of the prison operations. The warden reiterated the confidential nature of the task.

"You have my word," Frank assured him once more. But what the hell was the job itself? Something very serious was happening in this man's life, but what was it? "Sir, whose stone am I carving?"

"Let's walk across the street, and I'll show you," Mr. Jameson said.

Odd stick indeed. Frank followed him, though; stood when Mr. Jameson stood, walked to the door behind him. He had not yet agreed to the commission—only to keep the matter a secret. There was no harm in following the warden to the mystery work-site. Frank grabbed his bedroll and tools, but the warden stopped him. "You won't need those right now. They're safe here; you can pick them up at the end of the day."

This made no sense, but Frank complied. At the very least, he might not need the tools if he didn't take the job. And he could hardly envision anyone affiliated with this office wishing to steal his moth-nibbled bedroll.

Empty-handed, Frank followed Mr. Jameson across the street. He looked up at the armed guards patrolling the top of the stone wall and the towers at each corner, their gaze scrutinizing every movement both inside and outside the walls. They approached tower seven, the main entrance to the prison. It was directly across the street from the warden's office and jutted out of the prison's east wall at its midpoint. Reaching the door at the base of tower seven, Frank heard the guard on the inside call up to the key room in the tower above them. The massive door opened, and Frank followed the warden into a room within the entry tower. The door closed behind them. The slam of the door reverberated through the cold concrete room. It was dark, except for a couple of dim light bulbs hanging from the high ceiling.

Even entering such a place as a free man, the feeling of dread was unavoidable. This was a place designed to confine. Frank marveled at all the fail safes. The guard locked the door to the outside, then shouted something into a tube that ran up the wall. He connected the outer door key to a cable that was pulled up through a small hole in the ceiling. Soon the cable lowered again with a different key, which opened the door into the prison grounds. Frank and Mr. Jameson stepped into the daylight— a brief comfort, after the dark passage through the prison wall— and walked the short path to the main office building. Its drab white exterior contrasted with the dark red block-houses on its north and south ends.

Once inside the main administrative building, they were greeted by another armed guard inside a cage. Here the warden provided paperwork that apparently legitimized Frank's presence on the grounds. Looking over the warden's shoulder, Frank noticed the written explanation of his task: *miscellaneous repairs.* Curious. Well, the warden was not above telling a fib or two. After being cleared, the men were escorted to the deputy warden's office for a brief perfunctory meeting. The man didn't ask much, simply presented Frank with an identification paper that he would need to show each time he entered or left the prison building. The warden explained that Frank was to have an armed guard at all times to prevent anyone from bothering him. Then, the warden and Frank went back out through the door they had entered. At the base of the stairs they met Josh McMurphy, the armed guard who would escort Frank. McMurphy's face betrayed years of strain from dealing with society's worst. The warden explained that McMurphy was one of the only men who knew about the nature of Frank's project. The guard walked with them south across the prison yard towards the tower at the southeast corner of the wall.

The brick cell block towered above them as they walked south, turning west at the corner. Through the gap between the south cell block and the theater Frank could see the framework for the new hospital building taking shape on the north side of the yard. Here and there were prisoners in black and white striped overalls escorted by guards from one building to another. A few were working in a small garden area under the ever-vigilant eyes of the sentries. Prison work gangs were assembling and preparing to head out for the morning's chain gang activities. Several of the prisoners stared at the warden as they passed by, a cold, predatory look. Unnerving. Frank had met some hard men in his time, but he'd never seen expressions quite like that before. What on earth had he gotten himself into?

The large tower in the south wall held the Sally Port, the only gate through which vehicles could enter the grounds. A massive steel I-beam was hinged and locked across the interior gate, preventing anyone from trying to drive through it in a breakout attempt. At the foot of the tower, and just a few yards from the Sally Port gate, stood a twelve-foot by ten-foot shack with small windows along its top edge. One wall was a double door entrance with a heavy lock on it. McMurphy selected a key from the ring on his belt and opened the door for the warden and Frank. The guard closed the door and waited outside. In the dim light, Frank could see a sturdy wooden framework holding a thick, flat object covered by a canvas tarp. The warden flicked a switch on the wall, and a light bulb hanging from the ceiling glowed softly for a moment, then filled the room with a bright yellow light.

"This used to be a tool shed, when the admin building was built back in 32," the warden said. "I am glad they kept it around, it's perfect for this job." Mr. Jameson reached out and pulled the tarp off, revealing a three-foot by four-foot by four-inch thick slab of polished blue granite. Frank's eyes widened. He had never seen stone so beautiful.

"Where did you get this?" he asked. He touched the stone, brushed his hand along its smooth surface.

"Norway. The only place in the world where you can get granite like this." Mr. Jameson said. And then he began to explain. "I asked for you because I attended a funeral a year ago for Ruth Ismore in Helena." The warden described Ruth's stone, and Frank remembered it. "You carved that stone. I want you to carve just as fitting a memorial for my wife, the most beautiful and amazing woman I have ever known."

Frank stared at the warden. "I'm sorry. When did she pass?"

"She hasn't yet," the warden swallowed hard as the words came out. "She's very ill, and the doctors don't give much hope for her. She doesn't know that, though; I want her final days to be pleasant. Thus the need for secrecy." Mr. Jameson quipped that Frank might regard Deer Lodge as a big city, but it was a small town to him. He knew how word traveled from house to house. The warden wanted nothing and no one to frighten his wife. He fidgeted with his wedding band as he spoke. "And I want a stone ready for when the time comes; I don't want her in an unmarked grave, even for a day."

This was possibly the most unusual request ever made of Frank. He'd been paid extra to expedite the completion of a memorial in the past. But he'd never heard of anyone having a gravestone carved before the memorial's honoree was dead. He was not a superstitious man. This request, however, seemed like a real jinx. At the very least, it was downright morbid.

The warden was sincere, though, and touched by his own words—even if Frank felt troubled by them. Mr. Jameson sat down on a wooden crate next to the stone and confided how his wife was from Norway, how she dreamt of returning to visit her homeland, but how that could never happen now. "So I decided that I would bring Norway to her," he said. He reached into his jacket pocket and pulled a small booklet titled *Flowers of the World*. "Look on page fifty-three. I want that to be part of your inspiration."

Frank leafed through to the page and found a slip of paper with the warden's wife's name and date of birth on it, along with a dedication and scripture verse. The sketch in the book portrayed a delicate blue flower.

The warden bent down, reaching for something underneath the framework holding the stone. He stood and offered Frank a leather bundle along with a large sketch pad and pencil set. "These are for the work and for you to take home upon completion," he said and untied the cord around the bundle. "Call it additional compensation." Inside was a stone carver's hammer and chisel set with two-dozen chisels of varying sizes and types. Frank stared at the tools and the stone.

"Why are you hiring me?" he asked. "There are masons in Butte or Helena who could do this just as well, if not better."

"Not so, Mr. Redmond. You have a gift. Time dictates that it be simple and beautiful. A tall order. This stone requires your artistry. I want you to use your skill for me, for my wife."

Saying yes felt intimidating, saying no was hardly an option. "It would be my honor, sir," Frank said.

"I hope, by the end of this, you will learn to call me Bill."

"I'll try," Frank said with a half-smile.

"Very well; I'm sure you need time alone with your work," Mr. Jameson said. He'd be leaving, but McMurphy would be available for anything that Frank might need. Per the warden's instruction, Frank was to check in at the warden's office at the start of each day, and then McMurphy would meet Frank in the prison, escorting him to and from the old shed. The guard would also escort him to the lavatory in the theater, as needed, and would bring him a sandwich and coffee for the midday meal.

His instructions complete, Mr. Jameson left. Alone in the old shed, Frank looked at the stone. He sat on the crate and examined the flower in the book and the woman's name: Elisa. Artistry. He'd never heard his task categorized as that.

"Elisa Ingrid Jameson," Frank said quietly. The thought of carving a stone for someone still alive made him feel nauseous. Until he carved his mother's stone, Frank had never thought a whole lot about the people for whom he carved. The inscription for Elisa was sweet and typical, remembering her as a wife and mother. But the scripture was not one Frank had carved on a memorial before: Oh death, where is thy sting? Oh grave, where is thy victory?-*1 Corinthians 15:55*

None of it gave him inspiration for the carving itself. His usual scrollwork and wild flower motifs seemed paltry now. What was this woman like? What would she want on her stone? Had the warden asked his wife? No, he couldn't have. He didn't even want her to know she was dying. That seemed a kind gesture on the warden's part, at least on first glance. What a good man, a kind husband. But something about it didn't sit well with Frank. The man was playing god, wasn't he? Letting his wife think she might recover, all while he commissioned her gravestone.

Here lay the stone. Here stood Frank. He'd agreed to the job and, come hell or high water, he had to complete it now. He moved the tools, setting them on the top of another crate that was in the room. He stood before the stone and thought of where the most basic elements belonged. Soon an image formed, as it had so many times before, each element like a single brush stroke on a painting. Her name and the dates of her life, of course, and the scripture verse. The Norwegian flowers certainly, but they couldn't be the focus. Not on a stone so beautiful, so large. Once the rough arrangement was in his mind, Frank instinctively took the nub pencil out of his coat pocket, then returned it. He picked up the brand new sketchpad and opened the tin that contained a dozen new pencils. The pad was three times the size of the small one he kept in his toolbox and the largest he had ever held. Frank selected a pencil out of the set and began to draw. First, the flower. Over the next hour, he filled a sheet with seven sketches, various perspective views of the blue-petaled Nordic flora. Content with his rendering of the delicate details, he looked at the stone and envisioned the two areas where the flower could grow.

The glassy smooth surface sparkled with multiple shades of blue; such a large stone, so striking. On a fresh sheet of paper, with the stone in mind, Frank began a rough sketch of the entire work. He kept the graphite lines loose and flowing, vague shapes allowing his imagination to fill in the details. Time passed quickly, his focus broken by McMurphy knocking on the door before opening it to hand Frank a sandwich and apple. Frank barely tasted the food as he ate, his focus still on the drawing. It wasn't right. He'd never had such a hard time. The Ismore stone, the one that the warden had lauded, that design came to him immediately. The carving itself was hard work, of course, but the idea, the image, that was the easy part. This was the first time Frank struggled with such a thing. He wrestled on through the afternoon, fleshing out three more possible designs— all of which seemed lacking. It was a relief to hear McMurphy knock on the door to announce the end of his workday. Hopefully a good night's rest would bring him the answer.

Frank grabbed his coat, tarped the stone, left the sketchpad on the crate, and turned off the light. McMurphy locked the door and escorted him to tower seven and the door to the free world. Frank stopped at the warden's office to grab his bedroll and old tool set. The warden was gone, but the secretary, who introduced herself as Maggie, was waiting for him. She handed him an envelope containing his pay for the day. It seemed heavy. Frank peeked in it as he folded and tucked it into his jacket pocket. The additional three dollars, the coins he'd refused that morning, were in there as well.

"How was your first day?" Maggie asked, not at all unkind. In his nervousness that morning, Frank had not realized the refined gal at the desk might be a kind and friendly soul. He wasn't sure how to answer the question, given the confidentiality of the work and given the fact that he didn't think it went all that well. "Good, good," he said and grabbed his things. "Thanks," he said holding up the toolbox. Maggie had her coat on. He should open the door for her. Only he couldn't because his hands were full, and she had the keys and needed to lock up. She wound up holding the door for him. Yet another flustered moment on Frank's part.

Office locked up, Maggie turned to Frank and explained where the boarding house was, and told him the location of a diner where a tab was set up for his meals. The boarding house was on the way to her own home; she'd walk him there. She glanced over her shoulder, then narrowed her eyes at a few men loitering near the prison gate.

"What is it?" Frank inquired.

"I don't like how they look at me." Maggie said of the men who had gathered in the search for work at the prison, rail yards to the west, or the state highway department a few blocks away, or just a handout.

He fell in step with her then, as any gentleman would, walking at her left—closer to the street and obscuring the view for the toughs on the other side of the street. She smiled her thanks and set about at a brisk pace.

"I heard you're from the ranchland north of Avon," she said. "It must be lovely there."

Frank said it was, but couldn't think of anything more to say on the matter. Maggie was apparently not dismayed by his silence.

"You have family up there?"

"My wife, Abby, and my father Clay."

"And you have children?"

This was one of the reasons Frank rarely spoke to anyone at any length on the rare occasion he found himself in a big town. People always had to ask those same questions. Who's your family? How are your children?

"It's just us three," he said. For once in his life, he knew how to change the subject. Before she could pity him or wonder aloud how they ran the ranch all by themselves, he asked, "Do you know the warden well?" He did genuinely want to know more about the man.

"Well enough, I suppose. He helped me get the job at his office after my husband died," Maggie said. She explained how her husband had been a carpenter who had once completed some repairs on the warden's home across the street from the prison. A few months after that, her husband had fallen from a ladder while working on another house. He had passed away two days later. They had only been married a year, and she thought she would need to leave the community, to return to her family in Wyoming, though she didn't want to. Mr. Jameson approached her with the secretary position. It was good pay, and the job would last even after a new warden was appointed. They needed some consistency in the office. She could take care of herself. "It was the only good thing that came out of that time," she said.

Frank didn't know what to say. It was obvious she was still very sad over her loss. He wanted to comfort her somehow. "My mother passed away a year ago," he said. "It's been a hard time for my father."

She looked at him funny. "And you?" she asked.

"Pardon, ma'am?"

"You. It's been hard on you too, hasn't it?"

Frank was stunned at the question. People did not speak with each other like this back home. No one said things like that in Avon either, and there were some gossipy old coots who loved to pry into your business there.

Maggie backpedaled at his silence. "I'm sorry, Mr. Redmond. I've always been too forward. I hope you're not offended."

"No, ma'am."

They walked in silence then. Thankfully, the boarding house was on the next block. Maggie rallied as she wished him a good evening. "You seem like a decent man, Mr. Redmond. Mr. Jameson is a good judge of character, and his summoning you says a lot," she said. "I hope whatever you are doing for him is worthy of his trust."

"I hope so too," Frank said. He tipped his hat to her and headed into the boarding house. His mind whirling and not feeling keen on possibly falling into more conversation at the diner, he settled for a quiet bowl of soup at the boarding house kitchen. His room was upstairs, already a little uncomfortably warm. He opened the window and waited for the night air to make it cool enough to sleep.

That was when the hypothesizing began. Compared to his days at the ranch, he had not worked particularly hard that day, and so he was not all that tired. He lay on the bed alone with his waking dreams—how the divorce would play out. His dad would disown him, probably, might even ally himself with Abby and move with her to Portland where she had a cousin. Even John might disown him. Men who left their wives were not held in high regard by the valley. Well, to hell with them; they thought poorly of his family for having no children. They'd think poorly of him for leaving. Talkers and gossips claimed God had cursed him; it hardly mattered what he did or did not do at this point. What he knew for certain was that his present life with Abby was a merciless thing. She wasn't happy, either. It was hardly kind to stay on with her.

If this carving job went well, if word got around the region that he'd crafted the Jameson stone—if he ever got the damn thing done, that is—maybe Ross Undertaking Parlor would take him on as an employee. No, wait, Deer Lodge was too close to his old home valley, to the ranch. And the town was too small to make a living just carving stone. Maybe if he was as good as the warden seemed to think, he could move to Butte or even Denver and make some real money. Maybe he'd meet a nice lass there, someone like Maggie. She wasn't too bad. A little pushy, but sweet.

Now there was a comedy. How could he, a threadbare rancher, even entertain the idea of courting a woman who likely had a yearly salary more than he'd ever made in two good years? He'd be making better money by then, of course. There would always be a need for gravestones. Moving to a big city, he'd miss the land and hate the crowds, but he would never again be poor. Likely or not, it was a pleasant little fantasy, and it helped him fall into a content and dreamless sleep.

That next morning, as he lay there remembering where he was, the previous day's happenings came into focus. His ambitious day-dreams seemed foolish. Listening to the street noise and the occasional train whistle outside, he realized he had taken on a project far too big for his ability. He had never before not known what to carve. He had never been so uncertain he would be able to deliver a finished memorial stone.

CHAPTER 6
MAY 28, 1935

Frank checked in at the warden's office for his second day of work, and Maggie showed him into Mr. Jameson's office. The click of her shoes on the hardwood floor resonated off the office walls. She did smell good. Abby always made fun of women who wore perfume; it was such a frivolous waste of money. She said things like that, because she knew they could never afford it, said it to make Frank feel better. Perhaps perfume was not a bad thing. In his new life, Frank would buy perfume for his wife.

The warden greeted him. His clean, pressed suit gleamed in the morning light compared to Frank's patched and frayed work clothes. He was as out of place in the office as he had been the day before. "Did you get some good ideas for the stone after I left?" the warden asked.

"I did, sir. I'll need another day before I start carving," Frank lied politely. He was about to suggest looking at his sketches the following morning, to buy himself an extra day, when an image came to mind—or more accurately, the lack of an image. He knew precisely what he was missing. "Where'd your wife grow up in Norway?" Frank asked. "Her home, what'd it look like?"

"I can do better than describe it with words," Mr. Jameson said. He pointed to a painting on the wall opposite his desk. Frank hadn't noticed it the day before, so distracted by the oak desk, the mystery job, the man himself. It was a stunning canvas. Like a window in time, the frame showed a fishing village next to calm, crystal blue waters, the walls of a fjord and towering mountains in the distance towered above it all. Little red and white houses along the shoreline stood out against the steel blue ocean, the verdant green landscape, the grey, snow-streaked mountains beyond.

"That is her home," Mr. Jameson said, his voice very quiet, as though he was talking to himself. "Elisa lost her parents as a young girl; she was sent to America to live with her aunt."

Frank walked over to the wall, closer to the painting, memorizing its details. Of course, this was what he needed. He was trying to make up such a scene with a sketch of a hillside meadow the day before, but that was from his own land. Elisa's stone needed her own homeland on it. It would be the most difficult relief scene he'd ever carved. All the depth and odd angles. God, the water. How would he carve water?

Frank heard the warden's footsteps as the man came to his side. "A family friend commissioned this painting and sent it to her some twenty years ago. I always thought it should be in her sitting room. But every time we moved for my work, she insisted that I have it in my office—to remind me of her." The warden nodded a few times as he continued, "It does serve that purpose well enough. When you meet her you will understand."

Frank stared at the warden, once again shocked at the man's words. "Meet her? Sir, I hardly think that would be—"

"No, I insist," Mr. Jameson said. He remained polite but bit each word. "It's important to me, and it's no trouble at all."

Trouble? Frank was more concerned that such an affair would be even more macabre than the very act of carving a gravestone for a living person. Actually meeting her, speaking with her, this was outlandish. But he had no idea how to argue with this man.

"We'll plan on your presence for Sunday dinner then," the warden said.

Baffled, Frank nodded yes. Mr. Jameson commenced to give him instructions for meeting him at his church after the service. He would drive him to his home from there. "For Elisa's sake, I rented a home outside of town," he explained. "The stairs in the warden's residence in town are too much for her. We like the quiet, too." Mr. Jameson welcomed him to meet earlier for the service itself. Frank realized then that he had a fine excuse for refusing both invitations. "I didn't bring my Sunday clothes, sir. This is all I've got," he said gesturing to his scrappy attire. The warden had to understand this. He didn't.

"God does not care, and neither does Elisa," he said, overly-cheerful about the whole matter. "I follow suit. Pardon the pun. There's no dress code for dinner with a friend." Then, guessing correctly at Frank's concern, he added, "We shan't tell Elisa the exact nature of your purpose here. I'll tell her I've hired you for some stonework in town, that you're a fine craftsman. That is all."

That was all there was to say on the matter. Frank agreed to meet Mr. Jameson at the corner of Milwaukee and Fifth, after the church service. Flustered, he looked back at the painting, trying to memorize a few more details, visualizing how he could use it on the stone. The warden was already at the door, ready to accompany him to the prison gate.

"If you don't mind, may I see your sketch before you start your cuts?" he asked.

"Of course; it's your stone, sir," Frank said, surprised that the warden would ask permission for such a thing. The fellow never said anything typical or expected. He seemed to assume the outrageous to be common, and in the same breath could treat a common request as the most delicate matter. There was something about this fellow.

Mr. Jameson slapped Frank on the back in a friendly manner. "Tell McMurphy when the sketch is ready," he said. "I don't want to be a nuisance now; I know how artists can be." Perhaps this was supposed to clarify things, but it didn't. Frank smiled in mock understanding. He wasn't sure himself what artists were like and couldn't see how he might be categorized as one. He was just a rancher who carved stone on the side to make extra money. As Frank stepped out onto Main Street he looked for cars before walking across to the prison entrance. He noticed a man wearing a suit on the street corner watching him. There was nothing casual in the man's stare. The man was watching Frank with decisive focus. Something was wrong. Only two types of people wore suits on a weekday in Deer Lodge: bankers and government people. This man didn't look like a banker. Frank actually felt relieved when the guard opened the door and let him enter the prison. But passing through the grounds commanded all of Frank's attention, and he quickly forgot about the strange man in the suit.

Back through the gate, back through the prison yard, back into the shed. Alone with the stone once again, Frank turned on the light and pulled off the tarp. The whole room took on a blue tint once the stone was exposed. It felt like the first time Frank had exhaled the whole morning. As imposing as the project was, he was at ease by the stone. This was where he belonged. And now he had the right image in his mind.

Frank incorporated the new ideas into a new sketch. He committed it all to paper: the waterfront scene framing the entire stone—the shore along the bottom, the fjord rising upward, the distant mountains at the top—just as it should be. There would be some understated scrollwork around the inscription. For the next four hours he worked with the pencil, erasing and drawing, over and over again, trying to project the Norwegian fishing village

71

onto an outline of the stone. He had always been attentive to detail, but now he aspired for perfection. He felt driven to please Mr. Jameson, even if he could not understand the odd man. He wished to create something worthy of Elisa, a woman whom he found both fascinating and disquieting. Even if she never knew why he was in Deer Lodge, who he really was, if Frank had to meet the woman this Sunday, he wanted to be able to look her in the eye and feel he'd done well.

When McMurphy delivered his lunch, Frank told him that the sketch was ready for Mr. Jameson's review. He was just finishing his sandwich when the warden knocked and entered the shed. The warden surveyed the sketch, looking from drawing to stone, making humming sounds. He stood to his full height and nodded at Frank.

"I approve," he said. He looked back at the stone, touched the spot where the dedication, the date of birth, and date of passing would be. "Would you be willing to come down and complete the stone, when the time comes?" he asked. "I prefer that every mark come from the same hand."

"Of course."

"Will you begin cutting this afternoon?"

"I will," Frank said. "You're welcome to come by any time to look at it." It was hard not to offer such a courtesy. Though Frank wondered, as soon as he voiced the words, if that was a bad idea. He'd never had anyone look at his work before it was complete. Not even Clay and Abby got to do that. Up at the ranch, unfinished stones were tarped and locked in the carving shed.

The warden seemed pleased by the offer, though. He left Frank then, to begin the task. The door closed, and Frank looked at the radiant blue granite. It seemed a living thing. He took the next two hours to redraw the sketch onto the stone itself, transferring each detail and wondering if he would be able to render it well once chisel met stone. Past works were ornate with deep cuts requiring much time. More recently—since 1929—most everyone wanted simple, less expensive stones. This stone was not common, and cost wasn't an issue. The real limitation was time. Could he? Could he possibly use the chisel as a pencil, the fine lines of the sketch turned into furrows in the stone? Perhaps he could avoid carving deep chasms into the beautiful stone, but instead trust the gleaming polished surface to contrast with clean, quick cuts. Frank hesitated, questioning his abilities for a moment. Unlike the pencil and pad, he knew there was no erasing a cut.

He unfolded the leather bundle and looked at the assortment of chisels. With the two-pound hammer and a small flat chisel in hand, he approached the stone. He'd start with the element most familiar to him: the mountains. With a deep breath, he placed the corner of the chisel and tapped it with the hammer, the first sharp ring filling the small room.

CHAPTER 7
JUNE 1935

At the end of the second day, Frank saw the man in the suit once again, this time sitting in a car south of the prison entrance near the formal warden's residence. Frank could see clearly that it was the same fellow. He looked away when Frank met his gaze. Whoever it was, he wasn't trying that hard to be stealthy. As it turned out, Mr. Jameson must've seen that Frank was being watched.

The next morning Frank stopped in the office, but Mr. Jameson seemed on edge. Their conversation was brief, and when Frank got up to head out the front door to the prison, Mr. Jameson stopped him.

"You won't be going that way any longer," he said. "Follow me, please." Mr. Jameson walked to the back of his office and opened a door that Frank had assumed was a closet. Steep narrow stairs led down to a small basement, where two lights revealed stone walls and two steel doors, one on the south wall, one on the west. Pulling a key from his coat pocket the warden unlocked the west door. Its mass required no small effort to swing it open. A long tunnel stretched out before them. A little too stunned to question the wisdom of doing so, Frank followed the warden in. Mr.

Jameson secured the door and led the way to another metal door fifty yards down the tunnel.

"Conley had this built when the walls were constructed," Mr. Jameson said as they walked down the dimly lit passage. "Few know about it and from now on you will enter and leave this way. McMurphy will bring you to the passage entry, and Maggie will let you out at the office."

"Why the secrecy?" Frank asked, trying to match Mr. Jameson's surprisingly cool tone.

"My position here is a political appointment. There are some who do not want me here, some who once benefited from past corruption. They'll look for any reason to justify my removal," the warden explained. "You aren't doing anything wrong, Frank. This is just a precaution."

The warden pounded on the door and a small panel opened to reveal McMurphy's face. He scrutinized them both, then un-latched the lock and opened the door. The tunnel went on further to intersect yet another passage. Who knew how long it was. Frank followed McMurphy up a steep set of metal stairs to a massive steel plate at the top. Climbing through the trap door, Frank found himself inside the key room of tower seven. The four times he had been in it before, he had never noticed the door on the floor. After McMurphy and the warden were through, the guard closed and locked the door.

Back in the shed, Mr. Jameson reviewed and approved Frank's work, then left for the day. Frank had so many questions but kept them to himself. Secret tunnels? What if carving this stone landed him in this very prison? Mr. Jameson's assurance that he was do-ing nothing wrong rang hollow. Even so, Frank knew he couldn't quit. Not now. He knew what the stone needed. He figured it would take a good two weeks of work, and he had almost a full week to think of its beneficiary before meeting her. Time and rou-tine were the cure to most ills in Frank's life. This was no different.

Though the town, the nature of the work, and the irregularity of the tunnel kept Frank a little on edge, he did settle into something of a routine. Frank's days in Deer Lodge seemed to have the slowest starts he'd ever experienced. Unlike his days on the ranch, where work began as early as humanly possible to avoid the heat of the day, here he woke early, but dallied over breakfast at the Montana Café, shared a second cup of coffee with his boss, took time to review the previous day's work on the stone. By the time he was carving, he'd been wide awake for almost three hours. He found this most agreeable. Frank made up for it by carving nearly non-stop once he started. Each line of the image encouraging— no, demanding, that he continue.

The expressed purpose of his morning meetings with the warden was to report on the carving progress. But there was never any substantial talk about the work itself, and Mr. Jameson followed Frank to the utility shed only twice more that week to marvel at the progress. The chats seemed more necessary to the warden, on a conversational level. He did not pry into Frank's life after the first few inquiries yielded very guarded replies. Instead, each morning Mr. Jameson shared a new story about Elisa, about their children. Initially bemused, eventually genuinely interested, Frank listened.

There was the time when they lived in Maine, Elisa, while holding their youngest daughter, slipped off a log and into a creek. The little girl was fine. The creek was not deep. Still, Elisa was soaked up to her knees. She emerged from the water laughing and insisted that they fulfill their promise to their children to get ice cream after their stroll. Standing in a dripping dress, Elisa ordered her treat without a second thought about the looks she was getting. Then, there was the time that she stopped traffic in Chicago to save a dog who had been hit by a car, not giving a care about her own safety. She nursed the dog back to health, and it lived with them till it passed away two years ago. Frank could only force a smile on that one. Why would anyone risk her life for a dog?

He was not sure why his boss needed to divulge these personal details, but so long as the conversation was not aimed at his own life, he was content to listen. Still, to learn so much about the woman for whom he carved weighed on Frank. She was a living, breathing soul whose death was approaching, and Frank would profit from it. Really, only when he was working on the carving itself did he have freedom from that thought.

Frank worked till six each evening. At the end of the day, McMurphy escorted him out the tunnel. Then he met Maggie in the warden's office for the walk back to the boarding house. Everyone else in the office had left for the day. Maggie said she was happy to wait for him as it allowed her to catch up on work, and the extra pay was not a bad thing either. So they walked together, and Frank's presence spared her the hassle of the stares and catcalls of the vagrants and construction workers. Frank let her left hand rest in the crook of his right elbow. A nice touch, but awkward.

He would have very likely entertained an affair with Maggie, if it had not seemed fully impossible. Frank was sure Abby assumed he was taking some liberties during this trip, and their divorce had already occurred a thousand times in his mind. The marriage was as good as dead. It was no deep moral conviction that prevented him; it was only the threat of humiliation. On their second little walk home, when Maggie thanked him for being "such a gentleman" the appreciation seemed genuine enough, but it was somehow condescending, too. She said the words the same way a woman might say them to a very young boy.

So Frank found these evening walks with Maggie far more uncomfortable than he'd hoped. Each afternoon he looked forward to seeing her. She was a striking creature after all, not astounding, but pretty in her own way—dark hair pinned into a bun, fine lines at the edges of her green eyes when she smiled. After a day of staring at the cool blue stone, it was a delight to look at this woman, and a small torment to do nothing.

Thankfully, like the warden, Maggie was well adept at carrying the spoken word. Not only did Frank wrestle with his own usual quietude, there was also so very little he could say. He was not permitted to speak of his work, and Maggie knew that. He had nothing to say about his life back home, and Maggie caught on to that quickly. So she spoke—and Frank chuckled, nodded, said "Oh?" now and again. She spoke about the "T" key sticking on her typewriter, about the new cobbler who came from Boston and had such an entertaining accent, about the letter from her mother in Idaho, about women shipped to the West to be wives to moneyed men, and how some of them went insane with their need to move back to a coastal city.

"You don't talk about your wife much," Maggie asked as they walked home Friday evening. He was about to offer his usual "Oh?" when the nature of the question penetrated his brain. What? Frank hadn't talked about *anything* since their brief exchange the first day, let alone about Abby. Maggie took his non-reply as invitation for clarification, "I imagine you miss her, being apart for so long."

A few footfalls later and finally Frank said yes—not a complete a lie. He did miss her cooking. More quiet. This time Maggie seemed to be stewing. At the boarding house, instead of their usual good-evenings, she turned and faced him.

"Do you blame her?" she pried.

"What?" What indeed. What the hell were they talking about? Blame who for what?

"Your wife. Some men blame their wives when they have no children."

Maggie had very neatly picked him up and turned him inside out. This woman, this stranger, this sweet, gentle thing. Frank was shocked not only at her words, but also at the powerful urge to hit her. He felt awful for that, disgusted. Astounding how spoken violence could be as provocative as a solid right hook. Maggie had just picked a fight with him.

"No. I don't," he said. "Abby blames God. I don't. I don't blame anyone at all."

"Oh? That's a rare quality in a man," she said, a skeptical smile playing at her lips. "It must be hard to run the ranch alone."

She was merciless! What was this? He'd only been kind to her all week. "It's hard work," he said. Then Frank discovered he had something to say. He measured each word carefully. "It is hard, but it's a waste of time to worry about the future. Don't get anything done by worrying." That was his mother's old sentiment, and it was true.

"Are you going to move your family here someday?"

Merciless and plain mean. "A waste. Of time. To worry," Frank repeated. It was well and good for a man to critique his own life and livelihood, but hearing such words from a stranger was reprehensible. Deliberate and cool, he said, "We won't move, if we don't have to."

It was Maggie's turn to look uncomfortable. "I didn't mean to upset you, Frank," she said. "As I mentioned several days ago, I am very forward. My best and worst quality. Will you forgive me?"

Frank furrowed his brow. He nodded slowly, not so much in receipt of the apology, but in slow consideration of the entire interaction. This gal was like a barn cat playing with her mouse. "Good evening, ma'am," he said and turned to head inside. He heard her call her farewell after him. She sounded sad, penitent. He did not look back. Women never failed to confuse him, and he needed his mind clear right now. He had a job to complete, the most important one ever.

The next morning, Frank was thankful it was Saturday. Maggie wouldn't be at the office. The warden was alone there, coming in only to facilitate Frank's entrance into the passageway, and to look at the stone once more. By now, Frank had rough-etched the entire scene, leaving only the inscription area untouched. After Mr. Jameson left, he began the detail work on the shoreline and fjord. It was time to work on the water, really the most daunting task of all. Mr. Jameson had asked how much longer the project would take. Frank estimated another week. But that really depended on how the water carving went—he might find he needed another three days just for that. He did not share that with the warden, though.

Frank let the task wash over him. Nothing else existed. Abby faded from his mind. So did Clay, and Maggie, and even the warden and his wife. It was rare he had such experiences when he carved at home—he never had such great swaths of time. By his midday break, Frank had learned quite by accident, that carving water was mostly about what you didn't do. His first tap into the sea, he noticed how the mark contrasted with the polished granite around it. Of course, it's blue, and it's already got a sheen! He didn't need to carve the waves themselves, only their shadows. The task suddenly became possible. And enjoyable. He settled into making the tiniest most delicate taps to highlight the sea's movement. The steel of the chisel grew warm from hours of holding it. The vibration of each tap penetrated his fingers, only dissipating when the sensation reached his wrist. Gentle and steady, they were the same strokes he'd use to craft rose petals. It wasn't new at all. By the end of the workday, he felt pleased with the water. It really did look fluid.

He even moved on from the water, began the detail work on the shoreline itself, the houses and trees. But a full week of leaning over the stone, a full week of holding the chisel and hammer—it was not something his body was accustomed to. His back and arms ached. His elbows were searing. The change in attention, from water to houses, had woken him up just enough to realize how much he hurt all over. He set the tools down, stood upright, stretched—really looked at the stone, the whole thing.

"Well, Frank, if you pull this off, it'll be the best you've ever done," he said to himself. He had no idea what time it was. Since he'd started carving, it was the first time he was thankful to hear McMurphy knock at the door, announcing quitting time. A break, a full day off, would be a very good thing.

McMurphy was his normal silent, stoic self as he escorted Frank through the tunnel and out of the warden's office.

"See you Monday." Frank said as he stepped out onto the front stairs facing Main Street. McMurphy grunted a reply before locking the door behind Frank, freeing him for the remainder of the weekend.

After such a focused day with the stone, Frank's mind was in a strange way, remembering some things, forgetting others. He even thought for a flash of calling on Maggie and asking her to a picture show at the Rialto. Only then did he recall the abrasive interaction he'd had with her the day before. No picture show then. He'd still be kind for his part, still see if she wanted him to escort her home on Monday. But he'd make no further gestures of friendship. For tonight, he deserved a beer after a long week of work.

After a quick bite to eat at the Montana Cafe, Frank walked down Main Street and entered the first bar he came across, the M&M. The end of prohibition two years earlier had opened a floodgate of finally legal drinking establishments. Not that Frank had been one to drink much, anyway. It was expensive for one thing, and bar-drinking required too much potential for unwanted conversation. A flask of Old Crow kept in the cupboard at the ranch suited his needs just fine.

That Saturday evening was different though. That was a lot of solitude, even for him. He felt both moneyed and almost amiable. He had been entirely alone most of the week. A pint or two at the M&M would do the trick. The one-room bar was full of cow hands, miners, rail yard workers, and a few ladies from town and the surrounding area. The men handily outnumbered the women in the bar by eight to one. Frank sat at a table in the corner, alone with his drink. After spending six days focused on one task, it was good to relax and watch the antics of the other patrons. About halfway through the third pint, he was feeling it. Frank was, admittedly, an utter lightweight. Drinking was such a rare luxury, and the beer's warmth was a fine sensation after such a strange week, such a rough year. In his fuzzy state, he thought very freely of Abby and of Maggie and of his mother's passing and the ranch's failing. But the beer took the edge off the sadness, and that was good. Having little practice with this pleasure, he failed to stop while ahead. Four pints in two hours and he'd left the realm of contented after-work buzz to the land of the truly miserable drunk.

The old bar maid cut him off, laughing at him, "Go home kid—you best lay down before you fall down."

Frank was just coherent enough to recognize the wisdom of this advice. In the continuum of drunken personalities, he was far more apt to spiral downward than ratchet up toward belligerence. Yup, time to leave. Standing up, he felt the room spin, his right hand reached in vain to find support. His left hand caught a bar stool and held fast, but it was several seconds before he felt stable enough to try walking. Each slow step drew him closer to the door. He thought of the way a newborn calf tried to walk in the snow. Yes, that must be what he looked like. This thought made him chuckle to himself. The laugh was nice, better than thinking about the ranch's finances.

Just then, a woman stood up from another table. She spun around to head to the bar, only to run into Frank. Their muddled encounter pushed Frank into a shuffle step to regain his balance, but sent the woman tumbling into the nearest table. Her own night of drinking must have left her coordination in a more dilapidated state than his. The table, unable to support the woman, tilted violently, sending beer glasses and an empty peanut bowl flying. A spray of golden liquid caught the dim light as it showered over the crowd. Frank found himself grabbed by the lapels by an irate man who emanated the stench of chewing tobacco and cheap beer. The man ignored Frank's slurred apology and threw him across the floor—an easy chore given his already questionable sense of balance. Tumbling into another table, the second ruckus caused the bar to erupt. The last thing Frank remembered was a fist careening towards his face, its owner sneering through a broken row of yellow teeth.

CHAPTER 8

JUNE 1935

The week since Frank had left for Deer Lodge had not been as painful as Abby feared it might be. In fact, she was relieved by his absence. His dark mood infused the whole ranch when he was around. She didn't realize how much she'd been coping till he was gone. It was a blessing to be without that heavy feeling—always fearing their next interaction. Abby remembered that not all her work each day was unpleasant; she noticed once more how beautiful the mountains were this time of year. She still ruminated about the past year, still pondered what she might do if Frank was still gone several weeks from now. But she didn't have to confront the great problem in person every morning and evening.

Abby was hanging clothes on the line to dry when Stanley Hart, one of the neighbor boys, rode up on a roan mare. Like most children, he rode comfortably bareback. He was on his way home from school in Avon. Stanley was in his final week of the six-week long spring session. Children would go back for another six-week stint in the fall, though some took advantage of the optional summer session that would allow them to advance a grade. School, like so many other activities, suspended for the winter. Stranger gave a half-hearted warning bark then pranced up to the boy and horse, his tail high. Abby was happy to see the boy. She always was; Stanley was a sweet heart.

"I didn't know ya had a dog," he said, reining his horse to a stop.

"We haven't had him long. His name is Stranger," she said and stopped her work. "He's friendly enough, if he approves of you."

Stanley slid off the horse, and Stranger did indeed give him a friendly welcome, tail wagging fast and panting mouth turned up in a doggy grin. "Seems that he likes you," Abby said, then finished pinning up one of Clay's shirts.

"Yeah, my ma says I got a way with animals, but she says that's cause I smell like 'em, come bath time."

Abby laughed. Stanley's mother had her hands full with five boys, Stanley being the youngest. The boy commenced to give Stranger a good ear scratch. The animal obviously felt no need to act as watchdog with this visitor.

"Mr. Morgan at the post office asked me to give this letter to you," said Stanley, reaching into his bib overalls with his free hand and pulling out an envelope. Abby walked over to Stanley, who was still occupied with petting Stranger. The dog leaned into him in contented bliss.

"Can I water my horse?" Stanley asked as he handed Abby the envelope.

"Of course," Abby said. "You know where the pump is." She looked at the envelope. If Frank had written it, someone else had addressed it. She didn't recognize the handwriting on the exterior. She started to open it, but suddenly felt she should wait till she was alone. Tucking the envelope into her apron, Abby watched as Stanley led his horse over to the trough and began working the hand pump. Water flowed into the basin, and the horse leaned over, taking long, deep pulls from the trough. Stranger put his front paws up on the edge and lapped the cool water as well, his head no more than six inches from the horse. The animals watched each other closely as they drank. The horse did not spook, but her ears twitched nervously.

Clay came out of the barn and asked Stanley if he'd checked on whether the new connecting rod had come in at the depot. The boy said it hadn't; he'd check again the next day. Abby knew Clay was eager to see the sickle fully repaired, but she wondered how they would pay for it if Frank didn't come back. Clay thanked the boy and returned to the barn. Stanley turned his attention back to Abby. "Was that a note from Mr. Redmond?"

"I believe so," she said. "I'll read it later." Abby grabbed her laundry basket and headed towards the house. She wanted Stanley to stay; she should at least compensate him for running errands for them, but she did not want him to ask anything further about Frank. There was one very easy way to distract the boy. "You look hungry," she said. "I have a batch of molasses cookies that needs to be taken out of the oven. Care for a taste?" Stanley had started a game of tug-o-war with Stranger, battling over a rope scrap they found by the pump. Stanley perked up at the offer, answering with an emphatic yes. Hands full, Abby motioned with her head for him to follow into the kitchen. "You can catch me up on all the town news while you have a couple of cookies."

Stanley yielded the rope to Stranger who looked a little forlorn at the sudden easy win. The boy tied his horse and followed Abby indoors. To keep the kitchen from getting too unbearable, she had left all the doors and windows open. So, the smell of fresh cookies wafted over them before they even went in. Stanley took a seat at the kitchen table and flashed his toothy, ten-year-old boy grin.

Abby pulled the cookie sheet out of the oven compartment in the wood stove, using her apron to protect her hands from the heat. She set the cookies out to cool, then brought the morning's collection of eggs over to the table and sat down across from Stanley. "So tell me what's been happening out in the big wide world," she asked as she gingerly placed the fresh eggs into a preserving tin. There were already several layers of eggs in it, covered with a clear liquid. Stanley told her all the news he'd heard up and down the road between Avon and Finn—which family had a bad cold this spring, which baby had just learned to walk, who was thinking of actually buying a tractor even though they weren't really ranchers anyway, but transplants from a wealthy set in Connecticut.

"Oh, I almost forgot," Stanley interrupted himself. "Mr. Totland got hurt real bad down at the depot last night."

Abby looked up from sorting the eggs. Mr. Totland had been with the Northern Pacific Railroad since 1912 and had been a friend of Abby's father. She shook her head as Stanley recounted how a couple of tramps had attacked the depot manager. Mr. Totland was alive, but laid up with a head injury. Crime was practically unheard of in their region, but occasionally they were hearing of the usually peaceful railroad tramps becoming violent. People were coming from the coasts, arriving in western Montana hungry and all the more desperate when they found no work in town after town.

"That's terrible!" Abby said. "Poor Mr. Totland. Did they catch the men?" Stanley shook his head no. It was the first time she felt uncomfortable about Frank's absence. The room grew silent. Abby was quick to get their minds onto something else. "Stanley, would you grab me that bottle of Water Glass from the shelf behind you, please?" The boy got up from the table and carefully slid the glass bottle out from between a tin can of Hills Brothers Coffee and a sack of IGA baking soda. He handed the egg preservative to Abby. She poured its contents over the new layer of eggs in the bucket. She would set the bucket in the crawl space at the end of the day, next to several other buckets just like it. The treated eggs could keep for months. They could be used during a time when the hens were not laying any. Or they were useful when Abby heard of another family that was strapped; she'd leave fresh eggs on their stoop and use the preserved eggs for her own needs. Abby closed up the bottle when she was done and wiped her hands on her apron, rustling the letter in her pocket. She handed the egg preservative to Stanley, who put it back on the shelf. Sweet boy.

"I suspect you want some milk?" Abby asked. She reached for a hard-water-stained glass and the pitcher of fresh milk, anticipating an affirmative answer.

"Yes, ma'am! I mean, please, ma'am," Stanley said, trying to contain his excitement.

"You are always the gentleman. If I ever have a son, I do hope that he's as polite as you." Abby poured the milk and handed it to Stanley, who thanked her profusely. He gushed more gratitude as she handed him two warm cookies.

With a mouthful of cookie, Stanley asked, "So why don't you have any kids, Mrs. Redmond?"

The Question always stung a little. But coming from Stanley, Abby considered it a high compliment. Her reply was well-practiced and friendly enough. "I guess God just doesn't want us to have any yet," Abby said. "Perhaps it's so we can spoil kids like you when they stop by." Stanley smiled; the answer made good sense to him.

"Now finish up so you can get home. I'm sure your mother is wondering why you are taking so long." Stanley stuffed the last of the remaining cookie in his mouth and emptied his glass of milk. He mumbled another thank you as he chewed.

When the boy headed back outdoors, Abby saw Stranger was there to greet them, hoping for a handout. "Almost forgot about you, Stranger," she said as she ducked back into the house and came back with three cookies—two for Clay and one of the burnt ones that had been on the edge of the pan closest to the fire box. Abby handed Stranger the burnt cookie. The dog stretched his neck out and took it with a dainty bite. Only when clear of her hand did he quickly gobble it up.

"Stranger is a gentleman, just like you, Stanley," Abby said, smiling at the dog. "Always polite. He doesn't dare bite the hand that feeds him." Stranger's tail swished back and forth as he looked expectantly for another. "No, these are for Clay," Abby playfully scolded the dog who still looked up at her with hopeful brown eyes.

Stanley untied his horse and used the side of the trough to hop up onto its back as he gripped its mane. Abby called to him and waved, "You be sure to tell your mother hello for me, and thank you for bringing the letter." Stanley waved his goodbye, then turned the horse toward the main gate. The skinny little boy was dwarfed by his horse. But he was confident and comfortable, galloping down the road towards his home. Abby took the two cookies to Clay, certain he needed a break. Stranger, now Abby's shadow whenever she was outside this week, trotted along behind her.

In the barn, Clay wiped his forehead and hands with a rag he kept in his back pocket. Taking the cookies, he munched slowly while Abby shared the details of the incident at the depot. She was concerned and said so, even though they were six miles from town.

"I wouldn't worry too much 'bout it," Clay said. "It's a long walk up this way, and we aren't the only folks on the road. Sides, I suspect if anybody came up here thinkin' about being up to no good, Stranger would convince them otherwise." Clay took another bite. "I'm gettin to trust his judgment of character."

"He took a real liking to Stanley," Abby said, somewhat comforted by Clay's words and confidence in the dog.

Clay broke off half of a cookie and gave it to Stranger, who took it as delicately as he had from Abby. "Yeah, I suppose we'll keep this mongrel around."

Abby bent down and petted the dog. "I don't know why you came into our lives, my four-legged friend, but I'm glad you're here," she said. "No matter what Frank thinks." Stranger gave Abby a quick lick on her wrist as she rubbed his velvet ears. She straightened and sighed. "Well, enough talk. I have laundry to finish and dinner to cook. Stranger, you coming with me or staying with Clay?"

Abby began walking out of the barn. The dog looked at her, then back at Clay to make sure he was out of cookies, then left the barn to catch up with Abby. Walking back to the house, Abby glanced to the west and saw a dark line of storm clouds. Another heavy spring gale was on its way. She might have an hour or two before it arrived, though; she finished hanging her laundry, knowing she would have to take it back down before the storm rolled in. At least it would dry a little and wouldn't be soaking wet sitting in the basket all night.

Back inside the house, Abby took the envelope out of her apron pocket and sat down. She opened it, revealing a two-page letter. No, it wasn't from Frank, but from an acquaintance in Deer Lodge—a woman whose family had lived in their valley until a year ago. When her husband lucked into work for a mechanical shop in the larger town, they cut their ranch losses and moved. Abby didn't know them well and was curious to know what her news might be.

As she began reading, her mind raced. She couldn't help but speed through the page, catching little scraps: I wish I was writing with purely friendly tidings... not one to gossip... certainly want to know, however, if a trusted acquaintance had similar information...For three evenings, I've looked out my kitchen window and I'm sure I've seen your husband...

With each sentence, Abby's lips drew tighter. She was not surprised. Not entirely grieved either. The letter only confirmed her suspicions. If Frank ever came back, she would be the one to leave.

CHAPTER 9
JUNE 2, 1935

There was no rest for Frank in the small cell he shared with one of the other patrons of the bar. That fellow was passed out on the bottom bunk. The two remaining cells contained the rest of the night's collection of drunks and scrappers who were snoring away their sundry mishaps. Frank's head hurt, not only from a decent hangover, but also from the punch and subsequent fall. It was almost seven in the morning when he heard keys, doors opening, then footsteps drawing closer to his cell. The door opened, and to his horror, there stood Mr. Jameson next to the local deputy.

"I see you had yourself some adventure last night," the warden said. His tone was stern, but he seemed to be fighting a smile.

"Sir...I can explain," Frank started.

"No need," Mr. Jameson held up his hand. "Barkeep already filled me in. No one's pressing any charges. But we do have several bars in town. Next time you might choose one not known for catering to Deer Lodge's most difficult clientele?" The warden was irritated at bailing Frank out; that was clear. But he seemed amused, too, close to laughing. He was not scolding him. He was taunting. Frank knew he deserved far worse than that. "What was that about Sunday clothes? Even if you'd brought your best, you couldn't do a thing to make that face look pretty now." Mr. Jameson maintained a straight face as he delivered that one, but the deputy laughed aloud.

Frank kept quiet. He followed the warden and deputy as they walked down the narrow hall to the front office of the Powell County Jail. The deputy overseeing Frank's release filled out paperwork at one of the two small desks that filled the front quarter of the building. That done, he gave Frank his coat and hat. Mr. Jameson let up on the gibing, looking on in silence, a small mercy during the humiliating process.

Outdoors, the lovely morning was hardly a comfort. Frank donned his hat, pulling the brim way down against the sun. The sky was robin's egg blue, and not a car moved on the streets. Beautiful. Frank's eyes ached like mad. He also had no idea how to get back to the boarding house. The warden knew that and waved him into his tan colored '34 Ford sedan. This was the most luxurious motorcar Frank had ever seen, let alone sat in. Under any other circumstances, he would have been thrilled at his good fortune.

When Mr. Jameson settled into the driver's seat, Frank attempted to speak. "Sir, if you fired me on the spot, I'd fully understand."

The warden snorted at that sentiment. "And then what? Finish carving that masterpiece myself?" He started the car and explained as he drove—how the deputy last night had recognized Frank's name, how everyone in the law enforcement community knew about the stone-carver working on some mystery project for the prison warden. Just as Mr. Jameson predicted, word had traveled fast, despite all his precautions. The local deputy, finding the situation delicious, took the liberty to call the warden late last night. What a humdinger to deliver that news: *your artiste is in my jail at the moment…*

"I can't quite envision you picking a fight, so I made a couple of calls," the warden said. "Marley at the M&M is a reasonable enough fellow even if he caters to toughs. It didn't take much persuading for him to realize you weren't at fault."

What a moment. His boss, on his most difficult job ever, had to pull strings to get him out of jail. Frank offered his profuse thanks and apology. The opportunity for crow-eating did not end there, though. Mr. Jameson did not see the night's events as any reason to cancel their plans for dinner.

Frank did his best to resist, "I can't imagine meeting your wife looking like—"

"You need to wash up, son," the warden interrupted. "That cut's probably not as bad as it feels." He looked back and forth between the windshield and Frank, scrutinizing his hire as he drove. "Nah, not that bad a bruise at all."

As they pulled to a stop at Mrs. Watson's boarding house, Mr. Jameson reiterated his insistence. "My cook is expecting to prepare a meal for you," he said. "I'm heading to my church service. Meet me in two hours at the corner of Milwaukee and Fifth. You know what my car looks like."

The man had just got him out of jail. Frank nodded in agreement and got out of the car. He avoided Mrs. Watson's condescending stare and headed up to his room to make himself as presentable as possible. What a relief to find the key to his room in his coat pocket, and his full week of pay still there as well. He scrubbed up at the washbasin in his room and put on a clean shirt and pants. He'd only brought three shirts and one change of jeans; he hadn't thought he'd need anything more. Hell, he didn't own much more than that. Well, he no longer reeked of beer. But with his patched knees and elbows, his clean clothes hardly qualified as presentable. The tiny shaving mirror on the wall permitted him a limited evaluation of his swollen lip. Scrubbing removed the dried blood, but there was no hiding the puffy bruise. Frank combed his hair and peered again in the mirror. It was the best he could do.

He checked his pocket watch. It would be another hour before he was to meet the warden. Not long enough to catch up on sleep. He had no desire to sit idly in the stuffy room, or face Mrs. Watson to ask about breakfast, but he also doubted any cafes were open on a Sunday morning. No matter, he didn't feel all that hungry anyway, and a walk might do him some good. He skirted down the stairs past the front desk, thankful he could hear Mrs. Watson back in the kitchen. He walked east on Pennsylvania and then turned on north on Fourth.

He walked with no plan other than to wake himself up and try to work out the aches in all his joints. There was no pretense that he might be able to clear his head; he'd given up that hope as soon as he saw the warden arrive at his cell that morning. Frank did mull over the whole mess, though. Even if the stone was pristine in its finished state, he had no idea how he could look Mr. Jameson in the eye again. And what if there was a flaw in the memorial? What if he ran into some material flaw in the stone itself? In his sleep-deprived mind's eye, he saw himself making a delicate tap on the mountaintop along the top edge of the scene. One tiny chisel tap and a massive fist-sized portion of stone pulled away from the slab, leaving a gaping wound in the blue granite. He had cements and stone powders he could use to patch such flaws in a common stone from his own quarry. But there was nothing he could think of to fix that gleaming blue granite.

Frank chewed on that bone as he wandered through town. Soon he found himself on Milwaukee Avenue. It would be good to make his way to the church. Perhaps he could find a bench outside where he could wait, preferably one that was shaded. No such luck. For lack of anywhere better to go, he wandered up the church steps and stood under the eave at its entrance. The doors were open. Standing to the side, he could look in without attracting any attention to himself. There was Mr. Jameson near the front, the back of his balding head, the collar of his dark brown jacket.

Yes, there he was, the strange man who'd bailed him out. The one who'd found him and hired him, promising the pay of over a month's wages to create a gift for his dying wife, the one who escorted him through a secret tunnel each day. It was impossible to discern whether this whole fiasco was a monstrous gratification of the warden's own pride—would he pass by the stone in years to come and pat himself on the back for being such a good husband? Elisa would never even see this gift.

Or would she? Frank's exhausted brain hopped about, developing a new horror scene to add to the carving-flaw nightmare. What if the warden was macabre enough to show his wife the finished gravestone? Frank pictured him cloaked like a grim reaper, wheeling his wife to his office where he'd stashed the finished stone, pictured her screaming in horror when she realized...

Get a hold of yourself, man, Frank chastened himself. He wasn't sure whether to laugh or kick himself for the screwball daydreams. He needed to be in good form. The service would be done in another fifteen minutes. *Look at the church pews, there's some fine scrollwork on the ends. Look at the stained glass, imagine the time that went into those four panels.* Yes, he could do that for a few minutes. He could admire someone else's work. Even if it was in a church.

Frank could count on one hand the number of times he had set foot in a church since he married Abby. The Avon community church, built back in the 1800's, never had a full time pastor. Services happened only when a traveling preacher came through. Some seemed sincere, but Frank had seen enough preachers who were, as far as he could tell, men who had a taste for wanderlust and had simply found a vocation to fund their travels.

Frank was no scholar, not by a long shot. But he was not uneducated either, and Clay had raised him to be rational. Both father and son had similar philosophies. Question and prod at all superstitions. Believe the things that are right in front of you. Don't waste time worrying about imagined fears—especially anything pertaining to an afterlife. Churches held some value in stitching people together, but that was about it. Clay had attended church only when Vivian prodded him. Frank had followed suit in his relationship with Abby. This was far from unusual in their region. Men did not move to Montana to become devout.

He remembered his father's chats about the matter. When Frank was young, his father had a tough edge; the boy regarded him with nothing short of fear. But Clay softened at times, usually when they were on a long ride into the mountains to find stray cattle. He waxed philosophical then, spoke to his son with a gentle tone. In his own mind, Frank called these moments Father's answer-to-everything talks. Of course, he never said that to Clay's face.

"Think of it this way," Father would start, as if answering a question, though Frank hadn't asked him anything. "Of all the things a man can learn about, religion is the most imaginative. People dream up whole lists of rules, make up long and crazy stories, and then say it's all given to them by a big man in the sky. They make up more rules to make sure they don't break the first list of rules. Men create theology like your pals at school make up rules for a new ball game. And they get just as angry when someone breaks a rule."

If there was a God, the big Fella was so big he couldn't hardly care about the piddly attempts humans made to try to placate him. Probably didn't give a rat's ass that some humans thought they held a monopoly on understanding him. Still, Clay did not openly criticize any church-goer—especially Vivan. He qualified all his disdain for religion: "If it makes a person happy and content, and no one is forcing me to follow suit, it's well and good by me."

As Frank gazed into the First Presbyterian Church, a few disconnected words drifted out to him. But it was his own father's voice that echoed in his mind. The congregation stood for the final hymn, and Frank scurried down the stairs and across the street, to stand under a tree near the warden's car. The congregants filed out. Mr. Jameson lingered outside, socializing, politely explaining how Elisa was not feeling well, and that she was sorry she couldn't attend. The warden spoke gently, smiling at each friend's encouraging words and well wishes. He chatted with the minister at length, and the two laughed about something the minister said. It was strange to watch the warden in this context, strange for Frank to think of all the interactions he'd had with the man. The fellow was so soft-hearted. How did he manage to run the state prison? The first warden had survived having his throat slit by an inmate in an attempted escape. The job was not for the meek.

Well, it was alright by Frank that the man did not live up to the image of a typical prison warden. Who knew how that morning could have gone if he did. And the bizarre day had just begun. At least Frank didn't fear for his personal safety or his job at the moment. Meeting Elisa was enough to worry about.

Mr. Jameson looked at his car and saw Frank. He finished his conversations and waved to another family as he crossed the street. "You came!" he called as he approached. "I thought you might skip out of town." Mr. Jameson gave Frank one last playful taunt, then turned apologetic about dallying after the service. "In the past, Elisa was the one who held me up," he said. "Apparently, now it's my turn."

On the drive, Frank settled into an almost comfortable silence as the warden chatted. He explained a little more about Elisa's health requiring him to move out of town and into the summer home of a friend, a copper baron in Butte. Smaller than the state-provided home, its peaceful location and the view were perfect for Elisa's health. It did the warden good as well. He found the drive soothing. The house was ten minutes out of town on land that looked out at Mount Powell west of town.

Mr. Jameson became quiet as they drove past Hillcrest Cemetery. There were hundreds of grey and white gravestones, and Frank thought of how the Norwegian granite would stand out amidst the dull stones and green grass. The warden turned off the county road and onto the driveway of a single level home that looked more like it belonged next to some remote mountain lake than overlooking Deer Lodge. Its stone and log construction resembled the hunting lodges of the elite that Frank had seen pictures of. Its size was well beyond that of a rustic cabin, with copper roofed living wings branching off from the main entrance. Frank had seen the mine owner's homes in Helena and Butte, the elaborate stone and wood exteriors. He'd never gone inside one, but he could guess what the interiors were like. This house was not like those mansions which had brightly painted multiple stories that shouted the status of the occupants, but it was still immense compared to anywhere he'd ever called home.

The heavy oak front door was already open; a short stocky woman about Mr. Jameson's age greeted them. This was not Elisa. The warden handed her his coat and told Frank to do likewise. As the woman left with their coats and hats, the warden explained. "Meghan is our cook and housekeeper," he said. "And Elisa's nurse. And our butler too. I don't know what we'd do without her."

Frank nodded as he looked all around. On every wall were Old West paintings by C.M. Russell and Frederick Remington and others that Frank did not recognize. The warden approached Frank, joined him looking at a portrayal of a cattle drive in a wide, dry landscape. "The paintings, like the desk in my office, are not mine, I'm afraid," the warden said. Frank was not thinking of the canvas's value or ownership; he was pondering only that his own cattle drives never seemed so eventful. A good drive was measured by how uneventful it was. No bucking, goring, or trampling. Preferably no riding far off route to gather wandering stock. Meghan returned to the room, and Frank left his thoughts unspoken.

Mr. Jameson excused himself to check on Elisa, while the housekeeper attended to Frank. She offered him coffee and showed him to a room just off the entryway. "Sunday supper will be in an hour. If you want, I have fresh pastries as well. Perhaps something to hold you over?"

Frank wondered how much his boss had told Meghan. Probably not much. She could deduce plenty from his rapscallion appearance. She was very polite despite the fact that he looked like someone who ought to be kicked out of such a house. Yes, usher him out and bolt the great front door.

"That sounds good. Thank you, ma'am," Frank said, feeling a hundred times more out of place than he had that first day in the warden's office. It was one thing to enter this house, yet another to be waited upon. The maid walked ahead of him into the reading room and pulled the drapes back from a large bay window. The room filled with sunlight. There were two chairs by the door with a small table between them. Across the room, by the window, stood a wing chair and an end table holding a well-used Bible and a small lamp. Judging by the pillows and the embroidered blanket on the wing chair, it seemed a place where Elisa might sit and read. Meghan left and returned shortly with a tray of coffee and Danishes, which she arranged in the sitting area nearest the door.

She left again without a word, and Frank was alone in the room with all the books and the window looking out on the lush green valley and Deer Lodge in the distance. He was alone with the breakfast tray, and he approached it as if it was an animal he'd seen in the timber. *Threatening? Not threatening? Edible? How to handle it?* Ah—coffee. It really was coffee. That was familiar enough, though it was in a porcelain cup that looked like it might chip if he set it down too hard. God, he needed to get through this day without breaking anything.

Even if the hot brew stung his cut lip, it was very good. Woke up his appetite too. He hadn't eaten a thing since supper the night before. The Danishes had a sugary jam inside. Wonderful. Halfway through one of them, he wondered if he wasn't supposed to be eating with his fingers. He looked at the tray, lifted a saucer, a small dish, a napkin. There were no utensils anywhere, apart from the sugar spoon. Satisfied he was not breaking some unknown rule, he polished off the pastry and gulped down one more. He had just finished wiping his mouth when he heard the warden's voice from down the hall.

"Good news," he called out then entered the room. "Elisa is feeling well enough to join us at the table, and she's excited to meet you." His hands were clasped together, as if in thankful prayer. "I told her that you are a stone carver whose work I admire. If she asks further, you can say you are carving an elaborate relief for a town memorial. That would be true enough, yes?"

"I understand," Frank said. Mr. Jameson sat down on the other chair, stirred his coffee and sipped it gazing out the window across the room. The man appeared to be catching his breath, so pleased with his wife feeling a little better, that he had nothing further to say. And for the first time in their interactions, Frank felt he had some very pressing words. He didn't think too hard about it—really, he might have stayed silent if he'd been better rested. Regardless, the question tumbled out.

"Mr. Jameson, I haven't asked before, I guess figuring it was none of my business, but why is Elisa dying?" The warden looked at Frank then dropped his gaze. He leaned back. "It's fine to ask. It's her heart. Why would that be the part of her that decided to fail her?" Mr. Jameson added a little more cream to his coffee. The spoon clanked against the sides of the cup. "We've travelled all the way to Seattle to see experts, but the doctors all say the same thing. Her condition is from a fever she had as a child. She told me she had always been sick, but I never noticed. All those years as she raised our children, she had tired spells now and again. But not like this. At times her heart beats so fast I swear it is going to leap out of her chest. There's nothing I can do but watch and hope it slows down to normal and she gets another day. A month ago, one of the physicians told me in private that there was nothing they could do." Mr.

Jameson sipped his coffee and stared past Frank. He took a deep breath. "Frank, I never told her exactly what the doctors said. I can't. I want her to be happy whatever time she has left."

"Do the doctors know how long?"

"Maybe a year. Maybe a week. Eventually, her heart will give out. They don't know." Mr. Jameson looked out the window. He stood, then crossed the room to the bookshelves, and removed a silver frame. He brought it to Frank. "I want you to see her when she was well and happy," he said and handed the portrait to Frank. Elisa stared back at him, seated on a settee with three school-aged children, a boy and two girls, standing to her left. Her blond hair curled and pinned up, the woman seemed very slight, such a fine-boned hand resting on the boy's shoulder. The portrait was a serious pose, but both children and mother had smiles teasing at their lips, as if they thought the whole affair was silly and over-done. Not unlike the way the warden approached life, holding a powerful position but ready to make a joke of it all.

"She's so sick now," Mr. Jameson said. "I should've done more to brace you for that." Frank wondered if the man regretted inviting him over. Maybe he was re-thinking, seeing the awkwardness clearly, how inappropriate it was. Mr. Jameson returned the portrait to the shelf. He turned to Frank and put a seal on the conversation, "Enough about that, this is a good day. It's a spring day in God's country, we have a friend with us, and Elisa has some energy. I have to be thankful for what I have, don't I?"

Frank stared at his coffee and nodded once.

"So tell me about Abigail," Mr. Jameson said. "You've worked for me for a week now, and I don't think you've said more than two words about her."

Frank wasn't sure how to answer. As soul-baring as Mr. Jameson had been with him, it seemed tactless to say anything truthful about his own present state, the inevitable divorce. He felt Mr. Jameson's eyes on him as he took too long to answer.

Finally he forced himself to speak, telling a little about how he met Abby at a social in Garrison. "She's a little like you and Elisa I think," Frank said, finding he could be honest, could answer the man's inquiry without saying too much. "She loves to read; Abby would be jealous of this room. She's lived in some nice places, too, but she's never been sore about living at our ranch. She's tough."

"It's hard to be away, isn't it?"

Frank furrowed his brow at his coffee, and Mr. Jameson took that as a yes. "I understand; my job takes me to Helena, and Elisa can't make the trip with me anymore. Each second I'm away, I feel that I am missing out on a precious moment of life."

It was possible that meeting Elisa would be the easiest part of this day. Bearing up under Mr. Jameson's sadness might be the greater challenge. Even if everything was right-as-rain in his own life, Frank was not one to comfort a grieving soul. His own mother used to say to him, "Feeling blue? Go wash the dishes." That was her cure-all for any bad mood. As far as Frank could tell, it did work. Sad about something? Work hard to take your mind off it—you feel better and get something done, too. Somehow this didn't seem like fitting advice for the warden.

Frank did the next best thing to prescribing hard work; he talked about it. "I haven't been too homesick, with so much to take up my mind here," he said. "It's been a privilege to work with such a fine material. I'm grateful for the workspace too-better light than my shop back home." Frank managed to guide Mr. Jameson out of the abyss. They spoke about their respective worlds, the warden sharing how, at times, he wished he could work outdoors—at least if the weather was nice. Frank admitted he'd enjoyed the break from working out in the elements. Mr. Jameson was smiling once more by the time Meghan announced that the meal was ready. In the dining room the large, dark-stained cherry table could have easily seated twenty. The three settings of fine china and glass-ware arranged at one end seemed half-hearted tokens.

Frank stopped, unsure of whether he should sit, and where. He braced himself for some good-natured mocking from Mr. Jameson. But the man put him at ease instead, standing at the head and explaining, "You'll be here, Frank, to my left. Both because my lady should be to my right and because she needs to be nearest the door because of her wheelchair. And as for all this," he said and gestured to the settings. "It's frivolous. Follow my lead; it's only dinner. One course. You'll survive." He went on about how, though his family was wealthy, he had never fully succumbed to the torture of proper manners—much to his mother's dismay. Later, Elisa often had to remind him of the finer nuances of etiquette when his work involved dinner parties and eventually compensation that included a house with paid staff. Elisa hadn't grown up with such things, but she caught on fast. In the past, their servants had discreetly corrected him on the proper use of a salad fork, or where to place his silver when he was done with a meal. Mr. Jameson confessed that he liked to sneak into the kitchen now and again and make himself a sandwich. "I eat it on the back stoop, looking at Mount Powell. It's pure pleasure."

A woman's voice called from the hall. "Gentleman, do you mind if I join you?" Elisa's Norwegian accent immediately identified her, but the voice was stronger, more steady than Frank had expected. Meghan pushed the wheelchair up to the table and stopped short with a touch of the occupant's hand and a whispered command. There was Elisa. He could see the woman from the photograph. She was still there—in her eyes and one insistent smile. Yet it wasn't the same person. Meghan removed a crocheted blanket from Elisa's lap. Frank stood reflexively—at least he knew he was supposed to do that when a lady entered the room. Mr. Jameson went to Elisa, touching her shoulder and kissing the top of her head. He told her how happy he was that she could join them.

"How do I look?" she asked, fussing a little with her blue silk scarf. She wore a belt of the same color around her white dress that seemed a size too large for her vulnerable body. She was not beautiful. Of course she wasn't; she was dying. Even through the forced smile she was not old enough to look so tired, her body absent the feminine lines of a healthy youth.

"Positively stunning," Mr. Jameson said. He clearly meant it.

Frank continued to stand through their interaction, unsure of when he should finally sit. He would've been more comfortable hiding under the table or behind the drapes. He continued to stand, and he watched as Mr. Jameson—who looked so large in comparison—helped the little bird move from wheel chair to dining chair. The effort clearly left Elisa exhausted, her breaths quick and shallow. Mr. Jameson returned to his seat, and Elisa addressed Frank after catching her breath. "At ease, Frank Redmond. You only have to stand until I'm seated," she said, no small amount of irony in her tone. "In my case, perhaps you never needed to stand at all."

"I was explaining to Frank how we're not entirely sincere in etiquette," Mr. Jameson said. The two commenced to poke fun at the very concept of a dining room. This did not give Frank cause to relax. In fact, it may have put him a little more on edge, given that their quips would be most entertaining to someone who knew their subject better. As it was, he put into practice the warden's original advice. He laughed when they laughed and agreed with each sarcastic remark.

Meghan brought out the pork roast and steamed vegetables. Frank's hosts spoke a memorized prayer he'd never heard before, and Frank joined them with a cautious amen at the end. He copied his hosts on how they unfolded their napkins and how they let Meghan serve them, how they held their silver and how they cut small bites of the roast. The food was good; that was a fine comfort, though Elisa ate very little. The Jameson's carried the conversation, sharing their stories with Frank—or toward him at least, their lives were so foreign to him. Mr. Jameson told of his political appointments over the years, and Elisa shared a tale of how their younger daughter, the artist of the family, revealed her talents with a crayon on the wall at the governor's mansion in Illinois when she was five. Elisa defended the child's actions by saying it added to the décor of the place. It took Mr. Jameson a month to patch things up with the governor's staff.

Frank slowed down his chewing to accommodate the fact that his hosts were taking more time to talk than eat. When their plates were almost clear, Elisa turned her conversational focus toward Frank.

"You own a ranch up north of Avon?"

"Yes ma'am," he said and felt immediately self-conscious. "And pardon my work clothes; I didn't come to Deer Lodge prepared for any occasion."

"Don't apologize," Elisa said, quite serious. "I grew up in a fishing village. I worked alongside my cousins. I'll have you know, I believe the only lessons worth learning, one can learn from the sea—or the mountains, for that matter. The rest are trappings."

Frank smiled. Her comments were not condescending. He could tell that much.

"My husband says you're quite the artist."

"I do carve stone, small jobs when I hear about them."

"Any sculpture?"

"No, nothing that fancy. Reliefs. Commissions like foundation stones, cornices."

Mr. Jameson came to his aid then, though the new subject wasn't any easier on him. "Frank, you should tell Elisa about Abigail. She'd love to hear about her."

"Oh, yes, your wife. What's she like?"

At that moment, right when Frank could have frozen in fear or stuttered a bland nicety, somehow the sleep deprivation and desperation conspired to loosen his tongue and mind. A suitable recollection welled up in him. He knew exactly the answer that would tantalize his hosts and still resonate true in his own thoughts. "Well, I made one very big mistake once," he drawled and took his time wiping his mouth. "I tried to be poetic and told her she seemed like a cross between a wildflower and a badger."

Mr. Jameson nearly choked on a sip of water. Elisa set her silver down, a genuine smile on her face. "Do explain, sir," she said.

"At first look you'd think a breeze would break Abby," he said. "She is a small gal. But she ain't frail. Stronger than most men I know." That was true, at least it used to be. "When I met her, I thought she was as pretty as any wildflower around. Then when I got to know her, I found out she ain't afraid a nothin', though. Just like a badger."

He realized as he said those words that Abby had grown afraid of something lately. She was afraid of him. He pushed the thought aside. The Jamesons were laughing; that was what mattered. He could hold his own with these two. He could.

"And how did your missus take that observation?" Elisa asked.

"She wasn't my missus yet at the time," Frank said. "And, no, she did not take it well so far as I could tell. She thought I'd said she looked like a badger. But she still married me."

Elisa laughed—then stopped, coughing. Mr. Jameson stood but Elisa waved him off. She caught her breath and encouraged Frank on. "How did you slip out of that situation?"

"I didn't. I tried to explain, but she thought I was making up excuses," he said. "Never heard the end of it from her. I learned to keep such comments to myself after that."

"Oh, your Abigail sounds like a strong woman," Elisa said with a nod of approval. "I hope that someday I get the pleasure of meeting her."

"I hope you can, too," Frank said, avoiding Mr. Jameson's eyes. "I'm sure you would both enjoy each other's company."

The ring of a phone in another room startled Frank, that technology not common in his world. The dark-stained wood pocket doors opened and Meghan informed Mr. Jameson that there was a call from the prison. He excused himself, promising to be back shortly. Frank watched Mr. Jameson leave the room. He fidgeted with his napkin, looked down at his plate. He could feel Elisa's eyes on him. Then she spoke.

"I know why you are here," she said. "Thank you."

Frank swallowed at the realization. Before he could apprehend the thought, let alone reply, Mr. Jameson returned.

"Trouble at the prison?" Elisa asked. Her husband shook his head no, saying everything was fine as he sat down.

Elisa let out a soft sigh, her energy waning. "Gentleman, please forgive me," she addressed them both, but her formality was directed mainly to Frank. "I have been under the weather of late, and I need to retire." Elisa delicately folded her cloth napkin and set it next to her plate. "If you will excuse me?"

Both men stood, and Mr. Jameson moved to help his wife transfer back to her wheelchair. He took her arm tenderly as she stood; the movement required monumental effort on her part. "Frank, it has been so enjoyable to make your acquaintance," she said, once settled into her chair.

Unconcerned about etiquette, Frank stepped around the head of the table and approached the couple. He reached out, almost afraid to let his callused hands touch the delicate one offered to him, afraid that somehow he might break her. She held out her right hand—not sideways to shake, but palm downward, a suggestion that he kiss her hand. Elisa's fingers were ice cold to the touch, though the room was uncomfortably warm. Frank kissed her hand, tried to make the gesture look as expected and natural as he'd seen it done in picture shows. It felt awfully sophomoric; he'd never kissed a lady's hand before, not even Abby's. He wished Elisa a good day, looking into her blue eyes one last time.

CHAPTER 10

JUNE 2, 1935

The sun was still high when the warden dropped Frank off at the boarding house. He had a whole afternoon free, but he was spent from the sleepless night as well as the encounter with Elisa. He collapsed onto the thin feather mat, not even noticing the uncomfortable metal springs underneath. Sleep was immediate and dreamless. When he finally woke, it was dark out. A cricket chirped somewhere. He felt very awake. He knew exactly where he was, very aware of all that had happened. A hell of a day. What he didn't know was what time it was. A little light filtered in from a streetlamp outside. He found his coat draped over the end of the bed, his watch in the pocket. By the muted lamp light he made out the time: shortly after midnight. Mrs. Watson had a liberal curfew—as late as ten in the p.m. and as early as five—but he was certainly stuck indoors at this point. There would be no late night walk for him, though that was precisely what he craved. He settled for placing the solitary chair next to the window, where he could feel the cool air. He sat and thought.

It struck him that he'd never talked much about Abby before, not to anyone other than his own parents. Who had ever asked him about her? Years ago, his parents did, but those were teasing inquiries that expected no plain answer. The little story he told Elisa had done something to him. He remembered his wife, remembered much he'd forgotten. He still didn't miss her, or long to return. No, that wasn't it. But he felt a tug akin to homesickness. Yes, it was much like the way he was beginning to think of the mountains, his mountains, after a week away from them. He felt that way toward Abby, too. Only it wasn't the wife that he had right now. Rather he felt homesick for the woman she had been when they were courting. He did miss that. How she put him at ease at the social in Garrison—she made fun of two other young women, who were wildly over-dressed. She called them "the queen and that large tropical bird." Back then, she spoke plainly with Frank and asked him about ranch life. One of their first whole days together was spent riding into the foothills to search for three lost cows before the fall cattle drive. She worked hard even then. He missed their second year together. After Abby's spirits had lifted some, after grieving for her father, around then she began to smile at Frank once more—those months before Vivian grew very ill. That was a good year, and Frank missed it like he missed the familiar jagged line of the Garnet Range.

Were he at home right now, mulling over these late night thoughts, he'd be sitting on the porch with his pipe. He had no pipe with him, but his thoughts filled the cool air as good as smoke. Here was God's honest truth: there was a time when he delighted to be with Abby, but he did not anymore. That was how his thoughts came to rest on Maggie. Despite the terse interaction on Friday, he thought of her: what a strained upward reach for him. It had a fearful edge, an irritation—it was all very similar to how he'd felt about approaching Abby six years before. The thrill at the possibility. How surprising it was that the woman even spoke to him, a nobody from nowhere.

So the fondness for Maggie was, in a way, sentimental. Yet Maggie was also something new. She spoke her mind more freely, and as Frank thought about it, he began to regard this as an advantageous quality. It was maddening trying to figure what Abby wanted. At least there was less guesswork with a woman like Maggie. Frank mulled over Friday's interaction. She'd said she didn't mean to upset him, even asked for his forgiveness. Perhaps she was not so scornful. Perhaps she was only nosy. He'd been brusque, turning away with barely a word. Perhaps he could speak with her Monday evening, patch things up. He had no serious illusions—he knew Maggie thought of him as a rough and simple rancher. There was Mr. Jameson to consider, too. The warden would not think highly of a married man pursuing his secretary. At the very least, Frank shouldn't do anything that put his commission under any further strain. Yet, it was an insatiable curiosity. How far might Frank reach to acquire even an admiring glance from Maggie? If he could inspire just that— just a look—he'd consider it a worthy and successful experiment. He'd take it as proof that there was hope for him when he started over in a larger town.

It was two in the morning when Frank grew sleepy enough to catch a few more hours of rest. He woke at breakfast time, not half as alert as he'd been at midnight. Awake enough to head into another day of carving, though. As usual, he met the warden at his office early. Mr. Jameson followed him to inspect the stone.

"How much longer, do you think?" Mr. Jameson asked as he stood admiring the work.

"Should be finished by Wednesday, Thursday at the latest."

"It's turning out so much better than I had imagined," the warden said. "You really have a gift, Frank. It is a calling for you to do this work."

Frank was growing accustomed to the man's high-brow compliments, though he didn't believe them. The warden left, and Frank escaped into the rhythm of carving. The detailing had begun. He could spend a full hour on the roofline of a single house or the veins of one leaf, and it seemed only minutes had passed. Frank let himself obsess over the stone. More and more detail emerged from the granite with each tap of the hammer. He used a miniscule file to smooth out the petals of the flowers that framed the Nordic scene. He sharpened the edges between polished granite and shadows in the waves, thought of Elisa's eyes the same color as the granite. Rock could flow, stone could wind like a vine. Given the wealth of time Frank had with this stone, he experimented with each tool, discovered he could craft much more than he ever had in the past. He was truly painting with the chisel; the stone was the canvas.

As the end of the day approached, the singular obsession ebbed away. Frank found himself thinking of walking with Maggie. As he followed McMurphy out of the grounds, through the tunnel, Frank's anticipation was tempered by the uncertainty of how Maggie might act given Friday's exchange. As he climbed up the stairwell to the warden's office, he could hear the sound of the typewriter. He stood next to Mr. Jameson's desk, listened to McMurphy lock the tunnel door. Smoothing his coat, he entered the front office. Maggie smiled. She asked for a moment to finish her typing. Frank rehearsed in his mind what he might say. He was sorry for sounding unkind. That was it, that was all he needed to say.

Her typing done, office keys in hand, Maggie donned her coat and walked to the door, opened it, and Frank followed her out to the street. His heart pounded. The tidy apology came out in a too-boisterous declaration: "I'm sorry if I came off as a horse's ass a few days back."

Maggie laughed and looped her arm around Frank's elbow.

"Apology accepted," she said. That was that. As they walked, Maggie talked about her day and didn't pry into Frank's. They parted amicably at the boarding house, and Frank spent his evening in lengthy consideration of Maggie's voice and perfume.

The next morning, Frank's conversation with Mr. Jameson was brief. The warden seemed preoccupied, but so was Frank. He needed to get to work to take his thoughts off Maggie. Mr. Jameson didn't follow him to see the stone, though he mentioned he might stop by later. With renewed vigor Frank started work, letting his mind get lost in the stone.

At Tuesday's end, he paused and admired his work. Even he had to admit it was damn good. Just another day or two and it would be finished, everything except the date of passing. Frank didn't want to think of anything so morose. Not with Maggie waiting for him. Seeing her only improved his already happy mood.

Back in the warden's front office, Frank heard himself ask Maggie to join him for dinner. He was far more shocked than she.

"I'd love to," Maggie said without hesitation. "Brown's Diner is just up the street a few blocks."

Frank let this sink in. There was no harm in sharing a meal.

Maggie had another idea as well. "I'm so glad you asked because one of the guards stopped by today. He can't use his tickets to the Tom Mix Circus, because his little son is sick. I wasn't entirely looking forward to attending alone."

"There's a circus?"

"Just tonight. What luck, huh?"

Walking up the street with Maggie on his arm, Frank was a different man. No ranch, no Abby, no troubles. He was thankful that Brown's Diner wasn't a fancy place, given his attire, but it was clean and not too crowded. Frank questioned the establishment's claim of being the home of the original hamburger, but he kept that to himself. Ignoring looks from some of the patrons, they ordered their meals, and Frank tried to let his shoulders relax. He shared that his work was almost complete, almost referring to it as a gravestone, but he caught himself.

As if Maggie could tell he needed to be put at ease, she told him a story worth a good laugh—how she had accidentally locked herself out of the office. The warden had been so scarce lately, she had to ask a prison guard to let her back in. They both chuckled, then went quiet. Frank was not good at this.

"Have you ever thought of moving away from here?" Frank asked.

Maggie thought for a moment then answered. "Yes, I have. I'm not from Deer Lodge. Though I feel welcome here, I don't have the ties that many other people have."

Ties. Connections. Or maybe chains. That was what Frank had with the ranch. How could he get free?

"How about you?" Maggie asked. "Ever thought of hitting the road for someplace new?"

Frank stammered to get out an answer with no success. Maggie laughed, then apologized for catching him off guard. Their food came, and for a moment, the question was forgotten as Maggie enjoyed a hamburger, and Frank dug into a plate of meatloaf and mashed potatoes. It was good, but even Frank had to silently admit it wasn't as tasty as what Abby made.

"At times I have," he said finally.

"Pardon?"

"At times I've thought of striking out for somewhere else." Frank thought of Jacob Thompson, the man up in Finn who had left his family. His disdain for the fellow waned; perhaps everyone had judged him too severely. Who knew what finally made Thompson snap. Maggie sipped her tea. Coy and careful, she asked about something else entirely.

"Did Mr. Jameson stop by to look at your work today?"

"No, actually. He said he would, but he didn't."

"He got a call around mid-morning and left. I thought he'd gone over to the prison, but he never returned, and the guard who let me back into the office this afternoon hadn't seen the warden the whole day," she said. "I'm worried Elisa is not well."

Frank was certain of it, but there was no sense in talking about the matter. He was thankful Maggie let the topic quietly drift away. They finished their meals, then left the diner, walking north up Main Street towards the fair grounds at the edge of town. They were in no hurry; it was only seven, and the Tom Mix Circus didn't start until eight, though the grounds were open to allow people to see all the sideshow acts. Maggie was not her usual chatty self; surely she was thinking about Elisa and the warden. As for Frank, his concerns about the Jamesons were neatly eclipsed by the feeling of Maggie's hand perched on his arm. Perhaps this was the answer. Perhaps he could start a new life. And maybe he wasn't looking for some future gal who was like Maggie. Maybe his future was latched onto him right now.

Maggie's face brightened when they approached the circus tent. "The poster said they had an elephant and trapeze artists," she said. "I can't wait." She had seen a circus before, when she lived in Denver. But Frank honestly admitted he'd never seen such a spectacle in his life. He had seen Tom Mix though. The famous silent film star was in the first movie Frank ever saw—a western of course, the only movie that appealed to him. He liked westerns for the simplicity. Good men did good things. Bad men did bad things, until stopped by good men. Too bad the real world wasn't so cut and dried. Apparently Tom Mix found the circus business more profitable than movies.

Maggie wrinkled her nose as they ventured into the fairgrounds and walked along the sideshow tents. "Not the most pleasant smell, is it?" she said. The stench of beast and fodder permeated the air, visibly irritating some of the women and children mingling around, including Maggie. But to Frank, it smelt of home.

Once in the big top, Frank sat wide-eyed, mouth open in amazement, as each act dazzled the crowd. Sahara, the five-ton elephant, began her performance, and Maggie pulled on Frank's sleeve, pointing at the pachyderm. Frank wondered how much feed such a creature required. Frank and Maggie clapped along with the crowd and cheered as the aerial dancing diva, Irma Ward, dangled high above the center ring. A thin rope and the grip of her delicate hand were all that kept her from plummeting to her demise. Each flip and twirl mesmerized Frank; the strength that such a petite woman had to possess was amazing. He felt Maggie's hand on his arm, so gentle, really a bit weak in comparison. Fine fingernails, though beautiful, would not survive such an act. Abby could. She had the grip of a vice when needed. She could hold on like that. Frank brushed the thought aside; Maggie was a fine gal, and it felt good to have a more delicate presence at his side.

As Irma Ward ended her act, Tom Mix galloped out into the center ring astride his magnificent horse, Warrior. His voice booming over the applause of the crowd, Tom announced the next act: The amazing Flying Arbaughs; Jim Arbaugh and his beautiful wife, Jessie. The petite Jessie bowed deeply with her husband before climbing high up in the trapeze rigging.

The woman pierced through the air on her trapeze. Frank's fingers nervously rubbed the corner of his jacket. Jessie Arbaugh built up speed with each swing until, to the gasp of the crowd, she released her grip and tumbled blindly toward Jim's waiting hands. For the next fifteen minutes, Frank's heart beat fast with each toss, each confident reach through the air, every time those hands latched onto each other. Maggie cheered, and Frank looked at her often throughout the act. As the Arbaughs prepared for their finale leap, Maggie grasped Frank's hand. She did have a strong handhold after all. It was only after the Arbaugh's final bow that Frank felt the pounding in his chest subside.

It was dark as they left the circus, and Frank walked with Maggie to her house. Stopping at her walkway, Maggie pulled her arm away and stepped back smiling. Frank stood there mute. It was foolish that he had feelings for her after barely a week. She thanked him for dinner and wished him a good evening, then headed up her walk, and disappeared into her house. The walk back to the boarding house did little to settle Frank's mind and heart. He went to his room and sat on the bed. A colorful myriad of possibilities somersaulted and leapt about in his head, but there in the center ring was Maggie.

⇥ ⇤

On Wednesday morning, Frank stopped at Mr. Jameson's office at seven, but the building was dark, the door locked. He waited for several minutes and considered walking across the street to the prison, when McMurphy opened the door from the inside. As they passed through the tunnel, Frank wanted to ask where the warden was, but thought better of it. McMurphy seemed the type of man to keep things close to the vest. Besides, Frank knew. With that heavy awareness, Frank began another day of finish work, filing and brushing the dust away from every chiseled form. By late afternoon, Frank felt the stone was complete. All that was needed was the final smoothing and buffing, removing barely visible ridges in the cuts. He'd use the smallest flat chisel in the new set. Standing back, Frank looked at the stone. He tried to see it from the warden's perspective, hoping it was worthy of the compensation and of the trust the man had placed in him.

The warden had been scarce for two days. When Frank met Maggie at the end of the day, he asked if she'd heard anything. Mr. Jameson had spoken with her on the phone that morning, but was close-lipped about the whole matter; he said only that things at home required his attention. "He had a message delivered later, which told me more. He had to bring Elisa to the hospital," Maggie said. She took Frank's arm. "I'm worried about her and Mr. Jameson, too. Elisa is everything to him."

Frank looked at Maggie, patted her hand. He didn't stop at the boarding house, and Maggie seemed grateful to have him accompany her to her door. They stood at the end of her walk, two sad and worried souls, two people worried about two others. It was heartening, at least, to have a little company.

The embrace was neither seductive nor devious. Frank was surprised at that. He'd thought, in the recent past, that if he ever gave real consideration to the opportunity to be unfaithful, it would be out of frustration with Abby. But his wife wasn't a part of his thoughts at all in that moment. He held the woman in front of him because he felt scared, and he knew she was too. Maybe together they might not feel less afraid, but they might be able to catch their balance, might not stumble on this stony path. That was all. He held her face in his hands and kissed her forehead, her cheek. He looked at her, saw the concern in her face, her eyes glancing away—not offended, but thoughtful.

Maggie leaned back and placed a hand on his chest. "That's good for now, Frank," she said. She touched his arms, took a half step back. No, not angry or offended. But very pensive. "Good enough for now," she said again. He wished her a good evening as she turned to head up the walk to her house. Maggie stopped, turned back and gave him a sad smile, the slightest nod. That was all.

CHAPTER 11

JUNE 1935

The coffee at the Elk Café seemed more flavorful to Clay than the coffee at home or anywhere else. He knew it was the same kind they had at the house, but that didn't matter; it tasted better here. It might be the company of the other old ranchers. They gathered in the small eatery in Avon every morning to discuss the goings-on of the world. Joining them was a perk of coming into town to pick up the new sickle part, and Clay was in no hurry to head back to the ranch. As his day was taking shape, this coffee might be the only good thing. Even his chats with the other ranchers in the Elk had been discouraging.

He'd stopped in at the café in part to feel out the possibility of selling the ranch, to give Frank and Abby enough to make a new start. Well, it wasn't going to happen this year, or anytime in the near future. Everyone he spoke with had the same story: land rich and cash poor. No one foresaw purchasing additional acreage anytime soon. Clay was just getting up to leave when Harold Granger walked in the door. When they made eye contact, Clay saw his friend and neighbor tighten his jaw and cut across the room to him, looking like a man on a mission.

"Glad I ran into you," Harold said and motioned for Clay to sit back down at an empty table. "We need to talk." Harold seemed clearly upset. They had been good neighbors for years, helping each other in good times and bad. Never before had he seen Harold so bothered. The waitress arrived, and Clay agreed to yet another cup of coffee. Harold waited for the server to fill his mug, then began.

"You know me, I'm no gossip, but I felt you needed to know this," Harold said. "Your boy is straying. Seems he's looking for greener pastures down in Deer Lodge with some gal." Factual and businesslike, Harold passed along the details about Frank cavorting around town with some dark-haired gal on his arm.

Clay said nothing when Harold finished. Harold seemed uncomfortable and repeated, "Hate to bring bad news, but it seemed you ought to know."

"Yes, I ought to," Clay said. "It was right of you to tell me."

Another patron hailed Harold. Clay told him to join the other fellas; he needed to head home anyway. A little helpless looking, Harold dropped some change on the table and left his friend with the news. Clay sipped his third cup of coffee and let the reality set.

Well, it might explain things of late. Abby had been of a mood to sour the sweetest buttermilk. Perhaps this was why. She must have found out somehow. Words traveled awful fast; it was surprising Clay was hearing about the matter only now. Such things never stayed secret for long. How could Frank do this to Abby? Clay didn't raise a two-timing son! He had half a mind to drive over to Deer Lodge right then and there and clean Frank's plow. Perhaps knock some sense into him. No, no… he should let it play out. Rumors were just that. What if Frank was just being kind to someone in need? That delusion was pleasant, but Clay knew better. The way Frank had been acting before he left was proof enough. His son was looking for an out, and from the sounds of it, he had found one. If Abby did know, why hadn't she said anything? Abby didn't used to be this way. Ever since Vivian passed away, Abby had become such a shrinking violet. Would she confront Frank this time? Should Clay do so if Abby did nothing? Too many questions with no answers. Clay decided to heed his own father's advice: *When you're up to your ears in shit it's best to keep your mouth shut.* Yes, stay out of it. See what happens when Frank gets back. If Abby does know and doesn't confront her wayward husband herself, then Clay would step in.

This news about his son was the last thing Clay needed. He was worried enough as it was. Now, the uncertainty of things made his stomach churn. If his son didn't come home, the ranch would fail. As strong as Abby was, they couldn't run the ranch without Frank.

Clay finished sulking over his coffee and left knowing full well that the fellas in town would continue their commentary on Frank and Abby and the truth that the Redmond ranch was limping along on borrowed time. It was the nature of old men to discuss such things at the Elk.

Driving home, Clay looked at the connecting rod that sat on the seat next to him. It had cost a lot of money and the equipment dealer warned Clay that no one was making parts for their antiquated machines anymore. They would need to get new implements at some point. Nice sales spiel. But it wouldn't do him any good; they could barely afford the parts they could find. New equipment was out of the question. The ranch's machinery was like Clay, old, worn out, and barely making do.

The ruts in the road jerked the wheel as Clay slowed down and turned up the drive to the ranch. Stranger's barking and tail-wagging welcome at least gave Clay something to smile about. Abby must be in the house; otherwise, the dog would be by her side. Stranger had certainly forged a bond with Abby, and the dog seemed extra attentive since her mood turned solemn.

Clay gave the big dog a head scratch as he got out of the car, then headed to the equipment shed to start working on the sickle.

Stranger tagged along. The news of Frank burned Clay's thoughts. He was annoyed enough about replacing the connecting rod by himself, but it was flat out infuriating to know what Frank was up to in the meantime. Clay took out his frustration on the equipment, hammering and muttering curses. "What the hell is my boy doing?" he all but shouted. Stranger flattened his ears and backed away, cowering. Clay stopped.

"I'm sorry, boy," he said. "I wasn't mad at you." Clay set the hammer down and knelt on one knee to pet his friend. Stranger approached slowly. "It's days like this that I prefer the company of a dog. A bit more loyal than us humans, it seems." Standing back up, Clay continued his work but with a mite less rage so as not to frighten Stranger. Slow and steady, he pried and pulled on the parts of the sickle, guiding the connecting rod back into place, then inserted the restraining bolt. Come what may, the sickle was finally in good working order.

⇥⊹⊹⇤

The next morning, there were no friendly greetings like normal. Abby didn't even look up as Clay came downstairs. Her eyes were locked on the stove as if willing flame to cook the eggs in the skillet. Clay was feeling way too old to get involved in the mess. But Frank was his son.

A whole day later, Clay sat at the table once more waiting for Abby to plate and serve his breakfast. She seemed even more sullen than she was the day before, if that were possible. She turned from the stove and brought a plate to him, practically slamming it down on the table. He stared at the scrambled eggs scattered about.

"You know about Frank, don't you," she said. It wasn't a question.

"No secrets in Avon," he said. "Apparently not in Deer Lodge, either."

Abby tightened her mouth. She sat down and nibbled at a piece of toast. What could Clay say? Frank was his son, his blood. Yet the Redmond name was already tarnished from the rumors. Frank might be gone for good, or he might come back and kick Abby out. Both were dishonorable possibilities that Clay didn't want to think about. Abby, little Abby, what would she do if her husband made her leave? The resolve grew inside of Clay. He wouldn't let it happen. Abby was like a daughter to him. If she had to leave, he would, too. If Frank ran off, Clay would stay at Abby's side.

"Abby, when Frank comes back I'll talk—"

"No!" Abby cut him off mid-sentence. "I'll do it." She got up and returned to the stove to clean the cast iron pan. "I'll do it," she repeated that resolution to herself two more times as she carried on with the scrubbing. Clay hadn't seen Abby stand up to Frank in years, and he wondered if she had what it would take. Of course, it all depended on if his son even came home. Clay finished his breakfast and got up to head outside to start the day's work. He paused at the door.

"Whatever play you make, Abby, I'll back your hand," he said.

She looked back over her shoulder, her eyes damp. "Thanks, Clay."

CHAPTER 12
JUNE 6, 1935

Thursday morning the warden's office was dark once more when Frank arrived. His concern for Elisa grew, but he found he was rattled by something else, too. He missed the conversations with Mr. Jameson; he missed his friend. He considered heading up to try to find him. No, he should finish his job. That was what the warden would want. Back in the old shed, Frank perfected and polished every miniscule notch, every sinuous line. The stone was done, though; he needed to stop. A little before midday, he began rebuilding the original shipping framework for the stone. It would be needed at some point. Plank by plank, he hammered brads back in, creating the wooden base that would cradle the stone.

A knock on the door stopped him mid-task. He turned, expecting to see Mr. Jameson, but instead it was McMurphy. Frank set his hammer down and leaned an unattached post against the stone. The guard said nothing, only strode over to Frank and handed him an envelope. Inside was a note from the warden with one line: *Date of passing: June 6, 1935.*

"Sir," McMurphy said, a question in his voice. "I'll let you finish."

Frank looked up from the note. "Yes, I—. Thank you."

McMurphy left, and Frank turned back to face the stone. All the memorials he'd carved over the years, all the dates he'd etched, even his own mother's—none had been physically difficult. The action of carving had never bothered him. He was sad when his mother passed; of course he was. But carving her stone was a good and honest duty. What was wrong with him right now? He set the note on the granite surface, fumbled for the pencil in his pocket and found his hands were shaking. He was shaking. Frank rested his elbows on the stone, held his head in his hands. With a deep breath, he straightened and began to sketch the date. Then, taking up the hammer and a small chisel, he made the final cuts into the stone. He worked through his usual midday break, giving the characters the same care he'd given every other mark on the memorial. It took him much of the afternoon.

After finishing the date, Frank looked at Elisa's stone one last time. His finest work ever, but he sensed only its granite weight. He finished pegging together the wooden shipping frame, then sat on an old crate, leaned back against the wall with his eyes shut. He thought nothing, had no idea how long he sat there. McMurphy brought another note at four. A few final instructions. He could pick up his last payment at the office. The stone would be picked up the following morning, and Frank was to oversee its transport and placement in the cemetery in time for the funeral at six p.m. Mr. Jameson wanted him to attend.

Frank tucked the note in his jacket pocket, turned off the lights, and followed McMurphy across the grounds, past the prisoners and other guards. Once inside the key tower, they descended into the tunnel. Entering the basement of the warden's office, there were no parting words between Frank and McMurphy, neither being in the talking mood. Frank climbed the stairs up to Mr. Jameson's office and opened the door and there was Maggie. She knew. She knew about the stone too, had known all along.

"Mr. Jameson was out of town when the stone arrived several weeks ago," she said as they walked out of the building onto Main Street. "I had to take the shipping invoice from the truck driver." She held tight to Frank's arm as they walked and she explained how she'd overheard some of his and the warden's conversations. But, she wasn't certain about the situation until the warden's children arrived by train on Tuesday, their visit arranged on such short notice. "Is it beautiful, her headstone?" Maggie asked.

"Did the best I could," he said. Something about her question irritated him. Couldn't tell why. Right at that moment, a simmering wave of opposition rose up within Frank. The stone, the funeral, Elisa, the warden. The whole town of Deer Lodge. All the trouble back at the ranch. He wanted nothing to do with any of it, didn't want to answer any more questions. His anger, his disgust with it all, had nothing to do with Maggie, but she was there at his side. Anyone near him at that moment would have been engulfed by the surge. Whatever warmth Frank had felt for her yesterday, he did not want to talk to her right now. Because he didn't want to talk to anybody. He looked at Maggie, hoped she did not want him to stay with her. The lovely woman was speaking, saying some comforting words to him, to herself. Something about the stone.

"If Mr. Jameson approved it, then I'm sure it's beautiful."

Frank stopped at Mrs. Watson's. He begged off walking any further, said he was beat tired. Maggie looked confused, then said she understood, hugged him. He tried to hug her back. "It's been a tough day," he said.

For no sensible reason he could figure, Frank Redmond wanted to go home.

⬅⬆ ⬆➡

Friday morning, Frank stood in the prison grounds observing as a large truck entered through the Sally Port gate and then drove over to the old utility shed. Guards stood by watching. A few prisoners working in the garden stopped their tasks, craned their necks to see. Everyone but McMurphy looked curious about what was in the shack—*What is it? Where is it going?* After thirty minutes of leverage and brute force, Frank and three men from the undertaker's loaded the stone onto the flatbed. After checking out of the grounds, this time through the main gate, Frank met up with the truck and jumped onto the back. He rode with the stone the mile and a half to the cemetery west of town. There, he and the undertaker's men spent another hour lifting and placing the massive stone, removing the framework, easing it onto a large, matching blue granite base. The stone had even more depth, the details sharper, now that it was in the sunlight. The waves were lovely; sunlight played off the polished portions as it would on the surface of real water. The fjord and mountains stood crisp and sharp, the flower petals were as fluid as the water, contrasting with the rocky scenery. The three cemetery workers took turns shaking Frank's hand, commenting on the quality of the work. Then they began their unsavory task: digging the grave.

Normally so sturdy, so unaffected, Frank watched the men, listened to their rough voices—the men were not crass, not inappropriate, but the scene was still loathsome. No gesture made in front of that stone could be reverent enough. How was it, that all they could do for their dead was to dig a hole? How could anyone take payment for that task? Frank found the men, and then himself, detestable. One of the diggers stopped and offered to give him a ride back to town.

"No," he said. "Weather's fine for walking." He wished them well and left. At the cemetery gate, he looked back and saw how the deep blue of the stone stood out in the sea of common white and gray memorials. Just as he knew it would.

As Frank walked, he thought of the Jamesons, thought of their marriage and his own. He considered the unfairness of the comparison, then grew angry with himself. Today was no day for self-pity. A new chant formed in his mind, as persuasive as the one that sent him on his way to Deer Lodge. The marching drums pounded in his head. *Never, carve, again. Never. Carve. Again.* It was a good solid beat, and it got him back to town.

His final pay envelope was waiting for him at the warden's office. In it were an extra ten dollars and a note thanking him for all his efforts, for his friendship. Frank looked at the money and felt nauseous. He could hardly refuse it though. Along with the note were the leather bundle of stone carver's tools and the sketch pad. Maggie told him that McMurphy had brought them over, figuring Frank had forgotten them. He had. Intentionally. He wanted to leave them behind now, never to touch a stone chisel again, but he knew that it would be an insult to Mr. Jameson. Picking up the tools, he thanked Maggie, asked her to thank McMurphy for all his help. He was ready to leave, but Maggie's gaze was heavy with questions.

"Will you stay for the funeral?" she asked.

It was the only inquiry he could answer easily. Yes, he'd be there.

"Are you coming back to Deer Lodge?"

What would he do in this town if he quit carving? He had intended to stop by Ross Funeral Services before his trip was done, see if they might hire him on in the shop. He had no desire for that now. Other than stone carving, what did he have apart from the ranch? "I don't know," he said. "I'm sorry."

She looked down at her hands. "Poor Mr. Jameson," she said. She swallowed then spoke with resolve, "We'll take good care of him."

The words seemed accusatory. Frank was leaving. He didn't have to face Mr. Jameson tomorrow and the next day. Maggie did. But, nothing could be done about that. "Thank you," Frank said. He did mean it. There was nothing more to say. Quite sure he'd never see Maggie again, he turned around and left the office.

Walking outside, with no task to be done, no schedule or aim, Frank remembered that he'd never left a message for anyone back home. He'd had no contact with anyone at all, not even to let John know when he'd need a ride home. He stopped at the boarding house and used the phone to leave a message at the McAllisters ranch. If he was lucky, John would get the note that afternoon, might even be able to come down that evening.

That done, he went back outside and walked along quiet side streets to the undertaking parlor. The owner, Ralph Ross, had provided Frank with his ranch-saving side jobs for the past six years. Ralph brightened when he saw Frank walk in. "My boys tell me you crafted quite the masterpiece," he said. "Took a fair piece a business from me, you know. Can't say that I blame you, given your commission."

The comment was an honest but friendly jab. Frank should have laughed, should have asked about working for Ralph more often. He didn't, though.

"I won't be carving anymore," he said.

"Retiring a wealthy man after the Jameson job?" Ralph thought this was a fine crack, but his smile faded when Frank made no reply. "I don't understand; you've done your finest work ever. Folks will ask for you."

Frank said two words, "I can't." Then he walked out.

On his way back to the boarding house, he stopped at Helens' Shoppe window. There were several dresses displayed on mannequins. Most looked very expensive, but there was one simple but pleasant calico that caught his eye. Only two dollars. Frank wasn't sure why he wanted to go home, but he knew that was where he needed to be. In the same way, he knew he needed to buy Abby that dress. This desire too, was inexplicable but certain. Whatever happened, whether they kept grinding along or he found a way to part company with her in a respectful fashion, he would treat her fairly. The woman deserved a decent dress, and right then he had the money for it. He couldn't remember the last time she had new clothing of any kind. Heading into the dress shop, once more he found his own attire made him look suspect. Frank blurted out a rapid explanation of his intentions and his budget before the shop owner could decide to throw him out.

Thus assured, the owner showed him several calicos in a range of sizes. "And your wife's size...?" she asked. How would Frank have known that? Flustered, he held up two hangers holding dresses that looked awfully close to Abby's stature. He picked the smaller of the two, not realizing he'd chosen a dress quite a bit pricier than the one in the window. Frank made the purchase, almost a whole day's wages—Mr. Jameson's wages at that—and scurried out the door.

Frank made it back to Mrs. Watson's just as the wind picked up. Like all weather in the mountains, spring thunderstorms were sudden to arrive, intense while around, and fast in passing. The rain began pounding against the windows of the boarding house. Frank sat and watched a battalion of showers roll over the valley that afternoon. Afterward, the air felt clean and fresh, and a few sun rays pierced through the clouds. The hills beyond town were beginning to green up. Frank sat in his room till it was time to head to the cemetery. He had no appetite for supper.

The walk took only twenty minutes, and he was glad he had no car. The roads both inside and outside the cemetery were lined with vehicles. Frank wondered if anyone remained in town. He watched from a distance, standing in a small pine grove in the cemetery. Everyone was dressed in their finest black suits and dresses. Maggie was there. She saw him, then looked away.

Frank was close enough to hear the priest and Mr. Jameson and several others who spoke about Elisa. Words and portions of words carried over to him, but he could not understand them. There was too much in and on his mind already. Full. Weighted. Impermeable. The people stopped their talking. They sang.

They became very still. The casket descended into the ground. The people hugged each other and dabbed eyes, and shook hands and touched Mr. Jameson's shoulders. The people drifted, lingered, left. Soon only the bereaved man remained. Frank could not approach him; neither could he leave. Then the warden saw him.

"Frank!" he shouted. The man actually smiled as he called him over and thanked him for coming. As Frank approached, the warden grabbed his right hand with both of his and shook it. "You did an amazing job. I know how pleased Elisa would have been. She is pleased; I know she is."

Frank mustered a trite I'm-so-sorry-for-your-loss-sir.

Mr. Jameson looked at him with gentle scrutiny. "Your work says more than any words can," he said. "It will be here long after you and I are gone." Mr. Jameson reached into his pocket and took out a small hand-carved wooden box. He handed it to Frank and said, "Here, I want you to have this. Open it."

Frank unlatched the brass clasp. Inside was a silver necklace with a delicate charm attached. A silver setting held a small heart-shaped piece of the blue granite, polished to a glossy finish. Mr. Jameson explained that he'd had it commissioned in Norway when he ordered the stone. "But it didn't arrive until three days ago. I wanted to give it to Elisa. She never got to see it," he said. He looked at the memorial, then back at Frank. "I think she would want you to give it to Abby."

Frank shook his head no, closed the box, and held it out to the warden. "You should give this to your daughter, or someone—"

"No!" Mr. Jameson stepped back and would not take the gift back. "I insist! Believe me, there are other items my children will hold far more dearly than this. They don't even know this exists, but you do. You have a connection to it through the stone, and I want you to have it. Please."

Frank stared at the jewelry box. Once more, with Mr. Jameson, what choice did he have? The silver alone must have cost more than he made in half a year on the ranch. "You've paid me far more than I deserve," he said. The wages, the tools, this necklace—Frank felt them all as a miserable weight. He would pay for the broken sickle. He would have money left over. His family would eat well long into the winter. And Elisa was dead.

"I hope you continue to use your gift to honor others as you have honored my wife."

Frank winced. He forced a smile, shook Mr. Jameson's hand, said goodbye. The warden stayed on at the grave, and Frank walked back to his lodging. Coming around the corner of Main and Pennsylvania, he saw John leaning impatiently against his truck in front of the boarding house. How strange it was to see someone from his valley here. It felt like he'd been gone for two years, not two weeks.

"Sonsabitches, where ya been?" John shouted. "I been waiting nearly an hour!" Apparently the neighbor-boy-pony-express had worked a little too efficiently. John had been waiting for at least an hour.

"I was at a funeral," Frank retorted.

"Funeral? Who the hell died?"

"The warden's wife. That was the mystery job. Another gravestone." Frank had no stomach for John's usual coarse commentary, yet he was his ride home. As courteously as possible, Frank excused himself to get his things, promised to explain everything during the drive home. He gathered his bedroll and clothes, the tools—both old and new, the paper package holding Abby's dress. The necklace was in his jacket pocket along with his wages. He turned in his key with Ms. Watson, then rushed out. Everything loaded up, John hurried onto the highway. He hoped to beat the dark, as his headlamps were little better than candle lanterns.

Frank spoke. All secrets about the job irrelevant now, he spoke freely about the gravestone and the eccentric but good-hearted man who had had him meet his dying wife. Even over the rumble of the engine, Frank could hear John whistle at that bit.

"Now that's a peculiar fellow," John said. "But decent?"

"Yes," Frank said. "A decent man." He told John all about the warden's office and his house and how he had worked in secret in a shed in the prison. On further prodding from John, Frank even explained the cut on his lip, the mishap at the bar. This got a whoop of approval from his friend. But Frank said nothing about Maggie. By the time they reached Avon, John seemed almost as somber as Frank. At least his friend had caught on that he wasn't in any joking mood tonight. The closer they drew to home, the more Frank wanted to get there. The drive home was a race against time, which they lost. The sun sank behind the mountains, casting grey shadows across the landscape. It was dark as they turned north onto the dirt road that led home. John slowed to a crawl, limited by the faint light of the headlamps. Getting home sooner wasn't worth the risk of a possible collision with a deer or a Black Angus bull.

Pulling up to the road to Frank's place, they saw that the main gate was closed. John hadn't had a chance to tell Clay or Abby that he was picking Frank up, so they were not expecting him. Still, it was odd for the gate to be closed. A neighbor must have been moving cattle up the road to summer pasture and closed it to keep them from getting into the other property. Not wanting to bother with opening the gate and having John drive the hundred yards to the house, Frank gave John a full dollar, said his thanks, and hopped out of the truck.

He grabbed his belongings from the back and crawled through the wooden rails of the gate, careful not to lose anything, especially the necklace in his pocket. Frank walked up the rutted road with his bedroll slung over his shoulder, his hands free to carry the tools and Abby's dress. As John drove away, the true darkness of the night closed in. The truck's headlamps had cast some illumination after all. Frank hesitated, letting his eyes adjust.

The wind had picked up as they left Deer Lodge, and now it was howling across their valley, rising sharply upward as it hit the continental divide east of the ranch. Its powerful current twisted the trees along the edge of the barnyard. Starlight and sliver moon-cast shadows danced along the ground and buildings. Frank went to the stone shed first. Even in the dark, he knew every step. He could see well enough the wooden latch that held the door closed. He opened it carefully, fighting the wind. He set the tools inside on one of the two wooden worktables, then pulled the jewelry box out of his pocket. He stood by the door and opened the box one last time; the silver glimmering softly in the moonlight. Frank thought about giving it to Abby, but its tie to Elisa was too strong. Not knowing what to do with it, but wanting to keep it very safe, he closed the little case and tucked it next to the leather pouch inside his toolbox. This he latched tight to keep the mice out.

Locking the shed door, he walked towards the house, trying to put the memories of the past two weeks behind him. He would do his best by Abby. And that began with attempting to not wake her and Clay right now. He could sleep on the small couch in the side room downstairs, let them discover him there in the morning. Yes, that would be the least obtrusive way to handle this late-night arrival. Frank began to unsling his bedroll from his back as he opened the screen door to the front porch. He had barely stepped inside when he was greeted by a flash of teeth snapping at his face and a massive shadow ramming into his chest. Instinctively, Frank grabbed and punched to fend off the assault. The package holding Abby's dress fell to the floor and tumbled under a bench. Frank fended off the beast with his bedroll, striking at him repeatedly. The animal was all but invisible in the darkness. A glint of fangs and a dull swath of tan fur. Finally, in the midst of the scuffle, Frank remembered the damn dog. Really? This was the beast his father had befriended? "Godamnit!" Frank shouted. "Clay, get the shotgun! Now!" As he yelled and beat at the dog, Frank caught a glimpse of lamp light inside the house. Abby appeared first at the porch door, with disheveled hair, and clutching a cast iron pan.

Clay followed right behind her in his long johns and an untied pair of boots. He did have his old double barrel sixteen gauge, thank God. Frank walloped the animal hard enough to get him to back off for an instant. "Shoot the bastard!" Frank yelled. The dog stood before Frank, the fur on his back raised up, his teeth fully exposed and vivid in the lantern light. His growl carried over the wind.

"Shoot him!" Frank yelled once more, both angry and plain fearful the dog would lay on a fresh attack any moment. His father had a clean shot. Now. But he did nothing. Frank realized then that the shotgun wasn't for the dog.

"Stranger, no!" Abby commanded. Frank had never heard her use such a tone before. "Back off! It's Frank." The dog immediately transformed from ferocious killer to obedient, though cautious, canine. The beast looked at Abby and wagged his tail. Then he walked up to Frank and sniffed him. Frank pulled back, braced for another attack, but the dog, content that the intruder was no longer a threat, walked over to an old horse blanket in the corner and lay down. Frank pushed his way into the kitchen and exploded into a profanity-laced tirade. He threw his bedroll, grabbed the shotgun from Clay, and headed for the porch. Abby stepped in front of him.

"Stranger was earning his keep guarding the house," she shouted at him, the same tone she'd used for the mongrel. "So don't you even think about shooting him!" Abby's eyes flashed with anger, her body as tall as it could be. She was a confident woman to begin with, at least she had been in the past, but this was something

Frank hadn't seen before. Whatever he was hoping for when he decided to go home, this sure wasn't it. He had jumped out of the frying pan into the fire.

Clay took the gun back and headed upstairs to his room, muttering something about folks having the decency to come home during the day instead of the middle of the night.

Frank picked up his bedroll and shoved it toward Abby. He pointed to the bite marks. "That could have been my arm," he said. "Maybe that's what you want!" He stomped upstairs, not even bothering to remove his boots or take a candle or lantern. He was hardly feeling ready to sleep, but he stripped down to his long johns, and got into bed, his back towards the center. It was several minutes before the light from Abby's candle cast a flickering glow in the room. He felt her sit on the narrow bed. The room went black as she blew out the flame and lay down next to him. Frank listened to her breathing. The anger did not melt, but the edges softened some. He was home. He had come back. God, what a piss-poor way to walk in his front door. Damn dog. He had to try to explain himself at least. Slowly he turned over, looked at Abby's back. He touched her shoulder. She stiffened.

She hissed a single question, "Who's Maggie?"

Frank's mind raced. How could she possibly—who told her? What exactly did she hear? He had to tell the truth, but how much? Calm, steady, he stated the one fact that was the most innocuous. "I believe that's Warden Jameson's secretary," he said. "Why do you ask?"

Abby told him of a letter from an acquaintance in Deer Lodge. She would not say who or any details of what the woman wrote— only that she'd seen him repeatedly with Maggie. Abby would not be cowed; Frank was the one who had to do the talking: *Yes, Maggie was a widow. Yes, he walked her home on occasion. No. Nothing came of it.* Frank knew he had little defense, but there was no reason for Abby to speak ill of Maggie. He spoke with confidence on that count. "The warden's secretary was worried about the rail yard workers giving her trouble when she walked home," he said. "That's all. Not any different from you keeping a guard dog, I suppose." Except the dog got more respect in this house.

Abby was quiet. He knew she didn't believe him.

She pressed further. "Do you have feelings for her?"

This was impossible. It seemed like Abby needed him to be in the wrong. The truth was, right at that moment, Frank felt no affection for Maggie. Or Abby. Or anyone. He no longer had any desire to patch things up with Abby, not when she treated him like this. If anything, he wanted to hurt her. For chrissake, he came back. He sure as hell didn't have to do that. His welcoming party was a raging attack from his father's new guard dog and an interrogation from his wife. "Yes," he said. "I was fond of her."

Abby didn't move. The only sound was the howling wind and a loose board rattling on the side of the house. Finally, Abby spoke. "I don't trust you, Frank," she said. "I don't want to live with someone whom I cannot trust."

Two weeks before, this news would have been just what Frank wanted to hear. Now he had no idea what to make of it. Frank rolled onto his back and stared at the dark ceiling. He said then, what he thought was a sturdy last-word observation: "There is nothing I can do that would make you trust me."

"One thing's for sure, shooting Stranger won't help."

What did he expect when he decided to come home? That Abby would be pleasant toward him? He'd been less than pleasant toward her for months. He didn't reply, let the argument end far from resolved. She was quiet now, and he was beat—from everything—though he knew he would not sleep. After countless ticks of the wind-up clock, Frank slowly got up, hoping Abby was asleep. Slipping on his pants, he pulled the suspenders over his long johns and grabbed his boots, then felt his way to the door, down the hall and down the stairs to the kitchen. Only then did he light a candle. Its slight glow did little to lift his mood.

The wind was dying down, the house sinking into silence. Frank donned his boots and coat and grabbed a leather pouch from the shelf above the coat rack. It held his rarely used pipe and tobacco. This was a night that required such comfort. Frank carefully packed the pipe with the sweet, thin-cut leaves. The pipe held firmly between his teeth, Frank took the candle and opened the door to the porch. The orange light of the candle just barely illuminated the space. Frank stopped when he saw Stranger in the corner. The dog raised his head, but otherwise made no motion. Refusing to submit to fear, Frank closed the door behind him. There were four chairs along the wall between the house and the porch. He chose the one farthest away from the dog. Stranger laid his head back down, his eyes watched Frank with sleepy interest.

Pouring the melted wax off first, Frank used the candle to light his pipe. The soothing aroma of the smoldering tobacco filled the air. He took a couple puffs and leaned back against the wall behind him. "A fine mess ya got yourself into this time," he whispered to himself. Breathing his thoughts aloud, Frank looked over at the dog, the beast who just a few hours earlier had tried to kill him. Now the mongrel lay content only ten feet away. The dog raised his head again, perked his ears at the sound of Frank's voice.

"What about you? You're part of the mess," Frank quipped. "What do you havta say for yourself?" Stranger titled his head inquisitively to one side. It was difficult to stay angry when he looked like that. "Seems Abby wants you 'round more than me."

Frank puffed on his pipe as he continued his one-sided conversation. "Can't say I blame her, I've been a horse's ass. You at least mind her." With each word, the smoke lingering in his mouth dissipated into the air. The dog crossed his front paws and rested his head on them. Frank remembered Abby's last words of the night and looked at Stranger. "Looks like you and me need to have some sort a truce." Stranger again raised his head. The dog's expression was different now, not inquisitive so much as serious, like the first time he saw the dog out on the hillside. Frank felt uneasy as his eyes connected with Stranger's. It wasn't fear. It was as if he was looking at a long lost relative. Recognition. Skepticism. Concern. Frank swore the dog knew what he was thinking, had some understanding of his words. Whatever the case, if they were going to get along, it had to start now.

"How bout you don't try and eat my face off, and I won't shoot you? That a deal?" Stranger's tail swept back and forth. Frank nodded and went back to smoking his pipe. "I'll take that as a yes."

Stranger rested then, closing his eyes. Frank smoked his pipe till the last of the fine leaves were consumed by the soft glow. He sat a while longer, stretched his back. As he bent forward, he saw the edge of the package that had fallen to the floor. He reached down and picked it up, brushing the dust off. No tears in the packaging; the dress was still safe inside. Pipe between his teeth, Frank took the package and the candle into the house, leaving Stranger to sleep. He thought of stashing the dress in the stone shed; what use was it now? But he set it on the table instead. Who knew how she might take it. She might burn it to spite him for all he knew. Come what may, he left it there. Maybe it would be received, if not in gratitude, at least in tenuous peace. That was all he could hope for.

CHAPTER 13

AUGUST 1935

Abby pulled the reins tight, bringing the saddle horse team to a stop. The smell of fresh-mown hay and horse sweat permeated the summer air. A glance behind ensured she hadn't missed any hay with the buck rake she was running, gathering it all up for the next stack. Clay drove the second buck rake team near the stack they were currently building, while Frank and the hired hands ran the beaver slide hay stacker. The two-story lodge pole frame nestled next to the pile of hay they were adding to, the long ramp rising up from the ground at an angle with its top hovering over the stack. At the base, the over stacker waited for the next jag of hay to be placed on it by Clay. Once Clay's buckrake had backed clear of the teeth of the over stacker, Frank coaxed David and Goliath, pulling cables lifting the comb-like stacker up the slide. At the top, it flipped the hay onto the stack where one of the hands spread it out with a pitchfork.

Yes, there was Frank. Still living with them. Here she was, too. And Stranger still putting up with them all. What a confusing summer. The morning after Frank's return, she found him asleep on the settee downstairs. She noticed the brown paper package on the table. But, her first concern was Stranger. She opened the porch door, and the dog's happy greeting gave her a little hope, though she still wasn't looking forward to coping with Frank's presence once more. At least he had not hurt Stranger or driven the dog off. Abby headed to the privy, and Stranger ran off to make his morning tour of the ranch. When she returned to the kitchen, Abby picked up the package and walked over to the wood stove. Whatever it was, it might make good kindling. Frank's snores in the other room gave her pause, and instead she left the package on the kitchen counter. Only later, after the men were both outside, did she take it upstairs to her bedroom and set it on a high shelf unopened. Time would tell if she would ever unwrap it. For now the twine-tied offering wasn't giving Frank a free pass.

That whole summer, Frank never mentioned the package, or any of the events in Deer Lodge. For the most part he was quiet. That hadn't changed. But there was nothing sullen or brooding in his way when he did talk. She watched him now, directing the hired hands and spotting Clay as he drove a jag of hay onto the over stacker. Frank was in his element working the team, running the ranch. He was in charge out in the field. He was not like that with her. On the whole he seemed utterly defeated. This could have given Abby great pleasure. It didn't.

Abby was astounded at how long she could live with the question, how every morning she could wake wondering if she might gather her courage to leave that very day, and then, that night, she still lay down in the same bed with Frank. Really, the ranch conspired to keep her there. At what point, in the course of cooking, mending, laundering, chicken-feeding, and pig-slopping, did she ever have a free moment to pack a suitcase? She also began to wonder if it was possible to know if any man was faithful. Perhaps no woman could ever be certain. Perhaps no man could be trusted. Such musings made her tired, and the act of leaving required energy she did not have. She was so close to packing her bags when Frank went to Deer Lodge. The letter pushed her to the brink.

The land won out in the end. Abby prayed and wept over what might be the right choice, but the ranch held her even tighter than her faith. More recently, tired resignation began to grow into a genuine fondness that held her fast—not so much for Frank, but for the land and for Stranger. Her life was here up Three Mile Road for lack of anywhere else to go. Living with this complicated man and his father—this was not the family she'd ever envisioned. But it would have to do for now. Besides, leaving would require parting with Stranger, something she couldn't bring herself to do.

Regardless, it was good to leave the house and work with the men, as it always was. Branding, haying, and fall cattle drive— these were the times that Abby got to feel she was a part of the ranch instead of just a cook. She adjusted her broad brimmed hat shading her eyes from the harsh August sun. She looked out over the field, noting how far they still had to work to get the hay up for the year. This hay would feed the beef cows when they brought them down out of the mountains to spend the winter in the pastures near the house. The Deer Lodge money had allowed them to lease more grassland from their neighbors, replace parts on equipment, and hire a couple of men to help get the hay up. At least some good had come from that awful time.

There were three stacks already, and they were making good headway on the fourth. Beyond the stacks, Stranger stood watch, panting in the shade of the aspen trees near the road. He had abandoned his efforts at mouse hunting; it was too hot. It had been entertaining to watch the dog follow behind the buckrake all morning. As the rake gathered the cut hay, it sent field mice scurrying across the stubble-covered ground. After spotting his prey, Stranger leapt high into the air and pounced down with his front paws like a black and tan bolt of lightning. The hours of mouse-chasing and the high summer sun finally took their toll on the dog, convincing him he was better off in the shade. Abby couldn't argue with his decision. She would prefer to be out of the sun herself.

It had been a long but profitable day. Abby had helped all morning with the buckrake, then rode her saddle horse home and back to the fields at midday to bring a large lunch basket to the men, then resumed her work alongside them. Typically, when it was only Frank, Clay, and Abby, it took three weeks to finish haying—if the weather cooperated. With the two hired hands, it looked like they'd be done in just two weeks. Frank and Clay had hired the men over at the depot in Avon, the usual location to find local day laborers and transients who needed quick cash. Droves of men came to the depot from the hobo camp near the stockyard, or jumped trains from Helena with the hopes of finding seasonal work this time of year. George was a rail walker, while Martin came from Rimini looking for work. Both were hard workers and seemed happy enough to have a few weeks of steady pay, meals, and a place to sleep.

There was one hitch. Abby didn't like how George looked at her as she sat with the men eating their midday meal. Stranger didn't seem keen on the man either, avoiding him as he made his rounds begging for lunchtime scraps. Well, Abby would have to try her best to ignore the leering. Any other replacement they found might act the same. Besides, George would be gone in a few days. She thought of mentioning the matter to Frank, or more comfortably, to Clay. But neither man would regard such a thing as warranting any action on their part. It was yet another little irritation to share with Patty the next time they met. Only a dear friend could understand such frustrations. Abby had met Patty six years ago when Abby first started dating Frank—Patty was the wife of Frank's pal, John. How Patty tolerated that loudmouth man was beyond Abby, but she was grateful for the friendship. Ultimately, it was that tolerance for John that gave Abby confidence that her dear friend, more than anyone else, understood what she was going through with Frank. It was a pity that they only got to see each other every few weeks during the summer, and almost never in the winter.

The sun was just over a hand's width above the mountains when Abby decided it was time to head back to the house and prepare the evening meal. She had started a roast when she stopped in at midday, so setting the evening table wouldn't be too difficult. Sunset would be in another hour, and then it would be a half an hour after that before the men got the beaver slide set up for the next morning's stack. It would be pitch dark before they got back to the house. Plenty of time to get her own saddle horse team put up for the night and care for the barnyard animals before the men came in to eat.

With a soft clicking noise and a flick of the reins, Abby directed her horse team towards the cottonwood tree where Stranger lay. At the sound of the team, Stranger's ears perked up. He stood and stretched in that head-down, rump-up manner that dogs stretch. It looked so satisfying. Abby stopped the team and jumped down from the uncomfortable steel seat. She wished she could stretch the way Stranger did.

Abby worked her way around the horses, disconnecting the tugs from the buck rake, hooking the loose chain up onto the harness for the ride home. Her team that day were Jane, her own beloved riding horse, and Buck, Frank's buckskin gelding. Abby led her white-blazed chestnut mare over to the shade of the cottonwood and returned to free Buck from the equipment. She grabbed a rolled up lead rope that hung from the steel hames and connected it to Buck's halter. She petted his head before she led him over to Jane, who was nose-to-nose with Stranger.

"Now, you two behave yourselves," Abby chided the two animals. Stranger looked at her with his tail wagging, and a happy dog smile. He came closer to get some attention. "Time to get supper ready. Stranger, you coming with me?" she asked, as she patted the dog. Without a saddle and stirrups, Abby would need to use a stump to get on Jane's back. She hooked the lunch basket onto a tree branch and finagled herself onto Jane while holding

Buck's lead rope. Once safely on horseback, she leaned over to grab the basket, took Buck in tow and headed home. Stranger trotted along behind.

Abby didn't need reins to control her horse. Pressure from her legs guided Jane out of the field and onto the road. It was good she wore her overalls instead of a dress, as the leather work harness and horse sweat made for a somewhat tricky seat on the ride back to the house. Still it was riding, and riding was always a fine thing—the rhythmic clop of Jane's hoofs, the jingle of the harness, the breeze pushing through the aspen trees. As the trees thinned out, Abby looked back and saw that the men had finished the fifth stack and were moving the beaver slide to the next location. The two-story pile of hay resembled a loaf of bread, the layers of dried grass golden in the sun. A six-horse team pulled the thirty-foot high lodge pole contraption. Almost every horse they owned, the Belgian team plus over half their saddle horses, were working in the field today.

Just beyond the third stack sat the dozen or so dilapidated buildings that were the remains of Blackfoot City. Near the almost-ghost town, there were a few small gardens tended by the few remaining residents who scratched out a living from gold panning or cutting wood for the railroad. Blackfoot City's downtown had long since become one of the Redmonds' best producing hay fields. They often found signs that a town had once been there. Every spring the dirt seemed to shed a glass bottle or rusted metal part—there was a stack of these finds in the gully at the edge of the field.

Abby thought of Patty as she rode. They were due for another visit. The last time they spoke Patty said that Frank had changed, but Abby didn't see it, her anger still clouded her view. When Abby challenged Patty on the matter, she responded in her confident southern accent, one of many traits that set Patty apart from the people of the western Montana valley. Patty had moved up to Montana from Tennessee over ten years ago and had made every effort to hold onto her accent among the 'uncultured' western-ers. Though thinking herself cultured and gentile, Patty had a temper; she was no one to be trifled with, and was always willing to speak her mind regardless of the consequences. And that was what she did when Abby refused to see any alteration in her hus-band's manner.

"I'm telling you Abby, the man is whipped," Patty said. "I don't think he would dare look at another woman now. He talks with you now, doesn't he?"

"Yes, but he's talked to me before. At least when truly necessary."

That got a scowl from Patty. "No, he talked at you, he never talked with you. I do believe the man sees you as a wife now, in-stead of just some person he has to live with."

It was not easy to hear that, but Abby had to admit her friend had a decent point.

Abby's horse whinnied to the other horses in the corral and brought Abby back to the moment. Yes, another visit with Patty was needed. Abby wanted to tell her about hay season, about the obnoxious hired hand, and about how Frank really did seem dif-ferent, how Patty had been right again.

As Abby rode into the barnyard, she passed by the stone-carving shed with its locked door. It had been that way since Frank got back from Deer Lodge in June. In her anger toward Frank, it had taken several weeks before she realized he hadn't mentioned any new stonework. It wasn't as though she had ever been allowed in the shed before. The dark room was Frank's sanctuary. She'd only seen glimpses of the finished stones as they left in John's truck.

Abby was not quite brave enough to ask Frank about the matter. But Clay was. It was just before haying season that her father-in-law confronted Frank. Abby never heard the start of the conversa-tion; Clay brought it up while he was outside working on equipment with Frank. She sure heard the end of it as Frank stormed into the house..

"Because I don't want to, that's why!" Frank barked at his father.

"I don't see any reason why not, you know as well as I do we need the money. If you can get another job like the one you just had, we'd be set for the year."

Abby stood back watching the two men, the hair on her arms rising.

"I said I'm done carving, and that's that," Frank said. "Leave it be." He headed back outside, leaving Clay standing there visibly frustrated.

"I swear at times I can't fathom that boy." Clay said, looking at Abby.

She kept quiet, but like Clay, wondered at the reason for Frank's abandoning the stone carving. She knew about Maggie, that much was clear, but what could that have to do with quitting stone carving? As much as Frank had softened in the last two months, he'd become entirely tight-lipped about stone-carving.

Abby knew a little about the Jameson stone up at the Hillcrest Cemetery, only because Patty told her the stories about it. It was the talk of Deer Lodge, not only for its beauty, but for the fact that it had cost the warden his job. Perhaps that was it. That news reached them back in July. While enjoying a rare outing to the Elk Café in Avon, Abby had watched Frank grab an old paper on a nearby table. Leaning over his shoulder, she read the article about the warden being ousted from his job. It was only the second time Abby had seen such plain fear in Frank's face—the first time having involved their over-protective mutt. The article explained a nit-picking investigation into the misuse of prison property. In the end, the warden resigned, supposedly moving to Colorado at the end of the inquiry.

"Are they gonna come for me?" Frank whispered as he put down the paper. No one ever did, but Abby could tell that Frank's concern about his role in the warden's ouster weighed on him. Perhaps that was why he refused to carve again.

Whatever the reason, there was the stone shed, locked up tight. Abby guided the horses into the side corral next to the barn. The shadows of the mountains slid across the valley as the sun sank deeper in the west. Still enough light to finish her work outside. Twilight set in by the time she pulled the harnesses, brushed the horses down, and fed and watered them. Stranger wandered off on his usual evening loop around the property. Abby had grown fond of talking to the dog; he followed her around on almost all her chores, with occasional breaks to hover over Clay. The dog disappeared only once in the morning and once at the end of the day, sauntering off into the hills and fields. His little patrols took him a good half hour.

The dog was nowhere to be seen at the moment. Such a quiet time of evening. She had to remember that there was much good in her life. The extra money, food in the pantry, a good hay season; she must sustain herself on these things. Abby let herself take a deep breath of the nighttime cool before heading over to the chicken coop. There she coaxed the birds into their coop with a trail of grain, then shut them in and turned to walk back to the house. Looking up, she jumped, startled to see one of the hired hands standing only a few steps away.

"George! You nearly scared the life out of me!" It was a reprimand, but she was courteous enough. No sense assuming the worst and provoking him. Still she felt the same flutter of disgust and concern that she had earlier when she caught him looking at her. "Why aren't you helping break down for the day?" she inquired, terse but businesslike.

"Came up to grab some tools," he said with a sly smile. He took a step toward her. "I've been all over and never seen a woman as pretty as you." In the fading light, Abby could see the small scar that divided his right eyebrow, the pock scars on his cheeks. He was an unsavory creature. Her skin prickled. She tried to swallow, but her throat was dry.

"Thank you, George," she said, biting each polite word. "That's a fine compliment." She tightened her grip on the grain scoop still in her right hand and looked for some way to dodge past him. He was the larger of the two hired men; she doubted she could outrun him. "I have to get supper ready, so perhaps you should get those tools now," she said, then continued with a little more warning in her tone. "Frank gets very impatient with hired hands who take too long doing as they're asked." She stepped to her right as she spoke, in an effort to move around him. The man, easily a foot taller, took a big step, blocking her path, then came another stride closer. Abby heart pounded; she could smell him now, only a few feet away. The day of work, sweat, and dust hung thick around him.

"What's ya hurry, Miss Abby?" George's twisted smile made his intentions plain. Abby looked for her escape. She stepped back, turned her head, hoping to see Frank or Clay. No luck there. The house was only forty feet away, but it seemed like miles. She had to try. George reached for her, and Abby struck at his hand with the grain pan. His wince bought her a few precious seconds. She screamed as she fled, fear driving her flight toward the back door of the house. *God, please let that damn door open smoothly this one time.* Abby had her hand on the knob when she felt George's body slam into her from behind, pinning her to the door. The impact knocked the wind out of her lungs, and the grain scoop fell out of her hand. She couldn't breathe, let alone scream. The awful man grabbed a handful of her hair, groped at her breasts. She tried once more to scream, but George covered her mouth. Rancid stinking hand. During one faltering inhale, a fearful resignation snaked around her feet, up to her knees. But then the rage appeared. Abby worked her left hand free and lashed out, grabbing and striking at George's face. In a lucky blow, her thumb caught his right eye. The bastard let go of her and stumbled back in pain. Abby dashed towards the front of the house, where she knew the door would open. She could hear George behind her. Whatever damage she'd done, he was still fumbling after her, still intent on catching her.

As she rounded the corner of the porch, there was a glorious sight: *Stranger, barely fifteen feet away.* She had never been as thankful for Stranger's existence as she was right then. Abby dashed past the dog, who set himself on a prompt course toward George. Ripping open the screen door, every instinct told Abby to get inside and lock the doors, but the deep, loud bark stopped her. She spun around and saw George faltering at the sight of the big, black dog. The animal's baritone voice demanded respect. With her hand on the fully opened door, Abby watched the standoff between man and dog. She felt, suddenly, fearless and perfectly safe. Stranger stared at the man, who still held one hand to his eye. Despite the injury, and now an irate guard dog, the imbecile showed no hint of leaving.

For several seconds, the two did not move. Stranger's normally wagging tail was held high and motionless, his body rigid, intent on the threat to his human. Abby straightened. She stayed there at the porch entry, watching. Having Stranger there gave her renewed confidence—and a very sturdy hate.

"Git, dog!" George sneered, raising his free hand in threat. Stranger stood like stone, body unyielding and tall; the attempt to scare him off had no effect. George stomped at Stranger, ready to strike at the dog. But his hand stopped, the man frozen by what he saw. Even from the side, Abby could see enough of the dog to understand why George stopped. Stranger didn't flinch, didn't growl or bark. Instead, the dog just smiled. The skin on Stranger's nose and forehead wrinkled up, and his lips pulled back. Brilliant white fangs shined in the twilight. Abby had never noticed Stranger's teeth before. The wolf-like canines curved menacingly, almost an inch and a half in length. Abby couldn't see Stranger's eyes, but she could see George's. Judging from the vile man's face, the look on the dog must have been terrible indeed. Every muscle in Stranger's body was tense, waiting for the slightest reason to attack.

"You should get those tools now, George," Abby said, words dripping with disgust. "I'm sure Frank and Clay are wondering where you are." Her stare was near Stranger's in intensity. The man looked at her. He looked at Stranger. The dog had not moved or changed his expression. George backed away and slowly walked to the barn. Abby and Stranger stayed put, watching until George had gone far down the road with a wooden toolbox. Only after he was around the bend did Abby collapse on the porch steps, her body shaking as she sobbed. Stranger approached her, concerned. She wrapped her arms around the dog's neck, and he licked her face, his tail swishing back and forth. After several deep breaths, Abby wiped the tears from her face and stood.

"Come on, Stranger," she said. "I want you in the porch while I get dinner ready." With trembling hands, Abby opened the door and let the dog in. With Stranger inside the porch, she closed the door and locked it. She would open it only when she could hear Frank and Clay in the yard. Then, a new fear came over Abby. She had no idea what to do next. She could not tolerate the thought of George being on their property and eating her food, not for a moment longer. But what if Frank did not believe her? Or worse, what if he didn't care? The fear of that last possibility grew as she set out the supper. All the familiar little tasks, she did them, but it was like someone else was doing them. Meanwhile, the real Abby sat on the rafter above the kitchen table looking down on it all. With her real self apparently taking leave, Abby was unable to make any decision regarding any facet of the matter: *To tell or not? When to tell? What specifically to say?* One needed one's truest self to make such choices. The questions went unanswered. The Abby seated on the rafter watched the Abby below lighting lanterns, setting the table, unlatching the door, and letting all four men in as if nothing had happened.

One by one, they came into the house for the last meal of the day. Rafter-Abby noticed that George would not look anyone in the eye. Stanger watched the bastard as he passed by, raising the side of his mouth to reveal the tip of one fang as a reminder. The other men didn't see the canine gesture, but Abby was sure that George did. The whole meal George said not a word. His eye was still red and irritated, but no one mentioned it.

After the men finished dinner, George and Martin retired to the bunk room in the barn, and Frank and Clay checked the horses one last time. Rafters-Abby came down then. She put all the scraps from the meal on one plate and added a couple slices of good roast on top. This feast went to Stranger. Out on the porch, Abby placed the plate next to the dog, and patted his head. He looked confused, then enthusiastically began to eat.

"I'd say God sent you as a guardian angel for me," she said. "Thank you, my friend, you earned this." Stranger swished his tail back and forth. In less than twenty seconds, the plate was licked clean. Abby went back into the house to finish the dishes. When Frank and Clay came back in from checking on the horses, Clay quickly retired to bed. But Frank stayed downstairs, and Rafters-Abby watched him watching her scrubbing the roast pan.

"Kinda quiet, you feeling well?" Frank asked as he took off his boots.

Abby-below nodded yes and kept scrubbing.

"You sure?" Frank came alongside her and put a hand on her shoulder. Rafters-Abby wanted to thank him for that gesture, but the woman at the sink could do nothing. She just nodded, though she did look briefly at her husband and give him a quick smile.

"Do you want some help?" he asked.

"No," said the woman at the sink. "Thank you, though. I'm almost done."

Frank patted her shoulder, then went upstairs to bed. Alone in the kitchen, Abby was suddenly terrified. She jumped back into herself and turned from the sink, expecting to see George standing behind her. Yet nothing but the empty kitchen greeted her. She looked at the door, saw it was unlocked, and rushed across the room to lock it, taking comfort in the sound of the metallic click. Knowing also that Stranger lay on the other side gave her the courage to turn down the lanterns and go upstairs—but only after checking the lock one more time. Frank was already sleeping when she entered their room, his rough snores the most welcome sound she could imagine. Climbing into bed, she moved close and rested a hand on his back. He barely stirred, but his presence was a little comfort. She tried to sleep, but images of the day kept flashing in her mind.

Morning came, and Abby dreaded heading out to the privy. She had been scared before during late night trips down the path, especially when the packs of coyotes were yipping and howling just up the hill. Yet, this morning she was terrified to unlock the door to the porch. With a deep breath, and clutching a small knife, Abby opened the door. Stranger pranced side-to-side in excitement at seeing her. The cool grey light of dawn was starting to fill the land. She stepped outside and was thankful that Stranger did not wander off on his usual morning romp. Instead, he stayed by her side as she visited the outhouse and escorted her back to the house. He knew. That wonderful guardian dog. Only after Abby had closed and locked the door did she see Stranger trot off to the fields. Abby set about making breakfast then. Her real self, the part of her that liked to read in the early morning, was once again perched on the rafter above the sink.

Frank came down first, his eyes heavy despite his deep, exhaustion-fed sleep. Haying season wore everyone down. He glanced at Abby when he found the front door locked—something they never did. He unlocked it, went out to the privy, and a minute later, sat down with his first cup of coffee. Rafters-Abby desperately wanted to tell him. She had to. Though the real Abby found it impossible to jump back inside herself, she did manage to stand behind the woman at the stove and gently nudge her into place, guiding her to sit opposite her husband. The soulless woman clasped her hands in front of her and stared straight ahead. Her eyes began to water.

Frank looked up from his coffee. "Abby... what's wrong?"

She struggled to say the name of the awful man. She had to; it all started there. "George—" she said his name but couldn't say anything more.

Frank set his coffee down. "What about George?" Frank's eyes were hard. "What did he do? Did he hurt you?"

Frank's tone made Abby wonder if he was mad at her. Would he be angry if she asked him to get rid of the man, if she insisted that he hire someone else? Would he think she'd done something to attract the wretch's attention? So many men blamed women for such things.

Real Abby gave herself a gentle shake right then. Come hell or high water, Frank needs to know what happened. If he blames you, well, you know for certain that you need to leave. She did not cry. Word by word, she told Frank precisely what had happened: the assault, the reason George's eye was all bloody, the way Stranger had saved her, and how the dog had accompanied her that morning. She spoke these things in the same way she'd set out dinner the night before—with her real self not entirely there. This made it much easier to recount the incident, but made it much harder to understand Frank's reaction. One needs one's soul in order to understand another's. Frank's face changed, concern changing into stern focus and then rage. His fists were clenched so tight, the color drained from them. Just then Clay came down and stopped, seeing his son's face, Abby's strange stare.

"Get the car, Dad," Frank said. "You're taking George back to the station." Abby was silent. She didn't know what to say, still unsure of what Frank was thinking. Her husband stormed out of the house. Abby saw Clay's face change as he made a rough approximation of the matter at hand. He grabbed his coat and headed out to the barn. Abby sat at the table, stared at the roasting pan still sitting on the counter where she had left it to dry. She thought nothing. Felt nothing. But soon the noise of conflict pierced the walls and windows of the house. She heard the sounds and sat very still. She could hear Frank's harsh yells and a body being slammed against the barn siding. She heard what must have been the bastard's yelps, but they were repeatedly cut short by the wallop of fist to flesh. There were sounds from Stranger, too—barks and growls and teeth ripping clothing. She sat very still. The punishment outside went on for several minutes. Eventually the car started; she heard it drive away.

Frank came into the kitchen, slamming the door behind him. Abby jumped. But she did not move from her chair. She looked down now, concentrating on the table, the grain of the wood. She noticed Frank's knuckles were bleeding as he walked past, and she heard him work the handle on the pump at the sink till water poured out. Abby listened to him wash and dry his hands. Listened to his breath; rushed at first, then slow and steady. Out of the corner of her eye, she could see him still standing at the counter, looking out the small window above the pump. He turned around and came to her. As his hand reached to touch her shoulder, Abby flinched.

"I'm sorry," she said, reflexive, sad that she had recoiled from him but equally worried about what he might say next. Frank withdrew his hand and, without a word, pulled a chair next to hers.

"You mad at me?" Abby asked, eyes still aimed at the table.

"At you?" Frank sounded shocked. "No. I'm mad at him. And at me; I wasn't here to stop him."

He reached toward her once more, but stopped short of touching her, merely making an offering of his hand. Abby looked at it for a moment, then unclasped her folded hands, reached out, and let her hand rest in Frank's. She couldn't look at him, but she could almost feel the warmth of his fingers. Frank cupped her hand with both of his.

"I'm sorry I wasn't here," he repeated, his voice cracked ever so slightly with emotion. Abby slipped back into herself, and she looked at Frank's eyes. There was no anger there now, only sadness.

There was so little time to dwell on what had happened. The two did not discuss whether or not Abby felt like she could work that day; both knew this was not a matter that could be debated. Frank did persuade Abby to eat something, advice she heeded as best as she could. When Clay got back, he ate his breakfast while Frank and Abby hitched up the teams with Martin's help. One hand shy, they would all have to work a little harder. Abby figured it was better that way; hiding out in the house alone would be far worse.

Abby drove a buck rake again, but worked close alongside Clay's team. Frank made certain that he or Clay accompanied her to the house to take care of meals. It meant a less productive day, but no one complained. Even Stranger stayed close to Abby's side. For Abby, the fear echoed all day, as it would for days to come. George's face flashed in her mind whenever she closed her eyes. But she felt safe with her kin looking out for her, with Stranger nearby.

That evening Abby noticed that both Frank and Clay didn't have much appetite, leaving half their meals on their plates—excessive contributions to the scrap bucket. Even Martin left some on his plate. When she asked, they all said they were full, but Abby knew it was their way of thanking Stranger. Her husband and father-in-law also made no comment when Abby locked the door before heading to bed. From that day on, even they made sure it was locked if they were the last ones to head to bed.

CHAPTER 14
OCTOBER 1935

Abby was out in the yard at the washtub, taking advantage of the unseasonably warm day. She was alone, but Stranger was with her. Frank and Clay were up on the mountain, trying to get the last of the cattle down to winter pasture before the snow started to fall. Frank was actually the one who made it a rule that the dog stay with Abby if both he and Clay were not on the ranch. Everyone was shaken by the incident with George. For Abby, the fear had eased some; there were moments now when she did not think of it. This was one such moment. She scrubbed one of Frank's shirts against the washboard and looked out at the horizon: not a cloud. Not ideal for putting the fields to bed; some moisture would be good before the freeze up. But it would make the clothes dry fast.

She was lost, not in thought, but in the familiarity of the task, the soothing boredom of it, when the horses gave the first warning. The herd in the corral next to the barn spooked and began whinnying. They pranced around nervously. Abby worried that it might be a bear, but Stranger was not acting like he'd caught scent of an intruder of any kind. Then she heard the noise: a low rumble, like a thousand head of buffalo running across the plains.

The dog let out a high-pitched whine, not anything like his usual guard dog confidence.

Abby dropped Frank's shirt into the water and looked to the east, trying to locate the source of the noise. All she saw was the aspen trees in their bright yellow fall color—nothing that would explain the low thundering. Perhaps neighbors were moving equipment from the dredge, or maybe someone was moving a herd of cattle. The rumble grew, the water in the tub shimmered violently, and then the ground began to shiver. The horses ran and bucked, and Stranger hunkered down low. Abby struggled to stay standing amidst the shaking. She heard something break inside the house. Then, as quickly as the quake started, it passed. Stranger still cowered, looking around with great concern on his face, his ears tucked flat against his head. Abby calmed herself, realizing she had just experienced her first earthquake.

"It's okay, Stranger. I think it's over," she said, more as a reassurance to herself than the dog. She looked to see that the horses were still in the corral and then headed into the house to see what had broken. A dozen pieces of dark brown glass lay scattered across the wood plank floor—the remains of an old whiskey bottle she had salvaged from the hay field by Blackfoot City. It had served as a flower vase for the past year. Abby swept up the pieces and looked around to make sure nothing else was damaged. The wood stove had shifted. Frank and Clay would have to move it back into place when they returned. Other than that, the house seemed sound.

She went back outside and found Stranger was still rattled. She petted the dog and considered the situation. There was little she could do about Frank and Clay but wait till they came home in the evening. If they didn't show up, she'd have to ask a neighbor or two to ride into the high country with her at first light. The tremor had been mild though; she was sure they were fine.

Gradually, Stranger sat upright and wagged his tail again. "Right as rain, dog?" Abby asked; then headed to the corral to check on the horses. Animals all accounted for, she went back to the washing. So that was what an earthquake was like. In addition to living through snowstorms and forty below and driving ranch equipment, she now had earthquakes to add to her long list of ranch experiences. Those things—the mutterings of God and nature—those she could handle. Those things made her feel stronger after she lived through them.

The animals reverted to their contented selves, and Abby washed and rinsed and ran the clothes through the crank wringer and clipped them all to the line, then set to work on some mending in the house. There were no more tremors that day, and Abby felt more invigorated than frightened. Still, it was so good to hear Frank's voice that evening. She was in her sewing room when she heard the horses on the road. She rushed to the porch.

"Everything alright here?" Frank called from the barnyard gate. Abby shouted back assurances that all was well. She crossed the yard to the men, eager to hear their news.

"We had a bit of a rodeo up top," Frank said as he got off his horse. "The horses were full of piss 'n vinegar. At first I thought they mighta' caught scent of a bear or mountain lion." Frank went on to describe how the earthquake caused a dead standing tree to tip over near them.

"Didn't get thrown, I hope?" Abby asked.

"Nah, it didn't last long," Frank said as he unbuckled the cinch on his horse. "I've had rougher rides in John's truck."

Clay countered, "Ya didn't look all that sure of yourself from where I was sittin." Clay pulled the saddle off his big Appaloosa as he continued ribbing Frank. "You was lookin a little peeky; might need to get you bronc riding lessons from the Bander sisters."

Abby smiled at the suggestion. The famous women bronc riders were regulars at the Deer Lodge rodeo every year. They were tougher than most men she knew. Though rumor had it, some rodeo officials wanted to make it illegal for women to participate in bucking horse competitions.

"I doubt they'd fare any better, if their horse was bucking over a bunch of rocks!" Frank said. They volleyed on about the quake, about the cattle they'd found and the half dozen still eluding them. They'd have to go back up in the next few days to find them.

It was good to hear them talk like that, the friendly banter. Frank had changed; Abby could see that now. They still had some of the Deer Lodge money left, but that hardly justified Frank's lighter mood. The ranch was still far from profitable. The question of when to sell still sat with them at every meal, voiced or not. Yet, Frank no longer griped about the matter. He did not speak of the future of the ranch in that heavy way that made Abby know she was the problem. There was an ease about him; there was laughter now.

≈++≈

The next morning, Abby shivered as she dressed and wrapped a hand stitched quilt around her shoulders and went downstairs. She breathed life into the stove embers. The first frost had hit two weeks earlier, and, since then, the nights were getting colder and colder. The days were sunny, but it took longer to warm up the house as the season progressed. Stranger seemed to be feeling the cold as well. His large body was curled up in a tight ball on his blanket in the porch. Poor dog; what a rough night after such a rough day. Abby hated seeing the pooch so cold; she needed to do something about it. At breakfast with the men, she took her chance.

"Seems so much colder every morning. With frost so early, we might be in for a cold winter," she ventured. Clay nodded his head as he chewed.

"I suspect it'll be a bad one," Frank said. "There was fresh snow in the trees when we were up top yesterday."

"Already?" Abby said and sighed. She did not care much for winter. But this news did play well with her plan for Stranger. "I suppose we're going to have to get ready for winter whether we want to or not. I just hate the idea of the animals being out in the cold." Abby's compassionate sentiment didn't even get a response from the men. They were barely listening. She cut to her point, "I was thinking we should bring Stranger's bed in next to the stove." She looked down at her cup, took a drink the moment her words left her mouth. It was easy enough to imagine the look on Frank's face. She heard Clay swallow and clear his throat. The old man didn't say anything, though.

"How's that, Abby?" Frank's words hung in the air for a moment. Clay took another bite, which Abby deemed wise on his part. She knew that the battle ahead might not be a pleasant one. It was important though. For Stranger; for her, too. *How kind and sweet are you, Frank? You came home, tail between your legs. But do you really care? About all of us?*

Abby repeated, forceful and eye-to-eye this time, "I said that, when winter sets in, I think we should let Stranger sleep next to the stove." Frank's eyes narrowed, then softened, then narrowed again. He was wrestling, that was for sure. For the first time in five years, Abby had the courage, the confidence, to make an outlandish request. Stranger was worth the risk. Frank set his coffee cup down and hardened his stare. No, it wasn't going to be easy.

"No dogs in the house," Frank was firm, but he kept his volume low.

"Why not?" Abby set her cup down. "He already sleeps inside the porch. What's the harm in letting him come in the kitchen to be warm? Just at night."

Frank sat back in disbelief. "Abby, this is where we eat! He's been a good dog, but he's still a dog. No one in his right mind lets a filthy, mangy mutt in his house." Frank leaned forward for emphasis as he spoke, but the edge of condescension didn't faze Abby. She sat up straight and set her hands flat on the table. She wasn't intimidated, she wasn't afraid. Did she love Frank? Yes. She was surprised at that; she loved him once again. But she no longer regarded love and obedience as entirely twined. She would stand her ground. She owed it to Stranger for what he had done for her.

"This is my kitchen; I do the cooking, not you. If I want a dog in here with me, then he will come in." Abby did not shout or scowl. She said her piece and crossed her arms across her embroidered apron. "He isn't much dirtier than you two are after a day's work."

Clay raised his eyebrows, but still kept quiet. Frank wasn't as restrained. "Abby, have you seen what that animal rolls in? Dear God, have you seen what he eats?" Frank was angry, but even more, he was genuinely disgusted. "He's filthy, and I forbid him from coming in the house."

Abby leaned forward and replied. "You only bathe once a week, and I share my bed with you. But to be clear, you won't let him in the house because he's dirty, correct?"

"Yes, he's filthy, and I don't see him being all that willing to take a bath, do you?" Frank brushed Clay's shoulder with his hand searching for assistance, but Clay just took another drink of coffee. He was not getting roped in.

"So, if by some miracle, Stranger could figure out how to take a bath, you would let him in the house?" Abby did not care how ridiculous that sounded. Never in a million years had anyone heard of bathing a dog. What was next, horse washes? Chicken scrubbing? But she was ready to give it a try, to win a point. Definitely.

Frank laughed. Not the warm laugh when he and Clay poked fun at each other. A pained, sarcastic laugh. "Fine, if Stranger learns how to take a bath, he can come inside the house."

"Very well, I'll give him a bath this afternoon," Abby said.

"I'd rather you not get your face chewed off," Frank said. He shook his head, both scorn and wonder in his eyes. But he did not shout. No threats, no fist-pounding on the table. He did not storm out of the house. That was something.

Frank finished his meal, grabbed his coat off of the hook on the wall near the stove, and went outside. On his way, he mumbled under his breath how Abby would want to bring the horses and cows in during the next blizzard. Abby sat back in her chair and smiled. She looked at Clay, who glanced sheepishly back at her.

Clay clicked his tongue, took one more thoughtful bite, then spoke. "Remind me never to make ya angry at me, Abby."

"I think you're wise enough not to do that," she said. "Frank's still learning."

"He's a stubborn one; might never learn. Vivian swore she was training me up till the day she passed," he said. "I guess she was."

Clay stood and headed for the door, then stopped before going out. "Frank said he was going to town this afternoon to pick up some parts. I can stay back. I don't think Stranger will be all that keen on your idea; might take two of us."

Abby thanked Clay for the offer. "I know I'll garner scrutiny for completing this scheme. But I'll never hear the end of it if I don't try," she said. "I suppose now I need to figure out just how we shall carry out this venture."

The afternoon turned out warmer than Abby expected, and she was thankful, as she knew the water would be frigid right out of the pump. She hauled her large galvanized washtub to the barn, deciding the best way to bathe Stranger was to corral him in an area where he couldn't escape. Abby hoped that he would be cooperative, but deep down she knew that the dog would hate the whole undertaking.

Once Frank was gone, Abby and Clay set up their dog-scrubbing supplies in the one empty barn stall that had a concrete floor. They normally used it for pulling calves when a cow had trouble delivering.

It was the most secure area in the barn. Abby also hoped the concrete floor would help keep Stranger, as well as herself and Clay, clean during and after the procedure. Abby and Clay carried buckets of water from the hand pump. They filled the washtub about half full and then set four buckets of water aside for rinsing Stranger after his scrub down. They gathered all the other supplies they thought might be necessary: raggedy old towels, a bar of Abby's homemade soap, a lead rope. Stranger followed them every step of the way, his curiosity getting the best of him.

"Well, Clay, I say we're as ready as we can be," Abby said as they stood outside the stall. Its solid wood walls and gate would prevent Stranger from escaping his fate, but if things turned ugly, it would also hinder Abby and Clay's escape.

"I reckon," Clay said with some hesitation. "I don't suppose you'd rethink this and just leave the dog outside for the winter?"

"No, Stranger's getting a bath today, come hell or high water," Abby said, furrowing her brow. She knew that she had to see it through.

Clay called Stranger over. The dog was lying by the barn door, watching them. At the sound of his name, he got up and trotted over with his tail wagging. Stranger followed them into the stall and looked expectantly at Abby, hoping for a treat or at least some attention. As the stall door closed, Stranger showed the first hint of concern. Cautious, but still curious, he looked around and sniffed the washtub. Abby and Clay approached the dog as he leaned over the tub to take a drink. The dog's ears pivoted toward them. Stranger straightened up, turned, looked at them, and backed away with his ears flat against his head. He clearly knew something unsavory was about to happen.

"Come on, Stranger," Abby said in a gentle sing-song, "Time for a bath." She bent down, put her arms around him to lift him into the tub. Realizing that her touch was not one of affection, Stranger squirmed, let out a yelp, and launched his nearly hundred-pound body out of her grasp. Abby had restrained calves as big as the dog during branding season. But cows didn't have teeth like Stranger's. Clay spoke softly to Stranger, trying to soothe the now-panicked dog. It didn't help. Stranger ran to the door of the stall and found his exit blocked. Frantic, he pawed at the stall door.

"Perhaps we should put a rope on him?" Clay offered.

Abby put her hands on her hips and sighed. "I really was hoping this would be easier," she said. Stranger continued to paw at the door and whimper.

Clay grabbed a lead rope, formed a slip loop, and took a step toward Stranger. Abby stopped him. "No, Clay," she said. "This was my idea, let me do it."

"You sure?" Clay asked, but relinquished the rope to her.

Abby just nodded and walked towards the frightened animal. Stranger dashed to the far corner of the stall, as far as he could get from the wash tub. Abby made her voice as sweet and non-threatening as possible. She told him it was bath time, and it wouldn't take long. She promised him molasses cookies. She reached out with the rope loop to slip it over Stranger's head, but the dog's demeanor changed as she got close. The look of fear in his eyes was replaced with an ember of disdain, and that ember exploded into rage. Stranger had been hunkering as close to the wall as possible, but now he faced her. Abby barely heard Clay's warning. As quick as lightning, Stranger lunged forward and snapped at her, though he stopped several inches short of her hand. Abby leapt backwards at the flash of teeth, shocked at Stranger's aggression. Clay, unable to see the altercation clearly, jumped over and grabbed Abby's hands to see if she had been bitten.

"I'm fine, just startled is all," she said. Stranger now stood with his tail to the corner and his body facing Clay and Abby. He looked bigger than normal, his hair raised up along his back. Abby decided to make one more attempt and took a slow step forward.

Stranger glared at her and pulled back his lips, revealing his fangs. Good God. The dog was giving her the same look he'd given to George. Abby stopped for a moment. Instead of feeling frightened, she felt anger building up inside of her. Abby hated to raise her voice for anything other than to sing hymns at church or to call Frank and Clay in for a meal. Yet, at that moment, her voice rang out like an avalanche.

"You ungrateful cur!" she shouted. "How dare you show your teeth at me! I'm the reason you're alive and still living on this ranch!" Stranger had never been so addressed by Abby, and the verbal assault had its intended effect. The dog slunk back, retracted his snarl. Abby leaned towards him and railed on. She called him filthy and mangy, told him he was getting a bath whether he liked it or not. She took a step closer, leaving Stranger with only a direct path toward the tub. Abby stood over him, pointing at the washtub to make her meaning abundantly clear. "Get your furry carcass into that tub this instant, or, so help me God, I'll tan your hide on the barn door!" Her fire-filled eyes locked with Stranger's. The dog had reverted to cowering pup.

"Get in there!" Abby yelled. "Now!" She effectively stunned both herself and the dog. Clay, too. Stranger looked at the door, at Clay, at the tub, and finally back to Abby. Out of options, he scrambled over to the tub and jumped into it. He stood in the cold water shaking, ears tucked against his head and his eyes looking away from Abby as she stomped up to him.

"If you even think of biting me, it'll be the last thing you do!" Abby gave one final scolding to the dog. "You hear me?" She began bailing water onto the dog who, surrendering his pride, submitted to the washing without moving once.

Abby looked back at Clay, who stood in the middle of the stall, dumbfounded at what he had just seen. "You gonna just stand there or you gonna help?" she asked, her voice still held a mean edge. "Hand me that soap before the mongrel changes his mind."

Clay grabbed the bar of homemade soap, handed it to Abby, and took over bailing water as Abby scrubbed the beast from head to tail. After fifteen minutes of washing and rinsing, they coaxed the still-shaking dog out of the tub. Stranger stood in the middle of the stall, water streaming down his sides and tail. Both head and tail hung down in shame.

"Looks like a drowned rat," Clay chuckled. Abby laughed and agreed, then shrieked as Stranger shook. A cascade of water droplets covered the stall walls and its occupants.

"I suppose we should have dried him as soon as he got out of the tub," Abby said. The worst of the chore done, she relaxed. At least Stranger would like the next part. The two humans grabbed towels and started to rub the water-logged dog. The attention did put a happy gleam back into his eyes. After a few minutes and several soggy hair-covered towels, Abby decided Stranger was clean and dry enough. Clay opened the stall door, and Stranger rushed out into the sunshine. Simultaneously, both Abby and Clay realized that might not have been wise. They ran out after the dog, fearing that he would roll around in dirt or something worse. But the dog just ran about the yard, stopping every now and then to shake.

"Well, that went better than expected," Clay said. "The trick'll be keeping him clean. Not sure I wanna do that very often."

Abby sighed. "No, neither do I. At least it's done, and he'll be warm tonight."

"There ought to be an award for what we just did," Clay said. "Who ever heard of a dog bath before? Could turn it into a rodeo event."

It was almost dark when Frank pulled into the ranch. Abby watched from the kitchen as he parked the car in the equipment shed, unloaded the parts he'd picked up, and walked across the barnyard to the house. He entered the kitchen and saw Stranger on his bed next to the stove. Frank grimaced. The dog looked like a defeated creature, his head down, not daring to rise up as Abby set the table. She noticed the dog looking at Frank with sad eyes, the tip of his tail moving slightly in a half-hearted wag.

Frank looked at Stranger, but addressed Abby, "Well, you aren't all bandaged up, so I assume the bath went well?"

"Oh yes, we had ourselves a come-to-Jesus moment," Abby said. "But after that, things went just fine." Frank looked at the dog and then back to Abby, but kept his mouth shut.

After supper, Abby fed the scraps to Stranger out on the porch, let him outside one last time, then ushered him back into the house and out of the cold night air. Turning down the stove damper and blowing out the lamps, she went upstairs and slipped into bed with Frank. He was already snoring. Abby was drifting off when she heard Stranger whining. Her first thought was that maybe he needed to go outside. Then she felt the shaking. Unlike the little quake they'd experienced the day before, these tremors were strong.

Frank bolted upright, wide awake. The rumbling grew louder, and the whole house shook. Outside, Abby could hear the horses shrieking, and Stranger began barking. There was glass breaking downstairs, and soon the smell of smoke. The stove must have separated entirely from the chimney this time. Abby and Frank struggled to get out of bed, fumbled with clothing, managed to light a candle. The earthquake lasted less than half a minute, but it felt like hours. Frank found another candle that had fallen onto the floor in the quake and lit it from Abby's.

They met Clay on the landing. He had a candle of his own. Together, they went downstairs to find Stranger cowering in the corner of the kitchen, the floor strewn with plates and tipped-over chairs. A layer of smoke hung near the ceiling, fed by the dislodged stove pipe. Clay and Frank found dish towels to protect their hands and reset the pipe and stove before the whole house could fill with smoke. Abby found one kerosene lantern that had not been broken. She lit it and handed it to Frank, who went outside with Clay to check on the brick chimney, the barn, and the horses. Careful to keep her candle away from the kerosene spills, Abby did her best to clean up the damages inside the house. Stranger stayed in the corner, shaking. The poor dog. Abby found her large clay cookie jar. Nestled in the corner cupboard, a half-full flour sack protecting it, there wasn't a scratch on it. She took out two molasses cookies and called to Stranger. Trembling, but trying to wag his tail, he came to her. He kept his head down and ears flattened but looked up at her with loving eyes. She handed him a cookie.

"I owed you one from the bath today," she said and patted the dog softly as he munched. "What a terrible day for you." She handed him the second cookie. "Thank God we're all safe."

Abby rubbed Stranger's ears, gave him one last pat, and went back to cleaning. Soon the men came back in, reporting on a small breach in the corral. Their rope-tie repair would hold for the night till they could set new posts in the morning. The chimney seemed sound, though. That was enough assurance to let the three retire to bed for a fitful night's sleep.

Some hours later, Abby woke. No quake, no strange noises. Only Frank snoring. So what woke her? Oh, now there was something—Frank was holding her hand. She wondered if he had been awake when he did that. Or had she reached out to him in her sleep? No matter. It did feel good. Holding very still, she let herself close her eyes and rest.

⊷ ⊶

It took several days for news to spread up the valley. The massive quake had been centered near Helena, over twenty-five miles away. The damages on their ranch were minimal compared to how the quake devastated that city. Given all the damages to shops and houses there, it was amazing that only two had perished. Of the cities nearby, Helena was Abby's favorite, and she was thankful that the big Catholic Cathedral was still standing; its beautiful stained glass windows and stone spires were a delight to see on the rare trip to the city. Also unharmed was the opulent Broadwater Hotel and Natatorium. But its swimming pool was fed by a hot spring, and the quake had somehow sealed off the spring. Water no longer cascaded over the boulders at the north end of the pool.

Years ago, Abby had entertained the thought of staying there with Frank someday. She never told Frank about it. To walk the fragrant gardens, to dine on such fine food, and to swim in the tile-lined pool—it was a foolish dream. Now Abby wondered how long the hotel could stay in business, without the spring to feed the pool. No matter. There was little time to ruminate over the quake. Another week later, the first big snow fell, its arrival heralding the long struggle of winter.

CHAPTER 15

WINTER-TO-SPRING 1936

The cold of winter set in hard and fast, though Stranger didn't mind much. His thick black coat was perfect for it. Any chance he had, he was outside lying on top of a snow drift, watching his humans at their daily chores. The dog preferred to stay outside, but the woman insisted he come in every night. Obedient, he would lie down on the rumpled blanket next to the stove. He would stay there till his humans went to bed, and then get up and head across the room to curl up by the door. The half-inch gap at the bottom allowed a steady flow of cold air over his body, keeping him comfortable till the stove went out. At the sound of stirring upstairs, he would move back over to his bed by the stove, making sure he was there before the woman came downstairs. He dared not challenge her since the bath incident.

Apart from cold baths, and the requirement to sleep indoors, Stranger liked his life on this ranch. He did his best to help—or at least observe—everyone during the daily chores. Stranger knew his duty was to keep watch over them all. He stayed close to the woman; she was his favorite, even if she did pour water on him sometimes. At least she had not done so since the snow and cold arrived in earnest. Stranger liked the old man, too. He kept a good distance from the younger man, though even that human did not seem quite so hostile anymore.

Sometimes the younger man would even laugh at Stranger's antics in the snow. The dog would start out running, then dive sidelong into a drift, head obscured in deep powder. He pushed his body along till he was completely buried, only to erupt up through the snow, his body plastered with powdery ice crystals. Just his eyes and nose showed through the blanket of white. The sheer pleasure of this game was more than enough reason for Stranger to repeat it day after day. But the laughter from the humans added to his enjoyment. Another delight was when the old man tossed snowballs, and Stranger would leap into the air to catch them. Even the young man tossed a few at Stranger, though he stopped when he realized someone else was watching.

The old man knew how to play, and the young man was learning. The woman didn't understand how hot it was to sleep by a wood stove in a fur coat. But that was all right. She was the provider of ear-scratching and cookies. So it was a good winter so far. Stranger was fed and had a territory to patrol and protect. He was as happy as a dog could be. He was meant to be there.

As winter transitioned into spring, Stranger's territory became more easily accessible once again. The mud that collected in his fur and on his feet caused some loud words between the woman and the younger man. Much to his dismay, Stranger found himself forced to stand still at the door while the woman picked up and cleaned each of his paws before she brought him inside each night. He tried to get away once, more than happy to stay outside, but the woman would not have it. A few stern words from her and Stranger was convinced to bear the humiliation of this new nightly ritual.

On one of the drier days in early spring, all three humans saddled their horses and headed into the high country. Stranger tagged along as always, enjoying the chance to mark new territory and keep an eye on his people. The higher they rode, the more the dog lagged behind, distracted by new smells and an occasional squirrel. Each time he realized his humans were not nearby, he trotted ahead to regain ground, making sure that they never were entirely out of earshot. Occasionally, the woman called to him, but whenever she did, he was already on his way to catch up.

As they reached the top of a ridgeline, the humans began following one of the barbed-wire fences, stopping to fix portions that were damaged. Stranger continued his exploring, but kept an ear pointed at his people. At one point the three humans spread out along the fence, each finding spots that needed repair. They dismounted from their horses and worked for hours, sometimes calling kind words to each other. The younger man finished his section first and, after speaking with the others, got on his horse to ride farther along the fence. Stranger watched and decided to follow him. The man, focused on the fence, was unaware that Stranger was tagging along.

Though he was thirty feet behind, the dog picked up the odd scent a few seconds before the horse did. His nose worked frantically, trying to identify it. The big saddle animal tensed, ears moving quickly and nostrils flaring. Stranger could see that the man was concerned by his horse's behavior, but couldn't guess the cause. The horse knew. Stranger knew. He had smelled this threat before; it wasn't good. A motion to the left caught the attention of all three creatures.

The horse spooked as two black shapes darted under a log, then climbed a tree at incredible speed. Stranger keyed in on that movement, but also saw the larger black form of the mother bear running towards the younger man and his horse. The dog lowered his head and launched himself towards the approaching

172

menace, just as the horse bucked and spun, throwing the man to the ground. Dog and horse passed each other in a blur of fur, saddle leather, hooves, and paws—the horse retreating down the fence line and Stranger heading towards the threat.

The man hit the ground hard; he lay motionless as Stranger streaked past, just as the fanged, furred beast closed in. The younger man was hurt, and the dog thought of his first human, the fall on the tracks. No time now. Stranger charged at the bear. His barks rang through the trees, but they were drowned out by the roars of the bear. She repeatedly struck at the dog, who circled and bit at her.

The smell of the woods, the horse, the bear—all filled Stranger's nose, each easily identified, even in the chaos of the fight. With every circle the dog made, he swept in and bit. The bear lunged back, but never fast enough to catch Stranger, who quickly withdrew and circled for another attack. With each of his attacks, the dog drew the bear farther away from the man. Stranger caught a glimpse of him—now struggling to get up. Good, he was alive then. The dog carried on battling the bear, while tracking the movement of the man. Finally, he saw the man get to his feet, briefly watch the battle, then turn to stumble down the mountain to safety. This was what Stranger had been waiting for. Once the man was out of sight, Stranger broke off the attack.

The bear had other plans. The sow had anticipated Stranger's retreat. She cut off his escape route, and Stranger could no longer avoid her rage. He narrowly escaped the bear's jaws, but a paw caught his side. Stranger yelped as he felt the claws rip through his fur and tear open the skin along his ribs, the blow sending him tumbling over rock and grass. The bear was nearly on top of him now; he had to get away, had to get out of this clearing, and back into the timber. Stranger leapt to the side then rushed towards a patch of jagged deadfall trees. He dove through a gap just big enough for him. The bear wouldn't be able to follow; she would have to go around the tangle.

Stranger worked his way out of the dense weave of wood only to find the bear coming along his flank, still in hot pursuit. Heading deeper into the timber, he ran as fast as he could, at times feeling the breath of the bear on his tail. Finally, finally, the dog realized the forest behind him was silent. The bear had broken off the pursuit.

That was when Stranger began to smell and feel the warm blood soaking the fur along his side. He circled back and limped out of the trees, down to the fence line toward his people. He grew more and more lame with each step, the muscles of his shoulder stiffening in response to the gaping wound. He had to hold up his left front leg as he made his way over the rocks and tree roots crisscrossing the trail.

The old man rode up first. His horse was winded and foamed with sweat. The man swung himself down to the ground, still holding one of the reins as he knelt to touch Stranger—who gave a half-hearted tail wag. The old man kept glancing up the mountain, making sure that the bear was indeed gone. When he saw the wound on the dog's shoulder and side, he took off his outer shirt and soaked up some of the blood.

The woman and younger man arrived. They must have caught the younger man's horse; both horses were breathing hard through flared nostrils. The woman cried out when she saw Stranger. The younger man took off his coat and joined the old man in fashioning a bandage. Oh, it hurt! The dog whined as the men wrapped his wound. But he knew not to growl or snap. The younger man climbed onto his horse, and the old man lifted Stranger up to him. The dog lay draped across the front of the saddle, and his humans spoke to him with soft voices. He squirmed a bit, both from the pain and the fear of being so high off the ground. He could see the woman wiping tears away from her face as they rode back down the mountain. With each step, pain shot through Stranger's side. He whimpered any time the horse stumbled or took a hard step down the rough trail.

Once back at the house, the old man and the woman dismounted, and the woman ran into the house while the old man took Stranger from the saddle, then carried him into the kitchen. Blood dripped from the soaked garments. The old man laid Stranger onto the blanket-covered kitchen table. A pot of water was heating on the stove, which roared with a freshly-stoked fire. The younger man came in and all three talked, looking at the dog, who wanted nothing more than to sleep and escape the pain.

The woman gently pulled away the cloth that covered the wound. Stranger yelped and arched his neck. He wasn't intending to bite her, but his teeth glanced against her hand. The woman stopped, and Stranger laid his head back down on the blankets. His world went dark as the old man wrapped a towel over his head. He knew who was holding his head from the smell of his hands and the familiar voice talking softly. With each touch on the wound, he whined and wiggled in an attempt to get away, but strong hands and calm words kept him still. He could feel the younger man holding his legs as the woman poured warm water over the wound, cleaning the blood way. Some other liquid was poured on the wound. The smell was awful, and it burned! Stranger yowled. Thankfully, the worst of the pain abated quickly. Soon he felt the woman's hands pulling at his hair on each side of the wound. Much later, Stranger would see the result of her work: how she'd tied strands of his fur together to seal the torn skin. She fashioned dozens of these delicate knots, until the wound was closed. Stranger felt soft pressure on his side as the woman used a cloth to blot away the remaining blood.

All three of his humans lifted him up and laid him gently on his blankets by the stove. Even though he usually found his bed too warm, it felt just right at that moment. Its smell and feel were comforting. Only then did the old man remove the towel from Stranger's head. The dog lay there panting from the stress and the still-aching wound. His people looked at him and talked with each other, and then the men left the house. Stranger could hear them leading the horses to the barn. The woman stayed inside and brought Stranger a bowl of water, but he didn't even lift his head. All he wanted to do was sleep.

The next morning, the woman was up first, and helped Stranger walk outside to relieve himself. With each step he whined loudly, and her face showed her concern. Stranger didn't want to do his usual patrol. He couldn't. He wanted only to go back inside and lie down next to the stove. For several days Stranger lay there, only getting up to go out for short periods. The woman or the old man would loop a towel under Stranger's chest and hold it to help him walk.

Three days after the fight, the younger man came into the kitchen while the others were outside. The man poured some coffee and sat down in a chair nearby. The dog didn't lift his head, but returned the man's gaze. They looked into each other's eyes for some time. The dog was devoted to the ranch, to his people. The younger man had finally realized this; Stranger could see it in his eyes. The man knelt down next to Stranger and reached out to pet his neck. Stranger didn't pull back. For the first time, he felt no threat from him. The human spoke two words and smiled as he stroked the dog's fur. Stranger lifted his head enough to lick the man's wrist and then closed his eyes to rest.

CHAPTER 16
JULY 1936

As spring flowed into summer, Abby had spent mud season caring for Stranger, watching him recover. That was a fine diversion during the days their road was impassable except by horse. Everyone was thankful for the rain, though; it was the one advantage of living in the foothills. The mountains made their own weather. Hay season would be good. So many other ranches in the wide, semi-arid valleys were faring more poorly.

Regardless, it was a week into July when the rainy streak broke, and Abby felt like she was coming out of hibernation a few months late. She had not been to town since before winter, and the cupboards and cellar were looking bare. The canning garden was coming along well, but it wouldn't be providing food for another six weeks. She tallied the last few potatoes in the root cellar, the remaining jars of beans she'd put up from last year's garden, and just enough flour for one batch of biscuits. They always had eggs thanks to their hens, and Frank occasionally hunted. But, Abby didn't like running so low on the other staples. A trip to the store was in order.

She double-checked her cash money stashes: a jar behind the almost empty flour sack, a box under her and Frank's bed, a tin on the mantel. She did not touch the pouch in the top drawer of their chest of drawers, though. That was set aside for haying season. Clay had been tiring so easily this past winter. It was clear that hiring an extra hand would be a necessity, not a luxury, this year. The cash they did have available amounted to just over forty dollars to get them through the summer. It would have to be enough.

July was like that: Everyone working so hard and coming home hungry. At the same time, crops weren't yielding yet, last year's stores were running low, and it would be two months before they sold this year's beef cattle. It was more complicated this year; Frank's continued refusal to do any more stonework hit them hard. When Abby worked on their books, she had to admit that they had become a ranch funded by other work. But, Frank wouldn't say a thing about the topic. He spoke with ease about anything else, but if Abby so much as glanced at the stone shed, he turned steely and walked away, as locked up tight as the shed's door.

Gathering the couple of dollar coins and loose change, Abby tied the laces on her purse. She would need to stretch it well enough to get them through until the cattle sale in the fall. Money in hand, she walked to the barn where Frank and Clay were cleaning and repairing harnesses for the draft horse team. Stranger was right behind her. The dog was finally back to his old self; the slight but persistent limp did not hold him back.

Frank looked up from replacing a buckle on the cinch on Abby's saddle. It had broken recently after catching on a tree branch while moving the cattle to summer pasture. Abby asked if either Frank or Clay were planning on going into Avon anytime soon. They weren't. She apprised them of the bare pantry and the amount she intended to spend. "Since the roads are finally dry, I think I'll take the car then," she said. The men were intent on their tasks and merely nodded their approvals. They trusted her implicitly on all matters pertaining to the kitchen and funds. Abby turned to head to the car when she saw Stranger once again at her side. She had an idea. Not entirely expecting the men to even hear her, she added, "Well, Stranger and I will be back in a bit."

The thought of having a little company on the drive cheered her. Ranchers that owned both a truck and a dog often allowed the pup to ride in the pickup bed. Abby didn't have that option, but she didn't mind the thought of Stranger riding in the back seat. She was heading to the house to grab her driving pillow—the one she used to help her reach the clutch—when she heard Frank trotting across the barnyard behind her.

"Abby, did you say Stranger's going with you?"

She turned around and nodded.

"In the car?"

"Would you rather I teach him how to ride a horse?" she retorted and crossed her arms. "Yes, I want Stranger with me, since I'm going alone."

"Don't think I've seen a dog in a car before. Back of a truck, sure, but not a car," Frank gave a slight smile and shrugged. "Ya might get some looks is all. Just thinking about your reputation."

"I'd put more weight on the worth of that dog than I would the opinions of others," Abby said. "Come on, Stranger, you and I are going to town." Abby spun around and headed off to the house, Stranger trotting alongside.

She took off her apron and left it in the kitchen, then found her driving pillow and grabbed one of Stranger's ratty old blankets. Heading to the car, she smiled at Frank, who stood at the entrance of the barn shaking his head. She opened up the back door of the car and tossed the blanket across the worn seat, then told Stranger to get in. The dog didn't even hesitate. He leapt into the car, smiling as he panted in excitement, tail swaying back and forth.

Abby closed the door, then got into the driver's seat. She put her pillow behind the small of her back so her short legs could reach the pedals, then got the car started on the second try. Stranger leaned over and sniffed at her ear. As the car lurched forward, the dog stumbled into a seated position. He still had a happy look on his face, though, when Abby looked back at him. She waved at Frank as she pulled out of the shed and he waved back, still shaking his head in disbelief. Clay joined him, the two watching as Abby rolled down the driveway to the main road.

It only took Abby the length of the driveway to encounter the first complication. She had rolled her window down since the car was warm and it was a lovely day. Stranger, enjoying a smorgasbord of smells, alternated between straining to lean out her window and leaving nose prints all over the back windows. It was a touch distracting having a giant dog face right next to hers every time he wedged himself forward trying get more fresh air. This was easily remedied. Abby stopped at the main road, got out of the car, opened the back door—*no, Stranger, stay inside*—and rolled one of the back windows halfway down. She heard Frank and Clay laughing, heard them continue to chuckle at the sight of Stranger's large black and tan head pointing out his window as she resumed her drive.

Abby found herself laughing as well during much of the trip. Stranger bounced from one side of the car to the other, barking at every cow, sheep, and horse he saw. He stood with his front feet on the bottom window frame, allowing most of his head and neck to lean out of the car. Abby could see him in the side mirror, his ears pulled back by the wind, his nose taking in the endless smells as they got closer to Avon. One of the McAllister boys saw them first. The boy was riding a horse, checking irrigation ditches. As she usually would, Abby waved as she went by, but the boy was too dumbfounded to wave back.

Pulling into Avon, Abby turned on Main to head to the Birdseye Mercantile. Traveling down the street, she saw people everywhere stop what they were doing to stare at the big black dog hanging out the back of the window, barking with joy. Feeling like she was driving a highly unusual float in Helena's Fourth of July parade, Abby stopped the car in front of the store, turned the engine off, and got out. She rolled the windows up enough that Stranger could not escape, then closed the doors.

"You stay and..." Abby struggled to give the dog an explanation for why she was leaving him there. He seemed a little anxious. She certainly couldn't bring the animal out onto the town walks, though. "Sit Stranger. Sit and watch the car." The command stuck well enough with its recipient. Stranger sat at his window and sniffed.

In the Mercantile, Abby picked through the items available, pricing each one in her head against the funds she had in her small purse. Flour was the first priority, then potatoes, then the canned goods. Once satisfied she had enough to get them through till they sold some cattle, she headed to the front counter with her full cart. The owner tallied everything up and placed the goods in two old orange crates. Abby had just finished paying when a young boy ran inside with a look of frantic worry on his seven-year-old face.

"Mrs. Redmond! We need to call the sheriff!" the boy exclaimed. Abby knew him from socials at the Avon Community Church. One of the Johnson boys. "There's a really big dog in the back of your car! He looks mean."

"He didn't bite anyone, did he?" Abby asked. She truly hoped that Stranger hadn't gotten himself into trouble on his first trip to town.

"Oh no, ma'am, he's just sitting there, but he's really big, and I don't think you're gonna get him out."

"I see. Well, I think all is well," Abby said. "That dog belongs to me. His name is Stranger." Abby smiled as she explained. The boy tilted his head to the side and gave her a perplexed look, similar to the one that the shopkeeper now wore.

"You let your dog ride in the car?" the boy asked, incredulous.

"Yes, why not? I had to come into town, and I figured he might enjoy the ride," Abby replied. "Besides, I don't know of any law that says a dog can't ride in a car, do you?"

The boy shook his head and wandered away, confusion still on his face. Abby turned to the shopkeeper to get her receipt. The man clearly disapproved of her, but she still asked if he would help carry out the crates. He obliged. But the usually jovial fellow was silent as he followed her out.

The moment they stepped outside the store, Stranger left his seated position on the back seat and hung his head out the window, tail wagging and tongue panting in excitement at seeing Abby. He stopped panting and gave the storekeeper a scrutinizing look as the man approached with the loaded crate and sack of potatoes. Abby opened the front passenger door for him, then distracted Stranger with an ear scratch. Groceries loaded, the storekeeper wished Abby a good day and went back into the store, shaking his head. A small crowd had gathered along the street, muttering to each other and pointing at the car with a dog in it. Ignoring everyone, Abby climbed in, started the engine, and headed for home, content that Stranger was happy in the sun and wind of the car ride. Abby decided to see Patty another time, one without a barking companion tagging along.

Any other time Abby would have been mortified at all the attention, even more so that it wasn't of the positive sort. That day, she held her head high and drove out of town not caring what they thought. She already knew from Patty that there was still plenty of gossip about Frank and Maggie. Maybe it was time to throw folks a new bone to chew on. Letting the dog ride in the car seemed an improvement from all the talk about the two-timing Redmond man. Had it been a year already since all that? How much had changed. Frank was still Frank, but more tempered in his manner. Even polite at times. She did like how he made the effort to give her a kiss goodnight no matter how tired he was. Abby was content with Frank's insistence that he hadn't had an affair, even if he did have feelings for the woman. Initially, Abby had accepted the situation in weary resignation. Of late, that acceptance had grown into forgiveness, an honest forgiveness. It wasn't right, what had happened, but she'd relinquished her longing for revenge.

Well, it was time to let Avon and the valley have something new to discuss. Stranger barked repeatedly as Abby turned through the gate and drove up to the house. Such a funny animal. She admired how much he enjoyed life. He didn't care that they were broke most of the time. Stranger enjoyed each moment for what it was. Smart critter. Abby parked in front of the house, and Frank and Clay helped unload the grocery crate. Abby didn't say a thing about the looks she had gotten in Avon, and the men didn't ask. She suspected they would hear plenty the next time they went to town.

Abby was a little dismayed the next day, when Patty sent John over to inform them that a traveling preacher would be giving a sermon that coming Sunday. As excited as she was to go to church, Abby had hoped that her next trip to town would be a few weeks out. She'd had some second thoughts about the wisdom of her dog-in-the-car adventure. It would be nice to let the worst of the talk die down. It was only three days till Sunday. It would be a big event by Avon standards, as preachers didn't make their way to their little town that often. So much of Abby's life was spent alone in her work at the ranch. The winters were the most trying, the weather making travel into town nearly impossible except by horse drawn sleigh. Spring, also referred to as mud season, wasn't much easier. As much as church was a spiritual act, it was just as vital as a social connection. Abby longed for that connection, and feared it, too. If only people could simply be kind to each other. Well, to heck with the gossipy ones. She was going to church, and people could say what they wanted. Besides, it would be a chance to see

Patty. This spring had been far more eventful for her dear friend. Patty had just welcomed baby number five into the world. Abby had seen the little boy only twice since he was born in May. Yes, it would be very good to spend time with them.

The service would take up much of the morning with a potluck afterward. Abby spent all day Saturday baking and packed an enormous basket of cookies. Even Frank and Clay—yes, they'd decided to attend this one—even they were looking forward to the break from work. The men took their weekly baths a day before normal to ensure they were proper. Sunday morning came, and after her chores were done, Abby bathed while Frank and Clay tended animals and got the car ready. She did her best to pin her hair up but fretted about what she was going to wear. All her dresses, all three of them, were so old. So worn. Frank came up to their room, changed into his Sunday-go-to-meeting clothes, and was ready to go. Abby held one of her dresses, still struggling to decide.

Frank stood at the bedroom door. "I think you would look pretty in that dress I got you last year," he said, then scurried downstairs. What dress? Abby looked up at the twine-bound brown paper package that still sat up on the shelf. She pulled it down, blew the dust off, set it on the bed, and unwrapped it. The green calico dress was lovely. Abby put it on and was surprised at how well it fit. She smiled at how its color matched her eyes. Heading downstairs, she rounded the corner into the kitchen. The smile on Frank's face was enough to make Abby blush. He hadn't smiled like that at her for years.

With Stranger watching the ranch, the three left for Avon. Abby tried not to worry about the potential rumors and instead thought about the joy of singing hymns again and seeing a few good friends. When they entered the church, the first few greetings were friendly and eased Abby's mind; no one mentioned a thing about the dog. Everyone was too busy complimenting her dress. Frank stood a little taller and a little closer to her. She liked that.

If Frank and Clay were in their natural element back at the ranch, here in the church service, Abby was in hers. Here she could sing and pray without a skeptical glance from Frank. If only Frank understood how her faith had helped her stay with him. Her faith, the land, and Stranger had given her the strength to endure this past year.

Whatever insecurities Abby felt as they drove to church, were washed away as the service began. The town's past talk about Frank, the concern that they might scrutinize her regarding Stranger—it was all forgotten for a blissful two hours of hymn-singing and sermon. This was church for Abby: for a moment a whole group of people thought only of goodness and sang with one voice. Perhaps that harmony could last a while. She liked to think it might.

After the service, the Redmond's made their way outside. A table sat under a large cottonwood, displaying a variety of sandwiches and baked goods and pitchers of lemonade and tea that the parishioners had brought for the social. Off to the side, several teenagers took turns feverishly working two ice cream churns. Their efforts would be rewarded by getting the first taste of the delicious treat. Frank and Clay headed off to talk ranching with some of the other men, while Abby chatted with Patty, who had her two-month-old baby with her.

Abby was happy to spell Patty's arms for a while. She was fairly well practiced at holding other people's babies, accustomed to the little surge of inner hurt. It passed, and then she was free to look into the child's deep dark eyes. Regardless, she didn't want her friend to bring up the topic of children. If anyone could be overly frank on the matter, it was Patty. There were no secrets between the two women. So of course Patty knew that Abby and Frank were on more than amicable terms, that there was, once again, no reason for Abby not to be pregnant. Abby adored her friend; but ever since this improvement, Patty had taken up a crusade to convince them to adopt a baby from the orphanage in Helena. As

Abby hummed a lullaby to little Michael, she could hear Patty's silent scheming. It was too lovely a day to bring up the topic. Abby derailed her friend with the only other concern that weighed on her at the moment.

"So, I suppose you heard about Stranger's car ride into town?"

"I don't think there is anyone in the valley that hasn't heard," Patty said, clearly amused by the whole affair. She carried on in a playful tone. "Let's see, Ms. Wilson is calling you 'the loco dog lady'. And Mrs. Thornton is speculating that you might end up like Poker Jim and his pet chickens." She took a breath before continuing. "Now, given the character of those two old coots, I'd say you've offended the right people!"

Abby stared at her friend. It wasn't half so funny to her. Patty took a more soothing tone.

"I say it's all bosh! I've met Stranger, I know what he's done for you. If you want to let the dog ride in the car, so be it, and to heck with any mudsill for thinking otherwise."

"Well, I'm glad at least one person doesn't consider me the loco dog lady," Abby said. She forced a strained smile; she wished she could be as devil-may-care as Patty. She'd felt that way the day she impulsively loaded Stranger into the back seat, but her confidence was waning now.

The two women chatted on about the baby, about the rainy spring, and Abby picked at a small sandwich. She'd lost her appetite. Talking about other things didn't help; she wanted to go home. She said her goodbyes to Patty and little Michael, then made her way through the crowd, trying not to read too much into people's looks at her. She found Frank and Clay with one of the McAllisters. She politely interrupted them and convinced them it was time to head home—even though the dessert table was yet untouched.

"I guess I do have a reputation now," Abby said.

"The loco dog lady bit? Yep, we heard," Frank said. "I figure it says more about the folks who yap too much than it does about you." He gave her an encouraging smile, but his words did little to comfort her.

Just as they were about to clear the crowd, Mrs. Thorton intercepted them.

"Abby Redmond, so nice to see you again," she said, grinning like a barn cat that had just found a mouse nest.

"A pleasure to see you, too," Abby said. "I hope you are well these days." She squeezed Frank's arm for support. Hopefully this encounter would be brief and courteous.

"You know, dear, I heard about your outing with your dog, and I do need to say something," Mrs. Thorton said. No, it wasn't going to be brief. Or kind. "I don't think God ever intended for dogs to be treated like humans. They're certainly not fit for riding inside an automobile. Perhaps if you stopped treating your dog like a baby, maybe God would let you have a real baby of your own." Mrs. Thorton spoke in all seriousness.

Abby felt like punching the old bat. She didn't. She chose her words and enunciated each one, mocking Mrs. Thorton's school marm tone. "As always, your advice astounds me. Perhaps if you treated others with Christian charity, God would let you have friends of your own."

Mrs. Thorton gasped. She had no cogent reply. It was Abby's turn to grin. She opened her mouth to retaliate further, but Frank interceded, hooking her by the waist and nearly carrying her away. Abby fumed, not only at Mrs. Thorton, but at Frank's interfering. Clay stepped in to distract the old gossip long enough for Frank to usher Abby all the way to the car. She protested, complaining that she had to get the basket that she had used for the cookies, but Frank was hell-bent on leaving. Then Clay arrived with the basket. Neatly defeated, she got in the car and stewed as Frank pulled out onto highway 141 heading north towards home.

"Do I really treat Stranger like a child?" Abby asked as she looked out the window.

Frank shrugged his shoulders, then ventured in a very cautious tone. "Well, you haven't tried to bring him upstairs yet," he said. "But yes, you do. A little." Frank's observation stung, not because it was cruel, but because Abby knew it to be true. In her mind, the dog had earned every treat, every act of kindness she gave him. Clay spoke up when they turned onto Three Mile Road.

"As far as grandkids go, Stranger is okay with me." Clay surely meant it to lighten their moods, but the comment drew a glare from Frank.

Back home, Abby hurried upstairs to change back into her everyday faded dress. Frank was just coming up the stairs to change his clothes when Abby forced her way past him on the narrow stairwell. She grabbed the tin pan that she used to feed the chickens and banged the doors open and shut as she stomped outside to the grain bins. With a full pan of chicken feed, she walked over to where the hens were scratching near her garden.

Abby grabbed handfuls of grain and flung them about, much to the chickens' delight. They darted back and forth, pecking at the grain and each other, each one trying to capture the choicest kernels. Abby ignored Clay and Frank as they left the house and headed over to the barn. She was the laughing stock of the whole town. She hurled a handful of grain directly at one of the bossiest hens. The fat bird ceased her bullying, but then feasted on all the extra grain at her feet.

With a shout, Abby threw the grain scoop at the ground. The remaining feed flew upward, and the entire flock scattered briefly, only to rush back in to resume their feast. Abby leaned against one of the clothesline posts and slowly slid down it until she sat on the ground, her legs tucked beneath her.

This was the way of things: a woman married, a woman bore children, a woman cared for those little ones until they were not little, until someday they cared for her. Abby could envision no other possibility, for she did not know that any existed. Other than

Vivian and her own mother, she knew of no other woman who had been married so long, had given herself to her husband as a good wife should, and remained childless. What was wrong with her?

She knew women who were very happy mothers and others who were mothers and did not want to be. She knew women who wished they didn't have so many. Abby had even heard of women who never married for they never wished to mother. But such a choice usually required great wealth or a specific religious vow. Abby was not any of these women, so what was she? Of course, there were plenty who feared having children during such thin times. There were days Abby herself was grateful there were no more mouths to feed, when their own larder was spare.

And yet, she wanted a baby. This woman, on this evening, with the ridiculous chickens all around her, she wanted a child. Here was the truth: the likelihood of *never.* "Why?" Abby whispered, looking up at the soft white clouds. She watched the clouds blur, closed her eyes, let the tears seep. Something brushed against her leg. Stranger. Of course. His brown eyes looked up at her with great concern. She stroked his soft ears. He wagged his tail, then looked past her over her shoulder.

Abby heard Frank's footsteps. The dog stood and walked a few paces away, sat down, and watched them. Frank knelt down beside Abby, put his arms around her shoulders, and kissed her on the cheek. "It doesn't matter," he said. That was all he said. He let her cry, and she let him hold her. He repeated those words again that night, when they made love. And, at that moment, he was right.

CHAPTER 17
MARCH 1937

Of all the things Abby hated, cold was in the top three. On nights like this, it was in the number one spot, pushing out snakes and liars. The only good thing about calving season was that the stove was kept burning throughout the night. That meant the house was one toasty refuge.

Everyone took turns checking on the cattle every two hours, and catching sleep in five-hour shifts. Whoever was on call was responsible for making a careful loop around the herd and looking for any cows that were ready to deliver. These needed to be moved to the barn as it was far too cold to let them calve outside. The barn was also safe from predators—coyotes and cougars mostly. Once a calf was dry and standing up, the cow and calf pair were moved to a smaller field behind the barn. This made feeding and checking the herd a little easier.

It was two in the morning and Abby's turn to survey the herd. She stuffed two logs into the firebox, then began to dress. This alone was a substantial chore. Over her long johns, she donned a sweater and a pair of Frank's jeans. The latter she cinched with a scrap of rope, tightening it a little less than usual. She knew she was pregnant, about three months along, she figured. Abby was also scared sick it might not last. She'd told no one. Not even Patty.

On top of that first bulky layer, she stuffed herself into canvas coveralls and an anorak. Last, she pulled on boots and work gloves. The whole ensemble made coordinated movement a challenge, but it would help fend off the deep freeze waiting for her outside. She dressed entirely by lantern light. Rumor had it, Avon might get electricity next year. But there were no plans to run electric lines into any of the rural valleys. Two of the neighbors had acquired small generators and battery packs to power an electric light or two in their barns and homes. That was a luxury the Redmonds were doing without. The lantern alone was enough to reveal thick frost coating both sides of the single-pane windows. It had to be below zero for frost to form indoors even with the stove burning hot. March might mean springtime everywhere else in the nation, but it sure didn't in their valley.

Abby wrapped a long wool scarf around her head and looked down at Stranger. He had been watching her bundle up. His three-inch thick coat must be uncomfortable in the heat of summer, but it was perfect for this time of year. Abby didn't bother asking the dog if he wanted to come along with her. She knew he did. Stranger was often content to stay inside when Frank and Clay went out, but not so when it was Abby's shift. Nothing could keep the dog from tagging along when she was making the rounds.

Even with her layers of wool and cotton, the harsh chill was enough to take Abby's breath away. With every step, the snow squealed beneath her boots, and with each breath, the cold air stung her lungs. She didn't bother taking the lantern with her. The clear sky and nearly full moon lit up the snow-covered landscape as if it were daytime. Trudging across the yard to the large field next to the barn, Abby crawled through the wooden rails of the gate, her garments making it hard to force her way through.

Once through the gate, Abby circled around the field. The cows were calm; they were growing accustomed to the regular visits.

The moonlight was bright enough to cast shadows across the blue-grey landscape. Darkness held a firmer grip in the trees at the edge of the field, but even there the reflected light of the moon and snow allowed for easy progress. Abby saw a fresh trail into a grove of pines. She followed it to make sure an expectant cow had not sought shelter there to drop her calf.

Trudging through the deep snow, Abby grew warm inside her layers, but she knew better than to open her coat. Stranger followed behind her, using the trail she was breaking, instead of wasting energy making his own. The constant muttering of the cows carried across the field, their soft calls a comforting sound as Abby trudged closer to the trees. She heard also the unmistakable sound of rail cars connecting far off in the distance. It was a unique effect of the winter air—the noise coming from eleven miles away at the Mullan Pass tunnel was as clear as if it were only a mile away. Stranger whined, and Abby looked back at him. His ears were back against his head. Earthquakes and trains. These were the only things that could cause fear in the dog.

"It's okay, Stranger," she cooed to him. "It's just trains." She was sure his response to trains had something to do with where he had come from. Leaning down, she scratched Stranger's head as much as her gloves allowed her to, then pushed on into the pine grove. There were indeed three cows in there, standing together for warmth. None were ready to calve, though. Abby headed back to the open field and walked another twenty minutes, inspecting the rest of the herd.

On her way back to the house, Abby paused to look up at the moon and at the shimmering hoarfrost that feathered every surface in the barnyard. God, what a beautiful sight! It was damn cold, but the beauty took the edge off her disdain for mountain winters. Taking care of the cattle felt poignant; strange to care for the lumbering creatures at a time when she felt subtle changes in her own form. Stranger whined and held one paw up in pain. The cold of the snow was finally taking its toll on him, even with his thick fur. Icicles formed between the pads of his paws. The only remedy was to head in and let the dog thaw out by the stove.

"I know, Stranger, it's too cold to admire the moon," Abby said and trudged on. Stranger did his best to keep up. Every few steps, she looked back and saw the dog holding one paw up and then another. As she got closer to the house, they crossed over their original trail out to the field. Abby could clearly see her prints and Stranger's in the snow. What surprised her was the third set of tracks that paralleled theirs. Stranger's frozen feet would have to wait a moment. Someone, or some critter, had followed them to the field. Bending closer, she could see that the wide prints were certainly not human or that of any cow. They were cougar tracks, and not more than thirty minutes old.

Stranger caught up after stopping to lick his frozen paws. Even he forgot about his paws once he caught the scent of the big cat. He paced back and forth along the trail. Abby looked around and was thankful not to see the shape of the hunter nearby, but it could easily be hiding in the clumps of bushes and trees in the rolling field. Calling Stranger off the cougar tracks, Abby moved towards the house, still over a hundred yards away. She kept looking back over her shoulder, both to look for the cougar and to make sure the dog hadn't taken it upon himself to hunt the cat down. As she squeezed through the gate, she felt a little more at ease. But she didn't feel safe until the door to the house was closed and locked behind them. Abby took off all her layers, and Stranger curled up on his bed licking his paws.

Sleep was precious; Abby debated whether to wake Frank or not. He was in the middle of his sleep shift. But, he'd want to know about the cougar. Abby added one more log to the fire, turned off the light, and went up to the bedroom. She touched

Frank's shoulder, whispered to him. Bleary, he woke and listened to her concern about the big cat. He was barely awake, but definitely not willing to wait till morning to take stock of the animal's damage to their herd.

"We'd better head out then," he said. Frank was careful to let Clay get all the sleep he needed, so the "we" meant Abby. She was a decent shot anyway. If they both headed out with Clay's shotgun and Frank's bolt action hunting rifle, they might have a chance to ward off the cat. Neither had any illusions about actually killing the animal; cougars were masters at disappearing. They might be able to give it a good scare, though.

Abby knew she ought to help. Really. But she loathed the idea of heading back out into the freezing night. Frank tucked in his shirt, pulled up his suspenders, and looked at her—she still sat on the edge of the bed, not making any motion to get dressed again.

"Please, Abby," he said. "You know I—"

"I'm pregnant," she said.

So that was how she told him. Poor Frank didn't believe her, then felt awful for not believing her when she insisted it was true. Then, entirely flustered, he had the fun of heading out alone for an unsuccessful cat hunt. His extra shift confirmed the cat's damages—one calf gone, one miserable cow. They shared that unfortunate news with Clay in the morning. But even Abby could not refrain from sharing the happier bit. Frank insisted that only the men would check the cattle at night from that point on. He'd take an extra night shift to allow for that. Abby didn't argue. The house was warm and cougar-free.

CHAPTER 18
MAY-JULY 1937

"Abigail Redmond, I swear you are glowing today!" Patty gave Abby a loving hug, then stepped back, admiring her. "Being pregnant suits you well, my dear. How are the dresses fitting?" With five children of her own, Patty had several extra dresses, which she was happy to loan to a friend.

"Just fine, thank you again for letting me borrow them."

Abby insisted on continuing to visit Patty—it was still easier for her to make the trip than for Patty to load up her brood or risk disaster by leaving them unmonitored. Besides, the recent spring rains made travel by car near impossible. The roads had turned to a sloppy gumbo. It was the perfect excuse for a horse ride—. Frank protested Abby's riding a horse at all, but she assured him that Jane was safer than the car, and the doctor said as long as she didn't feel any pain, she was allowed to ride. Women had been riding horses and doing ranch work right up till the birth of the child for generations. Abby didn't see the need to be different on that account.

"What is it now, five months? How is the back pain?" Pat asked as she grabbed a kettle of hot water to make tea. She held a fussy one-year old Michael as she worked.

"A little achy now and then, but it's good to be past feeling sick every morning."

"My girl, Sally, was the toughest," Patty said. "After such an easy first pregnancy, she knocked me off my feet. So sick, so achy. This was all before you moved here. I was alone most of the time and nearly bed-ridden the last two months."

"Bed-ridden? I can't have that happen; there's too much work to do."

"Don't worry, Abby, you'll be fine. Though I don't envy you come the summer heat. I know you're happy now, but you will be begging for that baby to be born come August." Patty was up to her usual tactless honesty. "So do you want a boy or a girl?"

"Frank is adamant that it is a boy. I say it's a girl just to get his goat."

"And you, what do you want?"

"I just want a child. You know that."

"Good. Here, practice," Patty said and handed her Michael. "And how is the baby's big brother?"

That meant Stranger. Abby had grown accustomed to the playful reference. In so many ways, it was true. The dog certainly knew what was happening. "That dog knew I was pregnant before I had caught on. He still won't let any men near me except for Frank and Clay," she said. "We have to tie him up when we have visitors, and then he barks the whole time. I don't dare take him into town anymore, not after last time."

Patty laughed; she knew about that misadventure. Two weeks earlier, during a sunny spell, the roads had been dry enough to drive. So Abby took the car to town with Stranger in the back seat. It was a common enough sight now; most people didn't even bat an eye. Even Mrs. Thorton had silenced her ridiculous sermonizing about the Redmond family after she learned that Abby was pregnant. Apparently, God had begun working miracles even for those whom He did not regard as worthy. Regardless, on that fine spring day in town, all was well until the store-keeper followed Abby out to her car and opened the door for her. Stranger leapt at him and left a nasty rip in the man's shirt. Abby was thankful that it was only fabric that Stranger's fangs tore into. As much as she loved the dog's companionship and protection, she couldn't risk anyone being bitten.

"I sure hope that once the baby is born, Stranger will go back to his old self," Abby said as Patty set two cups of tea on the table.

"He will. He's fine with me still, and he's doing great with my kids right now."

That was true. Stranger had followed Abby up to Patty's house and now lay near the fence where Jane was tied. Patty's girl and the three older boys often stopped by the dog amidst their playing, pausing to pat his head. Stranger loved the attention. The women chatted on as they sipped their tea. Then Patty brought out another homemade maternity dress to loan to Abby, this one a little larger. Saying their goodbyes, Abby, Jane, and Stranger headed home. Abby didn't know why, but her back never ached while she rode. If anything, Jane's steady, rocking motion seemed to soothe her tired muscles. How much longer could she ride? Would she end up bed-ridden like Patty did? Abby hoped not. Riding was one of her few true pleasures.

⇌

The season of cold rain, muddy roads, and cloudy skies slowly gave way to summer. As always, Patty was right. July's heat made the burden of carrying her child a tiresome chore. Abby realized that most of the women she knew had essentially transitioned from girlhood to motherhood in little more than a year. They had never really known what it was like to be a grown woman without children. But she had enjoyed years of being very comfortable in her own skin.

The contrast was stark—now that such comfort was gone. She felt like precisely what she was: someone else's house. Her body was not hers. Every task, every action was inconvenienced by pregnancy. And yet, she never lost her gratitude for the baby. Those summer days, her mind and body were a tumult of happy frustration. Kneeling down to take bread out of the oven, standing sideways at the sink, shuffling after a wandering chicken, hefting herself onto her horse's back, and dear God, trying to find any comfortable way to sleep in the lumpy rope-strung bed. Nothing was easy. Many daily tasks were outright painful. But, as she reminded herself every day, these particular frustrations were ones she'd desired for a very long time.

Frank doted on her now. Pregnancy suited him as much as it suited her, apparently. It was strange how she regarded his attentions. At first, the affectionate hand on her shoulder, the assistance in the kitchen, offers to carry the laundry basket—it was all a bit irritating. She was suspicious of him. The first time he offered to reach for the soup pot, she almost shooed him away. There was this vengeful part of her that wanted to shout, "So, I'm good enough for you now? Are you fond of me only now?" That wasn't the case, though, was it?

It doesn't matter. That's what he'd said that evening everything changed. She was sure he said those words again the night they conceived this little one. Abby believed him then and needed to keep believing him now. She'd come to receive his kindnesses with an honest grace. As spring faltered into summer, Abby wondered at how her body could hold up for another two months.

Frank had taken to scrubbing the cast iron pan after breakfast every morning. Of all the kitchen chores, that one was the most excruciating for her back. One morning, Abby was finishing her breakfast and looking out the window watching Clay play with Stranger. Frank finished cleaning the pan, set it aside, then joined her at the table.

"How's my son?" he asked, ever persistent in his delusion.

"She is well and good," Abby said, unfazed. "Danced all night long. She's sound asleep, now that I need to be awake."

Frank smiled, said he needed to head out to repair some storm damages on the barn siding, and headed for the door. Abby stopped him, calling him back to the window. "Look at your father and the dog," she said and stood to get closer to the window herself.

Together they saw Clay and the dog square off, no more than a few paces apart. Their eyes locked, both unmoving, except for Stranger's tail—which was high and wagging quickly. What sort of a contest was this? Clay blinked first and let his legs relax. His shoulders dropped. Clay leapt to his left and clapped his hands once. This had to be something they had done before. Many times. Stranger regarded the clap as some sort of cue, leaping into the air in the opposite direction. As soon as his paws hit the ground, he bounded toward Clay and slid to a stop at the man's feet. Stranger reared up like a horse, and Clay grabbed the dog's front paws, walking him about the yard upright. The dog panted in excitement, his tail swishing quickly as they pranced around in an awkward circle.

"I'd swear they're dancing," Abby said, keeping her eyes on the spectacle outside.

"I guess so," Frank said and laughed. "Too bad I'm gonna have to cut in on their ball. Otherwise that barn'll never get fixed."

"They look so happy, though. Don't they?"

Frank smiled, but turned to head outside. Abby watched until Frank broke up the little dance. Stranger trotted after the men as they headed to the barn, the dog's face still beaming a happy grin, tongue flopping out the side of his mouth. Abby promised herself that she would dance with Stranger after the baby was born. Just to see the dog smile.

The next day Frank and Clay took the car up to Finn to help the grass widow Thompson move her cattle to higher pasture. She was the one whose husband had left her six years earlier. On a whole, she managed to run her ranch well with the help of her two oldest boys. But, when needed, the whole valley rallied around her. Cattle-moving was such a time. Frank didn't want Abby anywhere near a herd of cattle, and for once, she admitted that was probably wise. So, she stayed back.

The men set off, and Abby set about caring for the chickens and checking the food stores. With her ever present canine shadow, she went down to the creek box. There was still a half gallon of milk, but the beef was almost finished. The quarter that hung in the screened meat shed was also slim. It was Frank's turn to butcher and share quarters with friends in the valley, and it was considered courteous to check in with the neighbors to see if they were ready for another portion of meat. At least she could take care of that task herself.

Abby changed out of her dress and slipped on her work overalls. She had lengthened the shoulder straps with bailing twine. Not pretty; but it worked. She walked out to the pasture to catch Jane and make the mile ride down to the McAllister ranch. The sweetest horse alive, Jane required only a whistle and a handful of oats to catch and then only a simple hackamore to control. Abby preferred to ride bareback, especially now. It was far more comfortable, and hefting the thirty-pound saddle was out of the question at this point in her pregnancy.

Using the fence to get on Jane, Abby set off for the short ride to the McAllisters' spread. She did feel a little sorry for herself, not getting to help with Mrs. Thompson's cattle drive. It was good to leave the ranch, completing this small errand of her own. Who knew when she'd have time for riding again once the baby came? Jane's steady hoof beats, the bright sunshine, the mountains in the distance, and Stranger romping alongside—these things filled Abby with a peace she couldn't duplicate in any other way.

The only impediment to her serenity was the sound of an approaching truck. There were logging trucks that made occasional runs into the mountains to fell timber for a few small mills near Avon. No matter, she had plenty of time to find a clearing in the underbrush where she and Jane could move off the road. Abby gave a bit more rein to Jane, directing her to the top of the ditch. She looked to make sure that Stranger was safely off to the side as well. The rig appeared around the bend behind them. Abby was surprised that the truck didn't slow down as it approached, the road being barely big enough for one vehicle. She returned the wave from the driver. Friendly enough fellow, but driving way too fast. Stranger tensed, looking like he might give chase after the truck, and Abby shouted at him to stay. Obedient and attentive, the dog looked up at her.

There was no way she could have seen the thick strand of binding wire poking out of the back of the trailer. As the end of the trailer rushed past, the tip of the wire caught Jane a few inches from her tail, like a sting from a massive hornet. For the first time in all the years Abby had owned her, Jane spooked. Abby yelped as the horse leapt forward; she managed to grab Jane's mane and hold fast. But, one of Jane's front hooves sank into the soft dirt at the rim of the ditch. The animal staggered, lurching forward and down. Abby went over Jane's neck, falling to the left and down into the ditch.

Stranger darted out of the way as Abby hit the ground, somehow still clutching one of the rope reins of the hackamore. Jane, uninjured herself, had calmed as quickly as she had spooked. The horse stood over Abby, docile but concerned. The dog, too, rushed over and licked at Abby's face as she lay there, her hand weakly pushing him away. Her vision blurred. The dust of the truck hung thick in the air as its noise faded away. The driver surely hadn't seen her fall. The wind knocked out of her, Abby caught her breath and tried to call for help. It was unlikely anyone could hear her; she was still more than a half mile from the McAllisters and in the middle of thick timber.

She lay in the bottom of the ditch, looking up at the blue sky beyond the trees. *Breathe*, Abby thought. *Breathe*. She touched her belly. Pain seared up and down her back. She could move though. Legs. Arms. Fingers. Nothing broken. With a groan, and some unhelpful assistance from Stranger, Abby rolled to her side, then managed to stand up. She stood still, just breathing. The ditch was soft. The baby would be fine. Still shaking, she carefully climbed out of the ditch and back up to the road. The house was close; really, she hadn't gone far at all. Holding the hackamore rein and with Stranger falling in line behind her and Jane, Abby began her trek back to the ranch. Each step was a painful declaration. Something was very wrong.

By the time she got to the barn, the pain in Abby's back had spread to the front of her torso. Still, she managed to remove Jane's hackamore and turn her loose with the rest of the horses. She fumbled with the gate latch but finally secured it. The pain was so sharp she felt like she could see it, like lightning at the periphery of her vision. Leaving Stranger outside, Abby struggled up the two steps into the house.

"This is not happening," she told herself aloud. The pain would pass. She was badly bruised, but that had to be all. She just needed to think of something else.

It was a kind of madness, the insistence that all would be well. In the kitchen, she even tried to measure a cup of flour to make a batch of biscuits. Abby convinced herself that if she could do that, if she could bake a little something, it would confirm that everything was fine. By the time the biscuits were done, she would feel fine. She wouldn't even have to tell Frank about the fall. He would not be happy hearing about something like that. No, it was best not to tell him. In another hour, it wouldn't matter.

Abby began folding butter into the flour, and the motion alone made her gasp. Her back, her torso, her arms—any movement made the pain blaze. It was blinding. She sat down in her rocking chair, but sitting hurt even more. Climbing the stairwell was insurmountable. Abby stayed downstairs, lay down on the settee next to her sewing machine. Her hands cupping her belly, she prayed then, in part to God, in part to Frank. *Please get home soon.*

CHAPTER 19

JULY 1937

K eeping vigil at the hospital bed, Frank finally succumbed to sleep. Despite the fear that had fueled him the whole night, despite the panicked drive the next morning, despite the hard-backed chair, Frank nodded off. He slept sitting upright, his hand still holding Abby's.

In his dream, he saw Abby on their wedding day, saw the mountain bluebell in her hair. Vivian had woven that flower into Abby's braid and then pinned a similar flower to Frank's lapel. It was all as it had been on that day. But in the dream, the flowers faded while the minister preached. The man would not stop speaking, and the flowers turned brown before Frank even had a chance to kiss Abby. Then the scene changed, and Frank saw Abby and his mother baking rolls. They were talking and laughing. Then flames began to shoot out of the wood stove, the house filled with smoke. He had to find them, had to get them out of there. But he couldn't find them in all the smoke. He couldn't find the door. Suddenly, Frank was outside of the house watching smoke pour from the windows. He tried in vain to open the door, to free Abby and his mom. Looking around, Frank screamed for help. He saw the door to the stone shed swing open. Then, in the shadows Frank saw Death, the towering black robed figure, bony fingers grasping a fearsome sickle.

Frank woke with a start. The hospital smelled like alcohol and sickness and blood. There was Abby, her unconscious form, her skin nearly as pale as the sheets on the hospital bed. He watched her chest rise and fall with her faint breaths. Several times he thought she had stopped breathing, only to have his heart lift at seeing her inhale once more.

The night before, when Frank and Clay arrived back from Finn, they found Abby in tears. She told them of her fall. Initially, Frank was angry, but the look in her eyes, the pain and fear so clear, silenced him. He wanted to drive her to Deer Lodge that night, but Abby insisted repeatedly that she just needed to rest. Not so. In the morning, she admitted the pain was much worse and she was bleeding. Frank broke practically every traffic law on the way to the town, pushing their old car to its limits. Abby began having contractions a few miles before they reached the hospital, and Frank struggled to focus on the road, the other cars, the people who had no idea how badly he needed to get through each intersection. As Frank turned east on St. Mary's Avenue he grabbed Abby's hand.

"It'll be alright." He tried to assure her, hoping she didn't hear the fear in his voice.

Turning into the half circle driveway of the hospital, Frank had barely shut off the car when he began shouting for help. He ran around the front of the car to help Abby out her door. Before Abby was even out of the car, two nurses were there to help. Frank frantically explained what had happened as they helped Abby into a wheel chair and rushed her through the front door.

Frank followed quickly, but was stopped by another nurse who said she needed some information first. As he watched Abby wheeled away to another room, Frank felt fear tighten its grip, the realization that both his wife and child might die. Information?

He needed to be where Abby was. He stammered her name and age, their rural address, repeated the details of the accident. What more did the nurse need? He tried to head through the door that Abby had been ushered through, only to be stopped again. The nurse touched his arm, asked him to move his car out of the drive, told him where he could park. His wife was in grave danger and he needed to park the car?

After coming back inside, the same nurse ushered Frank to a small room near the main entrance. In it were several comfortable chairs and book shelves. No, he could not enter the ward yet; he would need to wait here. Hours later, an old nun, one of the nurses at the hospital, sat down next to him. She spoke slowly, as one might to a child.

"Your wife is recovering. The child, a girl, was stillborn," she said.

"I need to see Abby."

"You will. But she is bleeding still, it might be an hour or two before you can see her."

Frank knew from delivering countless animals that this wasn't good. He stared straight ahead.

"You should get something to eat sir," the nun said. "Come back and I'm sure we can let you see her then."

As if to betray his own resolve, Frank's stomach grumbled loudly. He could not think of eating though, not now. "I'll wait here," he said. The nun exhaled loudly, then stood and left Frank alone in the small room. The chair was not uncomfortable; it reminded him of the one at the warden's house when he first met Elisa. Frank pushed that memory away. He looked out the window, watched the sparrows dart around in a large pine tree.

When he was finally allowed to see Abby, she looked as though she were dead. It made him think of how he'd helped move his mother's body after she had passed away. At first he was afraid to touch Abby. Tentatively, he approached the bed and held her right hand. Then he wouldn't leave. He wanted to stay by her side till she woke. The nurses eventually called the doctor to convince him that Abby needed rest, that he should let her be for a few hours. He could come back that evening.

Resigned, Frank walked out into the hot afternoon air, lost on what to do. Fixing equipment, working with horses, carving stone—all these were things that Frank had control over. He decided which task was done, where the horse would go; he was in charge. Now helplessness made his steps heavy. Still, he walked to the car. *Get a hold of yourself, Frank! You won't do Abby any good if you're a sobbing fool. First things first, get settled here.* Frank directed his mind toward work. He needed to get a message to Clay, then he did need to eat. Then back to Abby. He could do that much.

Frank used the phone at Gallagher's Drug store to call the McAllisters. Jessie McAllister was friendly as always when she answered, and Frank could hear her turn sad as he told her what was happening. To keep his composure, Frank kept the call brief. He said a quick goodbye after Jessie assured that the message would get up to Clay. With that task complete, Frank used what change he had to buy a sandwich, then walked back up to the hospital, eating slowly as he went. Then, he began his vigil.

CHAPTER 20

JULY 1937

When John pulled into the drive, Clay knew it wasn't good. There was no honking or waving of the hat. Someone had died. Clay steeled himself for the news. Abby had been in such a dreadful state when Frank had carried her to the car that morning. Clay didn't think a person could look so pale and lifeless while still breathing. John must be bringing a message left at the McAllisters.

John got out of the car and spoke quickly. "Abby is still alive," he said. "I got to tell you that first."

"The baby?"

John looked at the ground and shook his head. "I'm sorry," he said. "Frank's message only said that the baby didn't make it. Abby is alive, but not doing well. He'll be staying at the hospital a while."

Clay exhaled and closed his eyes.

"I can take some of Frank's clothes to him tomorrow, if you like."

"Thank you," Clay said. "Yes, he'll need a change of clothes. Cash for a room, too." The two men could do that much. Clay set about packing a small pack of clothes and other necessaries for his son. Thank God for such a decent neighbor.

As John drove down the road, Clay was left at the ranch in a silence he didn't think was possible there. There was still all the noise that was part of the landscape: chickens clucking and pecking, horses sighing in their low rumbling way, a cow up on the higher pasture calling for a wayward calf. What was missing were the sounds of work—hammering in the barn, clothes on the washboard, a friendly shout, a frustrated curse. Those noises were lost with the dust settling on the road as the car disappeared. Clay's family might be small, but they'd always been together on this ranch; for the first time, Clay was utterly alone. Stranger brushed against his leg, and leaned into the old man's knee. He scratched the dog's head before heading to the barn.

He had to keep working. Small repairs had already kept him occupied, kept him sane, most of that first day. With Frank and Abby gone, there was just more to do. At least the draft team wasn't needed for any task. He needed to keep irrigating the fields and complete final repairs on equipment in preparation for the hay harvest. Enough to keep him and his thoughts set in a straight line most of the day. Every break involved Stranger, the dog resting his head on the old man's leg, waiting for the inevitable ear scratch. Clay didn't even think about the action any longer. It just occurred out of reflex. The dog's head appeared, and the hand began to pet. The motion was calming, too, invaluable at such a time. The dog had no idea how helpful he was.

Late that evening, Clay tried to force himself to eat a bowl of cold stew. The pot had been left on the stove the day before. A single lamp barely lit the room, but it was enough to expose its emptiness. The baby was gone, and Abby's fate was uncertain, and Clay could do nothing. He gave up on eating and took the bowl out to the porch to let Stranger finish off. After one last ear scratch Clay headed to bed.

Lying in the darkness, the silence became distressing. Even Abby's old wall clock wasn't ticking. He gulped at the thought that it might have broken that very day. No, no, that wasn't it. Abby simply wasn't there to adjust the clock's weights like she did every morning. Clay missed its rhythmic pace; ever since Abby arrived at the ranch, that clock had helped him fall asleep each night.

Clay thought of Vivian. When they lost their first child, they at least had gotten to hold her, love her for a month before the fever took her. As painful as it had been, Vivian and Clay had had each other, Vivian's optimism helping both with the loss. "God will give us another child," she had insisted. It took years, but she had been right. Frank had arrived, giving hope that the Redmond name would live on.

Lying in his bed, Clay caught himself reaching across the blanket as if to touch his wife's hand. The old spring bed had always been too small when they were arguing and just right when passionate. Now it was too big, a reminder of Vivian's absence and of everyone gone this night. The window was open, and a chilly breeze filled the room. The nighttime cool usually helped Clay sleep, but not tonight. He lit his lamp and looked at his pocket watch. It was only midnight. He pulled on his pants and shoes, took the lamp downstairs, and then stood before Abby's clock. Checking his pocket watch once more, he raised the weights of the clock on the wall to get it working again and then adjusted the hands to the correct time. The steady tick-tocks resumed.

Clay looked at Abby's rocking chair, and next to it, the petite three-leg oak table that Frank had made for her shortly after they married. The table held two books. One, Clay didn't recognize; the other was Abby's well-worn Bible with the hand-stitched bookmark that Vivian had made. Most of what Clay knew of religion was from Abby and Vivian, and that knowledge gave him little comfort. Nothing really could. *God, I feel so alone.* Clay walked through the dark kitchen and opened the door to the porch. In the shadows, Stranger raised his head from his bed.

"Come on in, boy," Clay said softly. It was summer, surely the dog preferred to be outside. But Stranger got up slowly, stretched, and followed his master into the house. Clay walked back to the sitting room. Stranger's nails clicked as he walked across the wood plank floor, and the dog let out a loud yawn as Clay reclined on the small couch against the wall. Settling into the cushions, Clay pulled a quilt from the back of the couch and wrapped it around him. As if on cue, Stranger lay down on the floor next to the couch, close enough for Clay's hand to pet his neck till both were asleep.

CHAPTER 21
JULY 1937

The sun light that crept through the windows reminded Frank of how little sleep he had gotten through the night. The few times he did sleep he was greeted by nightmares. There was a visiting hours policy, but the nuns had bent the rules the night before. Once Frank planted himself in the wooden chair next to Abby's bed, he wouldn't leave. They let him stay, even brought him a blanket.

With dawn flooding the valley, the nurses' morning duties required that Frank leave briefly. Though they reassured him he could come back and spend the whole day with Abby. Leaving the patient ward, Frank walked down the long hall to the main entrance. He was surprised to see John there, his friend seeming rather agitated. Frank overheard a receptionist informing John that only family was allowed to visit.

"John! What the heck ya doing here?" Frank said and shook his friend's hand. The nun breathed a sigh of relief as the two men walked outside.

"How's Abby? The whole valley's worried sick 'bout her," John said, concern etched on his face.

Frank shared what little he knew, which didn't brighten John's mood any. "Why'd you come down here?" he asked.

"I stopped by your place and gave Clay the message from the McAllisters. Hated to bring that news to him, but I think he suspected it all along," John said. "Even Stranger seemed to know what was up; the dog didn't try and eat me when I got out of the truck."

Despite everything, Frank chuckled at that tidbit. John continued.

"The McAllisters and a few others are helping Clay out, if he needs anything. Clay had me bring ya this," John said and reached into his truck to pull out Frank's bedroll. "He said ya left in a hurry. There's some clothes and money; we all chipped in a bit, just in case you're here for a spell."

"Thank you. It means a lot." Frank looked around and realized how hungry he was. "You want to join me for breakfast?"

The helpless grin on John's face was answer enough. Though the man was a willow of a frame he could pack away groceries like no one else. John drove them to Brown's Café where Frank felt almost normal for the hour they spent over eggs, bacon and several cups of coffee.

Afterward, John dropped Frank off at the hospital. Frank asked him to let Clay know he'd call when there was any more news. With a strong farewell handshake, John set off. As the car turned the corner, Frank walked into the hospital, hoping that Abby had somehow gotten well while he was gone.

Her face was still ashen; her skin still colder than normal. But she was breathing. Frank thought only of that. Sitting in the chair, he held her hand and looked at her still face. The doctor stopped by about mid-day and spoke plainly about how much blood Abby had lost, how weak she was. It was not what Frank wanted to hear. It seemed that the doctor was just waiting, like Frank, waiting to see if Abby had the strength to pull through it. Frank knew Abby;

if anyone could survive this, it was her. He held onto that thought as the hot day faded into the cool air of evening.

Frank figured he would settle in for another night by Abby's side, but the nuns thought otherwise. "You need to find other lodging tonight, Mr. Redmond. The patients need their rest. You can come back in the morning," a younger nun told him. Her soft brown eyes were compassionate enough, but Frank could tell this was no light suggestion.

"But I stayed here last night," he protested. "I'll be quiet."

"Sir, I know we allowed that, but you need to go someplace else tonight. You need rest as much as your wife does. The hotel isn't far." When Frank began to protest again, she turned very serious. "Mr. Redmond, if you don't leave, I will call the police. Please don't make me do that."

Well, he wouldn't do Abby any good in jail. Grabbing his bedroll, Frank scowled and walked out of the ward, then out the main doors. At his car Frank weighed his options. The boarding house was a long shot as its rooms were usually booked up with rail workers. That left the Deer Lodge Hotel. A bit pricy at a dollar a day, but after a quick count of the money John had brought, Frank made the decision to go there. If he had to stay longer than a week, then he would have to come up with some other arrangement, but for now it would do.

CHAPTER 22
JULY 1937

The morning after John made his trip to Deer Lodge, he stopped by the Redmond ranch to check on Clay and pass along news. "She still hasn't woken up, but she's holding steady," he said. "If you need anything, Clay, just ask; everyone wants to help out. The whole valley knows." The man's voice was serious for perhaps the first time in his life.

"I do need some rivets from Schultz," Clay said.

John's eyes lit up at the chance to help. "We can head to Avon right now."

"Okay if Stranger tags along? He can ride on the flat bed."

John didn't hesitate to say yes. Clay patted the wood bed of the truck and, with a near effortless leap, Stranger loaded up. As they drove down the road he barked his excitement all the way into town.

John dropped Clay and Stranger off at Schultz' and then drove on to handle his own errands at the mercantile. Clay told Stranger to sit and wait on the stoop outside the shop, and the dog took his post while Clay made his purchase inside. A few minutes later, with a bag of metal rivets in hand, Clay found Stranger lying on the stoop, right where he left him.

"Come on, pup, let's go find our ride," Clay said as he started walking west towards the mercantile. Getting closer to the mercantile, Clay heard heated words echoing down the street. Rounding the corner to the front of the store, he saw the six bags of grain on the back of the truck and John next to it, toe-to-toe with five irate men. Clay glanced over his shoulder and saw that Stranger was across the street sniffing a tree, oblivious of the conflict brewing. As Clay got closer he deduced that the argument revolved around the Ophir Creek dredge operator's damaging some of John's fence when they had moved their equipment. The mining dredge had run its course and now was shutting down, leaving a mess behind. It was typical of such operations; make the money and run.

The odds were not in John's favor if this turned into a scrap. If any one of the brutes had been alone, Clay's money would have been on John. Even against two, Clay would still wager on John. But five-to-one just wasn't fair odds for anyone. With a bag of steel in his hand, Clay walked up to his friend's side, hoping his presence would calm things down. It didn't.

"What the hell do you want, old man?" The fellow standing opposite John sneered. The man's four companions flanked him, two per side, each trying to look intimidating. This didn't fluster John as far as Clay could tell.

"He ain't no part of this!" John said, putting an arm out to keep Clay from coming closer. "Now, when are you going to repair my fence?"

"That fence was already down when we came through!" the group's leader declared. "You got a problem with your own shoddy workmanship." The barb got a chuckle from the group, but only riled John.

"You listen here, you sonsabitches, you get your asses out to my place and fix that fence, or there'll be hell to pay."

"Hell to pay? From you or this old man?"

Old? Clay might have grey hairs, but he could hold his own with most, and given the happening of the past few days, he wasn't in the mood to banter with some hard case dredge operators. "Son, you'd be wise to do as John says," Clay said, calm and steady. "This ain't a fight you wanna start." He stepped forward, his fist gripping the bag of rivets. Not a very threatening weapon, but Clay had another card to play. During the exchange, he'd seen Stranger amble up behind the group as if not interested at all. Now the dog stood at the alert, only a few paces behind the five toughs. Clay had chosen his words with care. He wanted one of them to do something, hopefully only a shove or a finger poke. If a punch was thrown, then things would get messy. He hoped it wouldn't come to that. The big mouth of the group took the bait.

"Really, old man? Let's just see what you got." The man gave Clay a quick shove with his left hand. Clay saw John start to reach for the man, but there wasn't time for anything more. In a black flash, the group scattered as Stranger leapt in with loud barks and flashing teeth. Two ran behind the fender of a car, one jumped up on the back of a truck, and the other two retreated a good twenty paces away. Even John took a few steps back in fear. Clay just stood there smiling as Stranger looked at each man, teeth bared and growling.

"That, is what I got," Clay said. "His name's Stranger." He walked over to John's truck and called the dog. Obedient, but still tense, Stranger jumped up on the grain sacks. He kept an eye on the men. "If I were you, I'd fix that fence, otherwise, we might have to get the sheriff involved," Clay said, then climbed in the cab. John joined him, started the rig, and hit the road. Stranger let out several victory barks as they left.

"Hot damn! Did you see the looks on their faces?" John shouted as he drove. "I owe that dog some jerky, and you my thanks."

"Don't mention it," Clay said as he looked out the window. What a brave dog. If only Stranger could so easily drive all their other worries away.

CHAPTER 23
JULY 1937

Three days after Frank brought Abby to the hospital, she still remained unconscious. Frank held her palm in both of his, rubbing the back of her hand with his thumbs. He was starting to nod off when he heard another patient coughing, several beds down from Abby's. The noise echoed in the room, which held twelve beds in it, six to a side. He heard a chair slide against the tile floor and the footsteps of the nun who sat at the desk at the end of the room. Frank listened as the footsteps grew louder; the cloth curtains separating each bed did little to screen the noise. The footsteps stopped, not at the other patient's bed, but at Abby's. Frank turned his head, his tired eyes focusing on the old but caring face.

"Mr. Redmond, we are going to take your wife to another room for a little while. Go eat something, and try to get some sleep," the nun said. She had a gentle smile and spoke with genuine concern.

"Where are you taking her? Why?"

"She needs blood, and we have a good, healthy donor."

"If she needs blood, she can have mine," Frank said. "Tell me what to do."

Again the nun smiled at Frank's devotion and put a hand on his shoulder as a younger nun arrived to help move Abby.

"The process makes the donor weak and tired, and you are tired enough as it is," the old one said. "Please, go, rest for a few hours and come back. I promise to care for Abby myself while you're away."

Frank stood from his chair, but didn't move. He stared at Abby. How could anyone keep a promise to care for another person? How many times had Abby suffered because Frank had never lived up to his promise to love and protect her? Helpless, he stared on as they wheeled Abby away once more. Clutching his hat, he walked into the empty hallway. Grudgingly, he heeded the nun's advice to go back to the hotel and clean up, perhaps get some sleep. There was nowhere else for him to go.

Standing just outside the hospital doors, he let himself adjust to the fresh air, the sunlight. It had to be mid-afternoon. He looked away from the sky toward the trees lining the curved drive, their shadows providing a little relief for his eyes. Frank took a few steps along the drive, then looked back at the brick building, wondering which room Abby was in. He faltered, torn. No, he could go to the hotel. He would be back soon enough.

Walking west on St. Mary's Avenue, Frank made his way to Main Street where he turned north towards the hotel a quarter mile away. Lost in his thoughts, Frank barely looked up as he crossed Milwaukee Avenue. He had barely stepped up from the street onto the sidewalk when a woman's voice brought him back to the moment.

"Frank Redmond?"

Looking up, he saw Maggie. She was pushing a small pram.

"It's so good to see you," she said, sweet and courteous.

"You have a baby."

"Yes. I married again, a little over a year ago," she said, her eyes so happy. She pushed the pram a little closer. "This is David."

"Congratulations," Frank said. He pretended to look in the pram, focusing on the wheels of the contraption instead.

"You know, you are famous here. Everyone talks about the stone—they call it the Sky Stone. People have come all the way from Spokane just to see it." Little David started fussing. "I really must go. But you're doing well? What brought you to town?"

"A relative in the hospital."

"Oh dear."

"It's fine. The doctor says things will be fine."

"Oh good," Maggie said, and David began screaming in earnest. Maggie gave a hurried goodbye and headed past Frank, continuing east up Milwaukee Avenue. Little David's siren cry faded into the distance as Frank trudged on. His mind swirled, muddy with fear and grief, and now a nice helping of bitterness. Abandoning his plan to wash up at the hotel, he headed in the opposite direction, west on Milwaukee Avenue. He needed to leave the bustling downtown and clear his mind. His feet led him across the Clark Fork River and up a gentle grade, climbed toward the mountains to the west. Head down, he walked uphill until, out of the corner of his eye, he saw Hillcrest Cemetery off to his left. There was Elisa's stone. He hadn't seen it since the day of the funeral. Both hating it and irreparably drawn to it, Frank walked closer. There were flowers in a simple vase perched on the base. They were withered but they couldn't be more than a few days old. The stone's details were still crisp. The Sky Stone. The awful thing had only damaged everyone associated with it: Bill Jameson had to leave his job in disgrace; Frank had nearly left Abby; Elisa was forever gone. He saw clearly then why he'd quit carving, why it repelled him so. Elisa had died the very day he completed this stone. Not only did he profit from her death, he had practically caused it. Frank turned away from the shining memorial and headed back to town. He did stop at his hotel room after all, where he killed a full hour sitting on the edge of the bed, staring at the scrolling lines of a brass light sconce on the wall.

At about four p.m., Frank headed back to the hospital. He drove this time, hoping to avoid another painful encounter with Maggie. Abby was still unconscious by the end of visiting hours. He spent another fitful night at the hotel and was back at the hospital at eight in the morning—the earliest the nuns would allow the worrisome husband in to see his wife. She looked better this morning, not as pale, though still clutched by that deep, strange sleep. Once again, Frank sat on the wooden chair close to the bed. He pulled a letter out of his coat pocket. The hotel clerk had received it and passed it along to Frank as he left that morning. No stamp, this had come by helpful hands—likely the McAllisters and acquaintances of theirs in the city. It was from Clay. Frank opened it and read aloud:

Everything is going well enough. Got the water turned onto the north pasture. Tell Abby to recover fast. We need her here. Stranger doesn't like my cooking. The old mutt misses you both.

Frank laughed at that. How could a dog miss someone? It was true though. He could easily picture Stranger lying by the door looking to the front gate in patient expectation of their return. Frank finished the letter, returned it to his pocket, and looked at Abby. "Good to hear from Dad," he said. Nothing. Not an eyelid flutter. Not a flicker of change in her breath.

A man's voice at the door startled Frank. "I had always hoped to meet Abby, but not under such circumstances."

Frank turned around to see Bill Jameson. Older, leaner, but still the man Frank had once considered a friend. He stood there with a small vase filled with flowers.

"Bill—I thought you had moved to Colorado," Frank stammered and stood as Bill approached and shook his hand.

Bill set the flowers down on a table next to Abby's bed and explained. "So you heard about the investigation. Those investigators just wanted their own lacky to replace me. There was no fighting it. I did leave, but I couldn't be so far from Elisa for long.

I'm on the State Board of Pardons in Helena now. Two-hour drive. Not so bad."

The two men returned their attention to Abby. "I'm sorry to see you here," Bill said. "How is she?"

Frank shared what little he knew and how'd they lost their baby. Bill's face was pained as he looked at Abby's frail, unconscious form.

"How did you know we were here?" Frank asked.

"Maggie called me. She knows I come up every week to put flowers on Elisa's grave."

A harsh "shush" from the nurse at the head of the room motivated both men to step outside to continue their conversation. Standing just outside the door, they spoke a while longer. "She looks good. Really. She'll pull through," Bill insisted. "The waiting is awful though." Bill said he needed to go but might stop by the next time he came through town. They shook hands, and as Frank headed back into the ward, Bill called after him.

"You made the right choice, Frank. Second chances don't happen every day." With that, Bill headed down the hall. Frank's tired mind didn't readily perceive the meaning of those words. Right choice? It dawned on him that Bill knew about Maggie. He had known the whole time. Frank leaned against the wall and let his head fall back against it with a dull thud. Just then a nurse opened the door and told him that Abby was stirring. Shaking his head in wonder, he hurried back to Abby's side.

Her eyes were still closed. He sat down and took her hand in his. It did feel warmer.

"I'm back, Abby," he whispered. "I had to leave, but I'm back now, and I won't leave you again." He kissed her hand, feeling for the first time, hopeful that she might recover.

Her shoulders moved first, a weak attempt at a stretch. Then she spoke. "I was just resting my eyes is all," she said, her voice weak, but clear. Her body seemed so frail; he feared he might hurt her. Awkward and careful, Frank leaned over and cupped her shoulders in his hands and kissed her cheek. "You're awake, you're awake," he said. "Thank you for waking up."

Abby wrapped one arm around her crying husband. They held each other as well as they could till Abby groaned a little at the pain in her back. Frank helped her settle back into the pillows, then stood by holding her hand tight. Her eyes were wide open now.

"I lost our baby, didn't I?"

Frank nodded and squeezed her hand.

Abby stared at the ceiling for a moment. "Was it a boy or a girl?"

"A girl."

"I'm sorry, Frank. I'm so sorry; it's all my fault."

"No," he said, forceful. "It's not your fault. This is no one's fault. No one's."

She stared at the ceiling again. She did not look at him when she spoke this time. "I want her to have a grave stone," she said. "Will you carve her one?"

Frank thought of all the countless souls for whom he'd carved. He thought of his mother, and Elisa, and now his daughter. He told Abby then, about carving the stone for Elisa. He told her about meeting the Jamesons and how Elisa had passed away the very day he had finished the stone. Slowly, Abby turned toward him, meeting his gaze as he spoke. "That's why I locked up the stone shed," he said.

Abby squeezed his hand. "You have a gift," she said. "I don't care if you share it with anyone else, but I think you should share it for our daughter."

Frank nodded. He couldn't see how any great good could come of it. But he would do this thing. For Abby.

CHAPTER 24

JULY 1937

Each day that Frank left the hotel to go see Abby, he looked west down Missouri Avenue and saw the storefront for Ross Funeral Service. He knew his baby lay there in the back room. Now on the fifth day, he could avoid it no longer. He stopped at the hospital one last time to say goodbye to Abby, comforted knowing that she only needed a few more days rest. Then Frank drove to the funeral parlor and parked out front. Fingers tapping on the steering wheel, he hesitated. His last parting with Ross wasn't exactly on pleasant terms. With a sigh, Frank got out of the car, straightened his hat, and walked into the mortuary.

The bell hanging on the door betrayed his entrance. Ralph Ross looked up from a stack of paperwork, and Frank removed his hat.

"Frank Redmond! My friend, come in, come in. I'm so sorry for your loss. How's Abby doing?" Ralph stepped around the counter and shook Frank's hand with both hands. His face was a contradiction, a welcoming smile and honest concern twisting his mouth and brow.

"She's better, the doctor said she could come home in a few days," Frank said. "I figured I would come and settle up with you and—"

"Nothing to settle. Your daughter is ready. No charge. Call it a professional courtesy if you want, but really it is the least I can do."

"I don't know what to say."

"I have some paperwork for you, as you know." Ralph returned to the counter and pulled a file out. Frank had seen the forms before, acceptance of the body and state paperwork. It was hard enough to go through it, but to see the word "Unknown" under the deceased's name was almost too much for Frank. Signing quickly he closed the folder.

Ralph left the front room and returned carrying a small, simple casket, no bigger than a shoebox. He handed it respectfully to Frank. It looked so fragile in his big hands. Part of him wanted to open it, to see his daughter just once, but he decided against it. Frank thanked Ralph again and turned to leave. Ralph stopped him.

"Frank, I know this might not be the best time to bring this up, but I want you to know that the offer to carve for me is always open."

"I know," Frank said. "I'll think about it."

"That's good enough for me. Give my regards to Clay and Abby."

Frank carried the petite wood coffin to the car and laid it on the front seat for the drive to the ranch. When he got home, Clay and Stranger were standing in the farmyard, ready to greet him. His father gave him a sturdy hug. Wordless, Clay found a shovel, and the two men walked up to Vivian's tree. Together, they dug a small grave next to Vivian's and laid the little casket in it. All the while, Stranger watched. The old mutt seemed to know what was happening. Even back in the driveway, he had foregone his usual boisterous greeting. Now he sat, quiet and intent, as the men stood at the graveside.

With the last shovel of dirt, the men stopped and looked at the grave. "I suppose we should say something," Clay said, still looking at the small mound of turned soil.

Frank remained silent. If it was his dad's intent to get him to speak, Clay was fishing in the wrong hole. Frank had no words. Though it did bother him that he didn't know what to say. This was his child after all. Nothing.

Clay cleared his throat and made his best attempt at a funeral prayer, asking God to take the child and to love her. God? What did he have to do with this? Frank knew that God always came up at funerals, but this time it didn't sit well with him. If God was real, why was he looking at his daughter's grave?

"Amen," Clay said and put his hat on.

"Amen," Frank whispered.

Waiting for Abby to come home, Frank retreated to solitary tasks. Work and time. Work and time. The best healers for an injured heart. Clay left Frank alone mostly, but Frank could tell that he was under his dad's watchful eye. Even Stranger stayed close except when the dog took to making his normal patrols. The dog took special interest in the graves up the hill. Frank watched to make sure Stranger didn't disturb the baby's grave. He didn't. The dog would just lie up there, occasionally barking to drive away any ravens or magpies that ventured too close.

CHAPTER 25
JULY 1937

The jagged branching crack in the paint and plaster was captivating if you stared at it long enough. Abby had abundant time for such contemplation since Frank had left for the ranch two days earlier. The thin, dark, uneven path started at the corner of the wall and ceiling and snaked out several inches into the sterile white paint, which covered everything but the floor in the hospital ward. He had departed only after receiving assurances from half a dozen doctors and nurses, all repeating that Abby would be fine and just needed another week of rest. With Frank gone, Abby occupied her mind with the crack, the cloth curtains, the heavily starched bed sheets, and the periodical care from the nurses. Each day the nurses took Abby by wheelchair to the small hospital library where she was allowed to spend an hour or two reading, but she still spent most of her time in the hospital bed. The pain that had tormented her initially had lessened some. Now, only her back hurt when she maneuvered herself out of bed to relieve herself or to get into the wheelchair. Each day she felt stronger, though never whole. For seven months her child had been with her, a part of her. Now her baby was gone, and the abyss that remained in her heart left Abby feeling as scant as the walls of the room.

Many times during the night she woke, thinking she felt her unborn daughter moving inside her. Reaching down, she would touch her flattened abdomen and know it was just a dream. In the darkness Abby could hear the movement of a pen and the shuffling of paper at the far end of the room. The only source of light emanated from the nurse's desk. The ceiling crack was hidden in the shadows, but with concentration Abby could see its familiar path. It was then that she would pray, her lips forming soundless words. Mostly she asked why. Occasionally her anger unfurled in more desperate accusation, but it always ended with the simple question of why. No answer ever came.

So went the rhythm of her first few days alone in the hospital. Four days after Frank left, Abby was allowed to get up and walk short distances with a nurse at her side. Abby's time in bed had left her weak, and she knew that she had to move as much as she could if she was going to get strong again. On every journey down the hospital hall, the nurse guided her a little farther than the prior walk. When the nurse said it was time to turn around, Abby always insisted on ten more steps. For the next two days, Abby added these embarrassingly slow walks to her routine of personal care, library visits, and memorizing the ceiling crack.

One day, halfway into her second week in the hospital, Abby had just completed her midday walk when a man wearing a suit arrived in the recovery ward. He held two books and a small vase of flowers.

"Mrs. Redmond, my name is William Jameson, but you can call me Bill," he said.

So this was the infamous warden. Frank had told her Bill had visited once while she was still asleep and that he might stop by again. The man had a softer look about him than Abby had imagined. It was encouraging to think of Frank admiring the man. Bill stood with confidence, a man accustomed to power; Abby could see that. Yet, behind the wire-rimmed glasses, she could see gentleness, a genuine concern for her.

"I do hope it is alright to pay a visit to you and that these gifts will help with your recovery." Abby looked at the books: *One of Ours* by Willa Cather and the other, a fine leather-bound copy of Mark Twain's *Adventures of Huckleberry Finn.* Abby let her fingers run across the embossed leather; it portrayed a scene of a boy on a raft, polling his way down a wide river.

"Frank mentioned that you liked to read," Bill said. "These are favorites in my family."

Abby thanked him. The smell and feel of the leather cover reminded her of her saddle, of home. She hoped Bill hadn't made a special trip just to see her, and she said so.

"Oh, I'm in Deer Lodge once a week, as my job and weather allow," he said. "I like Elisa's grave to have fresh flowers."

Abby admired the sentiment. "I have heard of your wife's memorial, but I've never seen it."

"Really? We need to remedy that." Bill politely excused himself and headed to the nurse's desk.

Abby could hear them converse in hushed tones, then the voice of the doctor joined the conversation. The exchange eventually ended in friendly laughter. Abby heard footsteps approaching and the sound of the squeaky wheel chair. Bill appeared.

"Would you care to join me for a car ride this fine summer afternoon?"

"Would I? What, outdoors? In the sun?" Abby smiled for the first time since before the accident. Bill stood outside the curtains as the nurse helped Abby dress, then he wheeled her out to his car. The sterile confines of the hospital had been a far cry from the high mountain air and working outside every day. Bill helped Abby settle into the car, and they were off. She looked out the half-open window. It was so good to feel the breeze again. They took St. Mary's Avenue out of town.

"Elisa always enjoyed a nice drive," Bill said. "She swore they were more healing than any doctor."

Abby had to agree. As soon as the cemetery was in sight, Abby noticed the massive blue stone. There was no missing it. Bill drove into the cemetery and parked as close to the stone as he could. Bill opened the door for her and offered his arm to steady her as her slippered feet walked gingerly, respectfully on the grass.

There it was, the painterly landscape carving that had made her husband the talk of the town. It wasn't vain flattery; those compliments were well-deserved. "I can't believe Frank made something so magnificent," she said. The artwork before her seemed so removed from the man with whom she lived and labored. The hard, practical, stoic man she loved. The fishing village, the fjord, and the delicate flowers framing it all—the lines flowed as smoothly as a watercolor. She imagined Frank carving the verse as well: *Oh death, where is thy sting? Oh grave, where is thy victory?*

"He quit carving after this stone," she told Bill. "He needs to carve again. He is meant to do this, isn't he?"

Bill huffed. "Well, there's only one person who isn't convinced of that."

CHAPTER 26
JULY 1937

A week after Frank and Clay had buried their stillborn kin, Abby came home. Friends from across the valley were there to greet her. Frank was thankful for that, she needed support, and he wasn't sure how to provide it himself. He saw her face as she exited the car, watched her look toward Vivian's tree and the grave. What the hell could he possibly say? Patty saved him, taking Abby in her arms and hugging her tightly, then walking her to the house where everyone had prepared a meal fitting for her return. That same afternoon, after everyone had left, Frank walked over to the stone shed and opened the door for the first time in years.

Everything was just as he had left it. He swept away the dust and cobwebs on the granite slabs, then hefted the smallest one onto the wooden support frame. There was the tool box, and inside it was the leather bundle of tools that Bill had given him. No corrosion on any of them; the case had kept them safe and dry. The jewelry box was still there, too. Frank opened it and looked once again at the silver-embraced blue granite. He closed it and put it in his pocket. He would finally honor Bill's wishes and give it to Abby. Not now, though; the beautiful thing must never remind her of this sad time. Perhaps at Christmas. Yes, Christmas, he could give it to her then. He had never been able to afford such a fine gift; this would do.

Frank turned his attention back to the stone. They had not named their stillborn daughter. Instead, back in the hospital, Abby had referred to her once as Baby Angel. That was what Frank would carve. Taking out a brushing chisel and his hammer, he began to chip away at the rough stone face, each strike removing a jagged piece, slowly smoothing it into the flat surface on which he could carve. The sound of the steel striking granite, the dust of the stone, and the warm July air—he had missed these things. It was almost comforting to Frank. Perhaps he could carve again.

CHAPTER 27

SUMMER TO FALL 1937

For the moment, Stranger and his humans existed purely in the rhythmic sound of hooves on the ground. The uneven beat was overlaid with shrill whistles and yells as the riders did their best to keep the steers heading in the right direction. It had been two months since the woman's baby had been buried. Finally, the dog's people seemed to have a little energy again. Even the woman smiled as she spoke to the neighbor boys who were helping with the cattle drive. Stranger liked that.

The dog had tried so hard to make her smile in the weeks after her return, but she wouldn't. She spent time every day sitting next to the stones under the tree. When she wasn't keeping watch by the stones, Stranger tried to help by keeping the magpies away from them. She cried a lot, too, sometimes by the stones, sometimes on the back stoop by herself. Each time she cried, Stranger would lie next to her, head on her leg, letting her pet him until her tears stopped. Lately, she was crying less often. Stranger knew she was doing better when he finally succeeded in teaching her how to dance. The old man wasn't dancing with him anymore, and the dog really needed someone to play with.

Day after day, through the hot part of the summer, Stranger had approached the woman, dropped his head and front legs, and invited her to play. He would rear up on his hind legs, waving his front paws. She'd shake her head and continue her work. Finally, finally, one afternoon when a cool breeze came down the mountain, she paid attention to him. This time, when he dropped his front end and raised his tail like a flag, she had looked at him, at his eyes! He leapt up, bounded toward her and reared within an arm's reach. She had taken his paws and walked him about the farmyard. He could see the woman smile. This was good. Stranger knew that much about humans—their mouths told a lot about their moods. They'd had a good dance just that morning before the cattle drive. It had made the neighbor boys laugh, and Stranger was glad they were so pleased with the trick he'd taught the woman.

They were on the road now. The woman rode her chestnut mare like old times and worked alongside Stranger at the tail end of the herd. Stranger darted from one side of the road to the other, his presence motivating the cattle to keep moving. The hard-packed gravel road was bordered with fences, making the herd bunch up, which made it even easier to move them. There was nowhere to go but forward. Any steer that wanted to get away had to double-back past Stranger. The dog's intense eyes and lowered head were all that was required to convince the bovine to reconsider.

The two men rode at the flanks of the herd, the older on the left and the younger on the right. One of the neighbor boys was the one whom Stranger liked, the one who had always played tug with him. As the boy grew taller, and Stranger older, the dog was finding it more difficult to win the game. Perhaps at the end of the drive, the boy would play. Perhaps the woman would play again, too. It was a good day.

A car horn caught Stranger's attention. They had turned the herd south onto the main road and cars were getting more common.

But drivers were usually patient, letting the mass of livestock pass by or waiting for the drovers to make room for the car to squeeze past. This particular driver must not have been from around these parts. Otherwise he would know that honking during a cattle drive was fairly futile. Looking back, Stranger saw the driver pounding on his horn, waving his arm out the window, and shouting rough words. Stranger looked to his humans for direction on how to handle the intruder. When the woman swung her horse around and set a course for the car, the dog immediately followed. He sniffed around the tires of the car and listened close as both the woman and the driver exchanged heated words. Stranger moved around the back of the car so he could see the woman, but the driver could not see him. The man kept shouting and pointing this way and that. The woman did not raise her voice, but Stranger could tell she was very angry. With what appeared to be the final verbal volley, the woman turned her horse back to the herd, and Stranger followed. Then he heard the car door open. Looking back, Stranger saw the man step out of his car.

A memory flashed into the dog's mind—an angry man standing to his full height. Yes, the build, the hat, the arrogant posture was much like that of a railroad bull who had once caught Stranger and his first human sleeping in an empty boxcar. That man had kicked Stranger, pummeled his human, and tossed them both out of the boxcar.

This was the same kind of man. A bad man. Stranger's protective instinct rose up inside him. The driver stood by his car, yelling more harsh words at the woman. He took a step toward her. Stranger's fur stood up; he was about to lunge toward the man when the woman spun her horse around and galloped the short distance back to the car.

The horse skidded to a halt next to the now very startled driver. Before the horse even stopped, the woman leapt off its back and stormed up to the man, who was a good deal taller. She unloaded a verbal barrage at him, her right pointer finger jabbing him in the chest. Stranger rushed to her side, but wondered if he needed to intervene at all. He stood still; she was doing just fine without him. The man was stunned. He didn't even fight back. When the woman stopped poking him and put her hands on her hips, he had an angry look on his face, but he backed away, standing right next to his car. The woman got back on her horse, her face contorted in anger. The bad man looked like he might rally and try to follow her. But Stranger halted his movement with a single loud bark and a flash of his fangs. The bad man looked at the dog, then at the woman, then got back into his vehicle. Stranger waited till the door closed. Then he approached the car and marked one of the front tires. The driver yelled and opened the door to come after him, but he stopped when Stranger reminded him of his teeth. Stranger sauntered down the road to catch up with the woman. The herd had moved on a hundred yards or so.

The woman and the younger man were speaking with each other. As they talked, the younger man cast an angry glance at the car in the distance, which had resumed following the herd, but maintained a generous distance from the riders and cattle. The woman seemed more relaxed, but she still had a serious look on her face. She clucked her tongue, riding on to keep the herd moving. That left Stranger standing with the woman's husband and his horse. The younger man looked at the woman, then at Stranger. He chuckled. If the dog could have shrugged, he would have then. Perhaps the woman needed less from them than either had ever believed. The younger man shook his head. Then he turned his horse, galloping back to the side of the herd. Stranger cast one last glare at the car, and then continued with his job.

As soon as the road widened and the herd could thin out, the riders moved the cattle off to the side, allowing the impatient driver to maneuver his car around them. The man kept his hands on the steering wheel and stared straight ahead as he sped past. Stranger sent him several good riddance barks for good measure.

As they neared Avon, the humans grew more focused on keeping tabs on the cattle, and Stranger did his best to help. Once the herd was safely corralled in the stockyard, Stranger trotted off on his own to explore a little, though he never lost sight of the woman. All around cattle bellowed and screeched, humans shouted to each other as they sorted them into the holding pens. Meanwhile, cars rushed by on the paved highway that paralleled the railroad tracks. The smell of it all was like nothing else—all the scents of the cattle drive, but twenty times more, and layered with car exhaust and warm tar on the railroad ties.

In past years, Stranger's humans would turn for home once the cattle were corralled. But this year, they dismounted and tied their horses up to the fence by one of the loading chutes next to the railroad. While they spent an inordinate amount of time speaking with a big man wearing a big hat, Stranger explored cautiously. The wooden ties and rails were all too familiar; he stayed clear of them. Stranger startled when the sound of an approaching steam rattler hit his ears. His heart raced. In his mind, he saw his first human, the train devouring him. He whined and cowered away from the tracks.

Looking for an escape, he felt the comforting hands of the woman on his back. He could see the concern on her face as she talked calmly to him. Still, he wanted to flee, to run from the terrible beast and the dreadful memories. The woman stood up, and with the slight pressure of her hand, guided Stranger away from the tracks to the protective shade of a large pine tree. There she knelt with him and petted him softly while the train came to a halt, while the younger man and the neighbor boys helped load the cattle into the box cars. Once the cattle were loaded, steam burst from the train engine and, with a hoot of its whistle, it started its slow acceleration to the west.

CHAPTER 28

JULY 1938

Clay watched from inside the barn as Stranger finished his afternoon patrol around the ranch. As he had for the past year, the dog made a special pass by the two stones under the old fir tree just north of the house. The dog sniffed Vivian's stone and the smaller memorial next to hers. The animal never marked there; he seemed to understand the site's importance. Instead, Stranger made it his job to drive off the raucous magpies who liked to roost in that tree. The dog had an uncanny sense of things; it always amazed the old man. Sometimes he wondered if Stranger was more than just a dog.

It had been a year since his granddaughter was stillborn. Though Abby visibly grieved, Frank was more reserved. He stayed attentive to Abby but held his own grief close to the vest. Clay knew that onus. Why Frank and Abby had experienced the same loss was beyond Clay's understanding. People joked about the Redmond curse, how they were destined never to have big families. He couldn't help but wonder if there really was a curse, if somewhere back in the family tree, God had blighted them for some unknown sin.

Curse or no, Frank and Abby were closer now. Clay could see that. Even so, his mind was heavy with other things. Cattle prices remained low, and they still did not own enough land to grow their herd. Perhaps if Frank resumed his stone carving, there might be enough to survive. To slow the bleeding, Clay had sold off several acres of timber to one of the local mills, but he knew that cash wouldn't last them more than another year or two.

Stranger quit chasing the magpies and looked toward Clay. It was a delight to spy on the dog, but he always knew when he was being watched. Clay stepped out of the shadow of the barn, into the barnyard. The dog came running, tail high and happy. Clay scratched the dog's ears, then headed into the house. Frank and Abby were gone to Butte, an all day trip to pick up canned goods at the Safeway store.

Clay rummaged around the kitchen until he found where Abby stashed the sugar cookies. He grabbed a handful of cookies along with a collection of old newspapers he had scavenged from the Elk Café—a mix of Silver State Posts and the Helena Independent. He went back outside and, as he sat down in one of the four wooden chairs just outside the porch, Stranger came up to him.

"Work's done," Clay said. "How about you and I relax a bit and catch up on the news? Looks to be about a month's worth." The dog couldn't possibly understand, but Clay had developed a habit of reading the paper aloud to him. Handing the old mutt an occasional treat ensured his rapt attention. Stranger loved to hear any news story if he got a cookie at the end. Clay unfolded one of the papers and offered the dog half a cookie for starters. With great control and delicacy, Stranger took the treat. Only when the man's hand was clear did he make a quick snap of his jaws, devouring it one gulp.

Scanning the front page, Clay made a short humming noise before speaking. "A big train wreck over by Miles City. Fifty some people died when a bridge washed out. All those souls gone just like that," he said. His face tightened. He turned the page. "And Japan declared war on China." He scrutinized the other head-lines. "Seems there ain't any good news."

Clay peered over the rims of his reading glasses, looking at Stranger. The dog sat, so attentive. Not really begging though. Clay wondered whether the dog understood much more than any-one realized. He folded the first paper, set it aside, and scanned another. "Here's something. A Negro boxer knocked out one of those Nazis in New York. Bet that put a burr under that German bastard's saddle. Master race, my ass," he folded that paper down as well and offered the dog a little more commentary. "Mark my words, Stranger, trouble's brewing over there; another war's com-ing. I've seen it before. Lost my brother in the Great War."

Stranger stood up and wagged his tail, big doggy grin on his face. Well, maybe he didn't always understand precisely what Clay was saying. The dog clearly wanted another cookie. Clay obliged. Stranger munched on a whole cookie while Clay petted his head. "My friend, I envy you. Your only worries are if the scraps'll be good, who'll scratch your ears, and whether you can keep the mag-pies away," he said. Clay held up the paper and added, "The life of a dog sure beats all this." Stranger pricked his ears and tilted his head, as if understanding the change in the old man's tone. Clay looked at the barn and the mountains beyond and sighed.

Stranger moved closer, then rested his head on Clay's leg. Human hand scratched canine head out of sheer reflex. The old man stared off into the distance. "I thought I'd have grandsons running this place someday," he pondered. "Can't make it on a spread this size just running cattle, and there's not enough money to buy more land. Enough land for sheep, but it takes a big family to run sheep. We barely made it with just Frank, but by God, we made it."

Clay looked down at the dog, who raised his tan eyebrows. He took the dog's face in his hands. "You're getting a little grey yourself there, my friend. Can't stop time, can we? There's another advantage you got over us. You don't know what's coming."

The dog nuzzled his hands. "Sorry, pup, forgot my job there for a second," he said. The work worn hand resumed stroking the dog's broad head. Clay looked over at the memorials for Vivian and his granddaughter. The small stone marking the child's grave was the last one Frank had carved. He'd opened the stone shed only for that purpose, then he locked it up again. Even when Clay mentioned how much Frank's carving helped with the bills, his son refused. The boy stayed silent about that, but the state of the ranch's finances was no secret. They'd be selling in a year. Two at the most.

"This is my home, Stranger. You understand that much, don't you?" Clay looked at the dog, then winced. Pain gripped him behind his right eye. Clay rubbed his temples, stunned at the sudden headache. Then, as quickly as it began, the pain subsided. It wasn't good to think such sad thoughts for too long; only made your head hurt. Clay dug into his shirt pocket, pulled out the last two cookies, and handed one to Stranger as he ate the other. Enough of these worries. Nothing could be changed one jot by worrying, it certainly wasn't worth giving yourself a headache. Clay leaned back in his chair, tilting his hat brim to shield his eyes from the sun. When Frank got home, they'd have the talk about selling. It was time. But for now, a nap would do him good.

Stranger nudged Clay's hand, probably hoping for another treat. Clay opened his eyes, then grew confused at why his hand wouldn't move when he tried to reach for the dog. Words remained trapped behind lips that wouldn't work. *Dear God, what's happening to me?!* Stranger blurred as Clay felt the right side of his body grow slack. Euphoria and fear crested with the darkness. Stranger whimpered. The mutt's muted barks were the last thing Clay heard as he drifted away. *Oh, Vivian.*

CHAPTER 29

SUMMER TO FALL 1939

Abby swung the axe high over her head in a smooth arc, its head penetrating deep into the log and sending two halves tumbling to the sides. She had often split kindling as needed in the past, but the heavier wood chopping had always been Frank's chore. With Clay gone, she had to do work that pushed the limits of her body. Though it was summer, wood was still needed to cook and to warm the house when a cold snap rolled through. The long axe handle and heavy head made the chore all the more difficult, but Abby got it done.

Clay's death meant so much more work for both her and Frank. They barely had time to grieve. But, she did miss her father-in-law. Abby remembered the day clearly, the trip to Butte to buy bulk goods and the drive home. Foreboding overwhelmed her when they turned into the drive and Stranger wasn't running down from the house barking at their arrival. The dog lay at Clay's feet, head to the ground, not moving a muscle. Stranger knew. The helplessness of it all was the hardest for Abby—nothing she could do for Clay, nothing she could do for Frank as he tried to wake his father.

They had made it another year. Abby wasn't sure how exactly. Just Frank and herself, and an increasingly gimpy old dog. They ran the ranch with occasional help from friends and, when money was there, hired hands. Financially they barely survived. The annual sale of steers and dry cows in the fall got them through the winter. In spite of the sadness of losing a father and dear friend, Frank braved the stone shed and carved a stone that matched Vivian's—simple, plain, just like Clay had wanted. They set the stone in tearless silence. Then Frank closed the stone shed once more. Too much work to do with Clay gone—that was her husband's excuse.

The emotion faded; work demanded that it did. At least for the humans the pain subsided. But for Stranger, it seemed Clay's death had a heavier impact. Abby had never considered whether an animal could grieve, yet she saw it now. For the entire autumn and winter, Stranger ceased greeting her at the door when she came outside to work. Instead, he kept vigil at the graves under the fir tree and only came in for the night at Abby's insistent behest. If called, Stranger might join Abby as she helped Frank with the horses or completed some other outdoor chore, but he would sneak away at first chance to resume his watch at the stones. She couldn't blame the dog. She wanted to grieve longer herself, but couldn't. She let Stranger do it for her.

Only recently, in the past two months, had Stranger once again become more attentive to Abby. As he had in the past, Stranger now lay by the front door waiting for her to come out so he could follow her about the farmyard. He kept watch at the graves only if Frank and Abby left for town without him.

If there was any good from Clay's passing, it was that Frank and Abby needed each other more than before. Pride was gone; if help was needed, it was asked for. It seemed they spent more time together this past year than they ever had before. Together they could complete most any task on the ranch. But haying season was fast approaching. The fact that they needed to hire help was unavoidable. It would have been impossible to bring up the subject of stone carving a year ago. But Abby wondered if Frank might not consider it again. She had earned Frank's respect working with him so much; at least she thought she had. As she split the firewood, she planned her conversation. Breakfast would be best; he was the least exhausted then. Pancakes, yes, he loved pancakes. Abby would bring it up over a large stack of flapjacks.

⇒‖⇐

The next morning, Abby waited till Frank had finished two pancakes and had nabbed seconds. She sat down with her own plate. "We need hands to put up hay this year," she said. "At least three I would think."

Frank nodded in agreement, his mouth full, a dab of maple syrup on his chin.

"We don't have the money, not unless we find another income. I could try and do some quilting and sell it. Perhaps we could sell some cows early."

"The cows won't be ready," he said. "And when would you have time to quilt?" Frank shook his head no at both ideas. Good. Then he had to see the sense of her suggestion.

"Well, we have to do something. You made good money with your carving." There it was.

Frank just chewed. He didn't say a word as he finished his breakfast and went out to work. Abby took this as a very positive response. No initial objection; he was thinking about it. He really was. She cleared the table and went outside to help Frank hook up the teams.

For the next two days, Frank didn't mention the subject, but it was wildly apparent he was mulling things over. Abby knew the look—the distant stare at the table, the utter silence as they worked together outside. She had never seen Frank struggle so much with a decision. Back in the hospital, he had told her why he had quit carving. It seemed like there was more, there had to be. Finally he spoke over supper the second night. What he said wasn't what she expected.

"Carving makes me a scavenger, chasing death to make a dollar," Frank said. He looked to the wall as he spoke. "I've had nightmares where I'm walking next to the grim reaper himself, going house-to-house to take people. When I used to carve, I was tough about it. I didn't care. I don't want to be like that ever again. To anyone." He looked at her then, not angry, but weary.

"You won't," she said. "You can't."

"How can you know that?"

"You've changed, and it's not because you quit carving."

Frank was quiet for a moment. "Still seems like I'm helping death along."

"Frank, death doesn't need your help; we're all headed there," she said. "The stones are for us, the ones who keep living. We look at them, and we remember. That's what your carving does."

Frank was quiet the rest of the meal. The next day when he started the car, he said only that he needed to go to Avon to use a phone. Abby looked out the kitchen window when the car returned. Best not to press him for any explanation, not right away. She watched Frank get out of the car and head straight to the stone shed. No, she didn't need to ask him to explain at all. He'd obviously called Ross Funeral Service. He'd offered to carve again, and Ralph must have had an order for him right off the bat. The pay was enough to get the help needed to put up the hay for the year. They would survive.

For Abby, there was one more consideration heavier than their own subsistence. Heading into haying season, she saw a shift in Stranger's behavior again—clinging to her side, acting more protective than normal. He had done this before. She had missed the clue a month before when Stranger left his vigil at the graves to shadow her whenever she left that house. Even with grey muzzle and sore joints, Stranger resumed his duty as her guardian. That and her sudden intolerance for certain foods and smells, confirmed her suspicions. Abby didn't feel anything for the pregnancy, daring not to get attached. She didn't want to tell Frank. Not yet anyway. Since their daughter's death, Frank never again mentioned the topic of children. Perhaps he no longer wanted to have any. No matter, she couldn't hide it much longer.

Shortly after the exhausting days of hay season, she chose another morning on which to make a sturdy pancake breakfast. But, she lost her resolve during the meal. Frank was practically out the door when she stopped him.

"I'm pregnant," she said to his back and steeled herself for an unpleasant reaction. His hand was still on the handle of the open door. He turned and smiled, walked over to Abby and hugged her gently, then kissed her on the forehead.

"I was wondering about that," he said.

"Really?"

"You been eating like a bird," he said then added, "It'll be a boy."

He walked out leaving Abby perplexed by his response. No anger; no elation either. As much as she loved Frank, times like this frustrated Abby. He must at least be a little concerned. For the next week she watched him withdraw into deep thought yet again. The following Sunday, he spoke.

"We're gonna sell," he said, emotionless. "The Thomas ranch has come into money and wants our place for more pasture and hay." Frank was looking Abby in the eye as he spoke. There was no argument over the matter, for even as Abby heard it, even as she contemplated the reality of leaving their land behind, she knew it was the only option left. A phosphate mine had been started on the Thomas ranch across the valley. The demand for the mineral was high with war starting in Europe. That meant money for them to expand. The Redmond ranch was now marketable simply because there was a moneyed possible buyer. It was time.

"It's because I'm pregnant," Abby said.

Frank nodded yes. There was no way they could survive on the ranch another year—it wasn't just the money. It was the fact that they needed Abby to be able to work. The winter would be the worst as friends would be unable to get to their place to help Frank, and he couldn't possibly do all the work himself. "When?" Abby asked.

"Within the next month, I hope."

So that was it. They were leaving. The following weeks went like all the ones before. The only change was that Frank had to leave occasionally, meeting with the buyers and lawyers regarding the sale. And in every spare moment, Frank was in the stone shed carving. Ralph in Deer Lodge kept him busy, but so did a stone carving shop in Helena, one that provided monuments and many other large jobs around the region.

One day in September, Abby had finished feeding the draft horses and was walking back to the house when Frank called to her from the stone shed. Frank's voice didn't sound distressed, but she wondered why he would call her in. He'd never shown her his work in progress. She crossed the farmyard with Stranger tagging along as always, his age and old injury giving his gait a pronounced limp. The dog followed Abby through the doorway. Abby was nearly blind in the dark room. As her eyes adjusted, she could make out the grey stone resting on a wooden framework. Frank stood next to it, wearing a leather apron. Above the stone, a large pulley hung from a thick beam in the ceiling with ropes arching over to a peg on the wall. The room smelled of stone dust and sweat. Abby asked what Frank needed.

"Is this all spelled right?" Frank asked, handing his sketch pad to Abby. She marveled at the sketch of angels and poetic verse. As her eyes grew more accustomed to the dim light she read the words and spotted one mistake: *their hands,* not *there hands.* She asked for a pencil, corrected the word, and gave the pad and pencil back to Frank. Only then did she see the stone in its entirety. The drawing had been etched onto the stone, everything but the words.

"It's grand, Frank." Abby reached out to touch the stone but hesitated.

"Go ahead," Frank said. "You won't hurt nothing."

The cool granite was rough to the touch. Her fingers traced the cuts, noting the change in depths, the smoothed and polished areas, and how the dim light softened the edges. Stranger also inspected the work, sniffing the stone and its support frame before exploring the rest of the room.

"Do you need anything else?" Abby asked, her hand still on the stone.

"No, just didn't want to have the wrong spelling is all. Thanks."

"Her family will be very pleased," she said.

As she stepped toward the door, she heard Frank whisper, "Thank you."

Abby called the dog and walked back into the sunshine. Stranger walked with her back to the house. The sound carried across the yard and over the valley, that sharp ring of hammer on steel.

CHAPTER 30
JULY 2000

Abby turned toward the sound of the dog barking near the road. She touched her blue stone necklace and looked south across the long-vacated homestead. So familiar, yet the changes of time were evident in the fields and trees—vivid in the absence of the house, barn, and outbuildings that had once been her home. Her grandson's dark sable German Shepherd chased after three magpies in the field next to the trail. She heard the voices of her family as they approached the gravesite, her oldest son leading them, carrying Frank's ashes.

Frank had died seven years ago. The urn had sat on the mantle at their home in Helena until now. With encouragement from her family, Abby had decided to let Frank rest up at the old ranch site. He had wanted it that way; it had just taken this long for Abby to become comfortable with the idea.

Passing through the small gate in the fence, she entered the gravesite. Abby used her cane and the fencepost to lower herself into the grass next to the stones. She caught her breath. It wasn't easy, the effort of the walk and the simple task of sitting down on the ground, not easy in an eighty-seven year old body. Even with her oldest son driving as far up the path as he could to get her close to the graves, it still was a long walk for her. She leaned over and touched the stone marking Stranger's grave. The black granite stood out among the others, the detail of the carving so much more intricate than on the adjacent burial markers. She let her fingers move across the polished surface, cold to the touch in the shadow of the tree. Frank had put so much effort into the dog's stone, a revelation of how much the old mutt had meant to him. A perfect representation of Stranger's head was carved on the stone's face, the image watching over the three graves nearby. Below the carving were the words: *Here lies a dog named Stranger. You came to us unwanted, but left us beloved. October 1, 1939.*

Abby traced the outline of Stranger's face.

It had been cold the day he died, cold enough for Abby to see her breath as she walked up to the graves that first day of October sixty-two years ago. The ranch was sold; they were leaving in a matter of days. She had climbed the hill to give a last goodbye to Clay, Vivian, and Baby Angel. Stranger had shadowed her as always, his age causing him to lag behind, though. "Are you going to make it, old dog?" Abby asked playfully as she sat next to the stones. It hadn't been easy for her to sit down in the grass that day either, as pregnant as she was. The aged dog, panting heavily, lay down next to her with his head on her leg. What a pair they were.

She felt so bad for the poor old dog. She hoped he would be able to adjust to life in the city: A small yard to patrol instead of hundreds of acres. Stranger closed his eyes as she rubbed his velvet soft ears. She ran her hand along his side, feeling the scar from the bear attack so many years ago. The white hairs around it were stark against the black fur. She felt him breathing softly, letting her hand rest on his chest, feeling his heart beat slowly. She stared down to the ranch house and barn, with the valley stretching out beyond. "It's so beautiful here. I can understand why you like this spot," she said to the sleeping dog. "You can see the whole world, it seems." Abby watched a flock of starlings dart across the blue sky and dip down behind the aspen trees lining the road. She felt Stranger let out a soft cough. Then he took a deep breath, and then nothing. Stranger was gone.

Frank had carved the stone after they moved, using fine materials from the shop in Helena. They had returned the following spring and placed it over Stranger's grave. Abby took comfort in the assurances from the ranch's new owners—that she and Frank could always visit, and that the fence around the memorial stones would be maintained.

Abby's eyes clouded as she thought of Frank, and Stranger, and everyone else. The voices of those around her got all tangled up with the sounds of the past. The feel of a large dog's head on her leg brought her back to the present. Her hand instinctively reached down to feel the soft ears and pet the broad head. A hushed but commanding voice, her grandson, called to the dog, "*Schatten hier, hier!*" The German commands caused the dog to raise his head.

Abby raised her hand silencing the young man. "Don't. He's fine right here," she said. "Let him be with me. Let him be."

Troy Kechely grew up on a ranch west of Helena, Montana, where he developed a strong connection to the land and the animals he tended. That connection is evident in his narrative writing and formed the foundation for his debut novel, *Stranger's Dance*.

A nationally known dog behavior expert, he is the author of *The Management of Aggressive Canines for Law Enforcement*, which teaches law enforcement officers how to avoid the use of deadly force against dogs during routine and high-risk encounters. He has written short stories and poems about the bond humans and dogs share for *Dog and Kennel Magazine*, numerous newsletters, and canine rescue websites.

Kechely currently resides in Bozeman, Montana, with his two rescue Rottweilers, Bradum and Carly.

Made in the USA
Lexington, KY
07 December 2018